"If I take off tape, you promise no yell, no scream?"

I nodded.

She licked her lips, giving me just a peek at her tongue. "Too bad I meet Ricker an' not you in Saigon."

She positioned the knife, cutting edge up, just under my chin. Then she leaned over and kissed me, upside down. I did my best to respond.

"Mmmm," she said as she broke off the kiss. "Very nice." She pulled back the knife. Break off the kiss, then withdraw knife.

She put the knife down next to my head and reaffixed the tape, testing it throughly. Careful woman.

"Yes, very nice. But I must wait for Ricker to get back. He want to watch." She started up the stairs. "You MP, like Ricker. He say he let me be 'double vet' ran' tonight. You know what that mean." She laughed, like glass breaking.

A double veteran was in-country slang for GI who, after having sex with a woman, killed her.

She turned off the lights. I could still hear her laughing through the closed door.

Praise for *THE STAKED GOAT*

"Jeremiah Healy's original characters and clever plotting bring a new realism to the field."

—Gregory Mcdonald

"Loaded with action . . . uncompromisingly realistic . . . Healy's gusty style is a refreshing throwback."

—*Philadelphia Inquirer*

"THE STAKED GOAT is a taut thriller that grabs you and sets you running alongside its protagonist until you, like Cuddy, slump exhausted at the book's end."

—*Atlanta Journal and Constitution*

"Healy's people are so vividly drawn that even the most minor characters seem to climb right off the pages and into your living room. Nor does Healy stint on plot or action . . . even with advance warning you'll be totally unprepared for the final three pages. . . . Healy is one of the most impressive new talents we've run across in some time. . . . THE BEST NOVEL OF THE YEAR."

—*The Denver Post*

"First class. A plot that really works and good, unfussy writing . . . I read this one almost at a sitting, something I haven't done for a long time."

—Michael Gilbert

"Fresh and intriguing . . . characters so real you care about them."

—Tony Hillerman

"Besides being one of the toughest of the current breed of detective hero, this stand-up guy is also one of the most sensitive. That's a tricky combination to throw, but Healy has a great eye and a very steady hand."

—Cleveland *Plain Dealer*

"A fine thriller . . . Healy's prose is some of the crispest around. . . . He has what it takes to produce more than one winner and probably more than two."

—*Boston Magazine*

Catherine O'Brien

THE STAKED GOAT

Jeremiah Healy

PUBLISHED BY POCKET BOOKS NEW YORK

This novel is a work of fiction. Names, characters, places and incidents are either the product of the author's imagination or are used fictitiously. Any resemblance to actual events or locales or persons, living or dead, is entirely coincidental.

POCKET BOOKS, a division of Simon & Schuster, Inc.
1230 Avenue of the Americas, New York, N.Y. 10020

Published by arrangement with Harper & Row Publishers, Inc.
Library of Congress Catalog Card Number: 85-45034

For information address Harper & Row Publishers, Inc., 10 East 53rd Street, New York, N.Y. 10022

ISBN: 0-671-63677-4

First Pocket Books printing May 1987

10 9 8 7 6 5 4 3 2 1

Printed in the U.S.A.

For
Evelyn
and
Virginia

One

I SWATTED THE SNOOZE BUTTON ON MY CLOCK RADIO twice. The ringing noise didn't stop, so I picked up the telephone.

"Yeah?" I said.

"Shouldn't you be answering 'John Francis Cuddy, private detective'?" A gruff, hearty male voice.

I blinked at the time. "Not at 7:05 A.M. Who is this?"

"Or, at least, 'John Francis Cuddy, Captain, United States Army, retired'?"

"In a minute you'll be talking to yourself, my friend. Who is this?"

"Christ, John," said the voice through a deep laugh, "you always were a pleasure to wake up in the morning."

My head began to clear. "Al? Al Sachs?"

"The one and only."

"Al, it's been . . ."

"Actually, that's not true, not anymore. You know Martha and me got married four years ago. Well, I'm no longer the one and only, being the proud father of Alan G. Sachs, Junior, age two-point-eight years."

"Al," I said, getting upright and rubbing the sleep

from my eyes, "you're Jewish. You're not supposed to be naming your children after somebody still living. It's bad luck."

"Yeah, I know," said Al, "but Martha, she's Lutheran and my folks are all gone and I'll bet you've been to temple more than I have. Hey, remember that time in 'Nam, when you were going to some feast-day Mass to get out of being duty officer? I went to tag along and when the old man tried to stop me, you told him I was your technical advisor on the Old Testament readings." Al laughed for me. Kind of nervously, I thought.

"So what are you doing in Boston?"

"Making my fortune, John, making my fortune. I had a lotta luck with the Bs last night."

I had watched the game on television. "Al, you're crazy to bet on hockey in this town, even in favor of the Bruins."

Another nervous laugh. "Yeah, yeah, you're right. Listen, John-boy, I'm a manufacturer's rep now for Straun Steel. They're a Pittsburgh outfit that fabricates little steel gizmos for building construction, and I gotta go, I got an eight-fifteen appointment at a job site. Listen, whatsay we roll for drinks and dinner tonight, maybe eight-thirty, nine o'clock?"

"Where are you staying?"

"A place called the Midtown Motor Inn. On Hunterton Avenue."

"That's Hunt*ing*ton Avenue, Al. Also, it's a Tuesday, and Boston tends to close down early during the week. Want to make it seven?"

A quick cough and again that nervous edge in his voice. "No, no, can't. Got another appointment. Can you swing by my motel at eight-thirty?"

"Sure, Al, I'll see you then."

"Oh, and John?"

"Yeah?"

"Remember 13 Rue Madeleine." He hung up.

13 Rue Madeleine. As I put down the receiver, memories of Al bubbled back to me. The best, if also the oddest, guy I knew from the service. We went through military police training together. Not an altogether easy time. The Jew from CCNY and the Harp from Holy Cross. Tossed in with fifty or so Ivy Leaguers, West Pointers, and Old South military school graduates. At first, Al and I were more ignored than actively hated. Then we started to win a couple of friends by sheer force of personality, in which many of our classmates were sorely lacking. Our newfound acceptance wore thin on some hardliners who picked a fight with me one day in the TV lounge of the bachelor officers' quarters. I had decked a Yalie when a Virginia lad, who I later found out had prepped with the Yalie, swung a chair ungentlemanly close to the back of my head. The Virginian missed because Al had clouted him on the upper arm with the edge of his hand, thereby breaking a bone above the swinger's elbow. The battle was joined, as they say, with a West Pointer named J. T. Kivens siding with us. The real MPs eventually arrived, and the official box score went Yale/Virginia. Al, J.T., and I eventually found ourselves as street MP officers in Saigon. I heard that Yale and Virginia ended up guarding VIPs in some appropriately front-page battle sectors and conferences.

Al and J.T. had preceded me to Saigon by about eight weeks. Al was billeted in a former hotel converted into a bachelor officers' quarters. The connecting bedroom shared his bath and was available, so I moved in.

Beth and I weren't married then, and Al and I did our best to keep each other alive and sane. When we got back from the service, he was terrific about staying in touch. When we didn't reciprocate his happy-holiday card the year Beth died, he called me. He must have called every few weeks after that. He also called me after Empire Insurance fired me for refusing to falsify a jewelry claim, after I started to sink into the bottle, and again after I began to pull myself back out with my own private detective business. Then I stopped hearing from him, which I now realized I found surprising.

Al. He was the oddest guy I knew because you could never figure him out. One day he ran around literally putting tacks on everyone's chairs. When I asked him why, he said it was something he suddenly remembered he had wanted to do since grade school. Another time, on an R-and-R in Hawaii, he spent fully two and a half hours of our precious time going through a Honolulu telephone directory looking up the names of his CCNY classmates just in case one might have moved six thousand miles southwest. A third time, in Saigon, he broke down crying at the sight of a bunch of street orphans in rags because he said they were posed like a photograph he had seen of the starving Jewish defenders of the Warsaw ghetto.

But *13 Rue Madeleine*. An old World War II movie with Jimmy Cagney. Contrary to popular belief, we did not always get first-run (or even second-run) films in Vietnam. One night Al and I saw it. I remembered Cagney as an American secret agent caught by the Nazis in Europe and tortured for information. They were going to just dump him on the road as though he had been hit by a car or mugged. Cagney has the last laugh, though, because intelligence that he relayed out before his capture results in an Allied bombing raid that destroys the German headquarters in which he is being held.

After the movie, Al and I were drinking back in his room. Al said to me, "John-boy, if I'm ever captured by the other side, like Cagney was, and I figure they're going to fake my death, like an accident, you know, what I'll do is break my little finger, and then you'll know I was killed by them."

"Christ, Al," I replied, "what other side is going to be interested in a pissy-ass MP lieutenant like you who doesn't even deal with combat intelligence?"

Al went on as though he hadn't heard me. "Yup, I'll break my little finger so you'll know, and then you'll go after them for me like I'd go after them for you. To square things."

"What the hell are you talking about?"

"Evening things up. A repayment for all we've been through together. I get them if they get you, you get them if they get me. See?"

I told him I saw. I changed the subject, and I could not remember it coming up again.

Till his phone call.

Two

I HAD TO TESTIFY AT THE D'AMICO TRIAL THE MORNING that Al called me, so I did my best to push our dinner out of my mind. When Empire fired me, I was quickly blackballed in Boston insurance circles. Then I received some pretty good press from a case I worked on involving a judge and his missing son. Thereafter, a few heads of claims investigation began to call me for special assignments.

About six months ago, a worried fire and casualty company contacted me. They had been tipped that one of their insureds had hired an arsonist to torch a warehouse containing obsolete merchandise. The only problem was they did not know when. The Boston arson squad is professional but limited in personnel. It simply cannot stake out indefinitely a building where one act of arson might occur, while being crucified by the media for not nailing the perpetrators of twenty definite arsons that have occurred. Accordingly, the company asked me to watch the warehouse from 8 P.M. to 4 A.M., the most likely arson period.

Since the warehouse owner, one Harvey Weeks, obviously could not be let in on the surveillance, I checked through the neighborhood until I found a nice elderly couple whose house backed on an empty lot behind the warehouse. I was frank with them, and they swore that they would not tell anyone why I was there. Their name was Cooper. Jesse was black, Emily was white. They came north from Alabama to escape racist remarks, slashed tires, and occasional beatings. I suppressed a desire to ask if things proved better for them in Boston. They hated violence of any kind, and they agreed to let me use one of their closed-off back bedrooms that faced the warehouse grounds. It wasn't perfect, but no one observer can watch all four sides of a building except while hovering in a helicopter above it. The Coopers insisted on leaving me food and fixing the old daybed in the room. I goosed the head of claims investigation for twenty dollars more per week than he wanted to spend on them.

The first seven nights passed without incident. The arson squad had run a discreet check on the nightwatchman. His name was Craigie. He was seventy-one, nearsighted, and straight as an arrow. With my binoculars, I could see him outlined in the reflection of his battery lantern, the warehouse owner being too cheap to use floodlighting. Craigie was as punctual as a steeple clock, and I began to feel that I knew him as well as I knew the Coopers.

My hosts extended their bedtime so they could have tea with me before I went upstairs. They both wore cardigans off the 2-for-$5 rack at Zayre's. Jesse was one of the first black marines in combat in World War II, losing most of one hand to a Japanese grenade. Emily had retired from teaching fourth grade in a non-Catholic parochial school. The whole time we talked, rarely more than twenty minutes a night, Emily would hold Jesse's good hand. I did my best not to think about the times Beth and I had kidded about what we would be like when we grew old.

On the eighth night, Craigie made his nine, ten, and eleven o'clock circuits, lantern bobbing. No lantern at 12:00, or 12:05, or 12:10. At 12:15, I was dropping over the security fence at the back of the warehouse. I had a highbeam penlight in my hip pocket, and a .38 Smith & Wesson Combat Masterpiece in my right hand. I followed the perimeter of the warehouse until I found a window ajar. The owner was no more lavish on alarm systems than he was on searchlights. I edged the window up and stepped through, into the warehouse. I tried to slide the window back down, but at the first squeak I stopped. While my eyes were adjusting to the darkness, my ears picked up a soft, flapping noise above the industrial hum all large buildings, however vacant, produce. The flapping sound grew closer, the sound of running feet.

He might have had me if he hadn't tripped over a wooden pallet some forklift operator had failed to stack. He cursed and stumbled just as my adjusting eyes picked him up, fifty feet to my left.

"Freeze!" I yelled, dropping to one knee.

He said something as he let fly two quick shots. In the quiet darkness of the warehouse, the firing sounded and looked like atomic bombs launched by a flamethrower. One slug thumped harmlessly into a bale of something three feet from me. The second ricocheted two or three times, whining crazily through the dead air above our heads.

I pulled the trigger of the already cocked weapon. I cocked and fired again before his scream from the first registered on my ears. I thought I heard the skittering clatter of a lost weapon, too. Just to be sure, though, I circled around and came in on him from ninety degrees off where I had fired.

He was curled like a fetus on the cold floor, rocking side to side with his left hand high on his right shoulder, and his right hand on his thigh. He was moaning, "Jesus, Jesus." I flicked on my penlight and caught the dark outline of his revolver ten feet away from him.

I moved over to him and held my weapon against his temple while I quickly and unfruitfully patted him down. He was bleeding freely from both wounds.

"Where's Craigie?" I asked.

"What the fuck are you talkin' about?" he said.

I shined my penlight into his face. He was thirtyish, heavy features, curly black hair.

"The nightwatchman, where is he?"

"Man, get me to a fuckin' hospital!" he yelled.

I put the ball of my right foot onto his wounded shoulder and pressed about as much as you would to ease forward twenty feet in bumper-to-bumper traffic. The lump on the floor emitted a nerve-curdling scream and flopped left to right like a gill-hooked sunnie.

"You tell me where the nightwatchman is or I'm the only surgeon you'll ever see."

"Oh sweet shitting Jesus, man, he's in the back, in the back!"

I took off for the back, scoffing up the torch's weapon on the way. I got sixty or seventy feet when a wall of flame whipped up in front of me. I jumped back, lost my balance, and went down in a heap on my left elbow. It was bruised but not broken. By the time

I got up, the flames were three feet closer and impenetrable.

"Craigie," I yelled, "Craigie, can you hear me? Craigie?"

It was like asking after coal pitched into a furnace.

I walked back toward the torch, rubbing my left elbow.

"Christ, get me outta here. Get me out!" He was yelling before he could have heard me coming. "Mother of God, sweet Mary, get me out, get me out!"

I grabbed him by the left arm and yanked him over to face me. Although it was barely forty degrees outside, and not much warmer inside when I had entered, the sweat from my fire-sided forehead was pouring down my nose and into my eyes.

"Who, fire man," I asked the lump. "Who paid the price for this one?"

"What's wrong with you, man? Get me outta this place. Please God, fuckin' Jesus, get me out!"

"You're talkin' like a baked potato, fire man," I said softly. I looked behind me, then grabbed his hair and twisted his head to assure him the same perspective. "That flame looks twenty, maybe thirty feet closer than it was the first time I asked the question. You can't outrun it, fire man. Now who was it paid your price?"

Lump's face was contorting. I've yet to meet a torch who wasn't scared blind, and rightly so, of uncontrolled flames. "The owner. The bastard owner. Weeks. Harvey fuckin' Weeks! For God's sake, man, get me out, get me out!"

I dragged him by the bad arm till the screaming,

actually one long scream, stopped. Then I slung him over my shoulder and headed for the window. The Coopers must have heard me going down their stairs, because the first lonely siren hit my ears just as I shoved him through the window.

The lump's name turned out to be Joseph D'Amico. I attended his bail hearing three days after the fire, Joseph himself being under guard in a hospital room. His lawyer's name was Thomas Smolina, a short, fiftyish man in a blue polyester suit that affected a Glen plaid. The lawyer was trying to persuade Judge Harry J. Elam, then chief justice of the Boston Municipal Court, that his "Joey" should be released on $20,000 bail, cash equivalent. The "cash equivalent" part meant that instead of a bail bondsman putting up $20,000 for a nonrefundable premium of $2,000, the D'Amico family, arrayed in the first row of the courtroom, could put up two thousand cash themselves, thus saving the bailbond premium so long as Joey showed up at the trial. Smolina argued that the D'Amico family, solid citizens of Boston for thirty-nine years, provided the sort of stable base that would ensure that his client would attend the trial. Lawyer ticked off each family member, who stood up and nodded to the judge as his or her name was mentioned. Smolina reached Joey's brother, Marco, a man about my size and build in a black turtleneck. Marco nodded and then, as he sat back down, swiveled his head to glare at me. I smiled politely and thought that Joey's lawyer should have screened Marco from the family portrait presented to the judge.

Judge Elam thanked Smolina and turned to the assistant district attorney. She stood and began speaking without needing to identify herself. She pointed out the defendant's track record of four missed trials, one for armed robbery, one for arson. She mentioned Craigie's blackened and cottony body, escalating the expected indictments to felony/murder. She also mentioned codefendant Harvey Weeks' suicide attempt upon hearing the police come knocking at his door. She felt $250,000, no cash equivalent, was more appropriate. In the front row, Mother D'Amico began to whimper, none too softly. Marco put his arm around her shoulders and pulled her close to him, none too gently.

Judge Elam asked Smolina if he had anything to add. "He's not a bad boy, your honor. And he's from a good family," said lawyer, gesturing with a sweep of his hand that reluctantly included Marco.

Judge Elam set bail at $250,000, no cash equivalent.

I wanted to speak briefly with the assistant district attorney, who had in front of her three or four more manila files to deal with that morning. I stayed seated and debated waiting for her to finish. The D'Amicos, lawyer in lead, came down the middle aisle. Father D'Amico was consoling his wife, Marco hanging back a bit. As Marco pulled even with my row, he paused and leaned over to me. He muttered, "If I was you, I'd have somebody else start my car for me," and then continued on.

I decided I would wait to speak with the assistant district attorney.

She was about 5-foot-8, slim in a two-piece, skirt-and-jacket, gray suit. She had long black hair pulled into a bun. From where I sat in the courtroom, I could see her face only in partial profile. She handled two more bail disputes and a short probable-cause hearing before the luncheon recess. Everyone stood as Judge Elam left the bench. As she reached my row, I fell in beside her.

"My name's John Cuddy," I said, "and I'd like to buy you lunch."

She looked up at me, then down at her watch. "Nancy Meagher. I've got twenty-five minutes and I brought a sandwich."

"Can I have half? Or both?"

We stopped and she smiled. "You're the PI who shot D'Amico, right?"

"That's right."

"Shame about your second bullet."

"You've been reading about me."

"Yes. And wondering how much pressure you had to apply to pal Joey to get him to admit Weeks hired him."

"It was within constitutionally permissible limits."

She glanced down at her wrist. "I now have twenty-four minutes but still a whole sandwich. Halfsies still O.K.?"

"You bet," I said.

We sat in her shared cubicle. Her officemate was out.

"Don't superior court prosecutors usually cover bail hearings in heavy cases?" I asked.

"Usually," she replied, neatly tamping a bit of errant tuna into a gap in the corner of her mouth. "But I've been here nine months, and I'm good." She smiled without showing her teeth. An open, Irish maiden face, with widely set, soft blue eyes and a straight slim nose. A smattering of freckles that would reach epidemic proportions with summer's sun. As a girl, she must have been cute. As a woman, she was damned attractive. I felt a little glow.

"Good tuna," I said.

She wiped her mouth with a patterned paper napkin from home and pitched it into a wastebasket.

"What's on your mind, Mr. Cuddy?"

I had no napkin so I used my handkerchief. "D'Amico. More precisely, brother Marco. Syndicate?"

She shook her head. "Peripherally, at most. He's a numb-nuts, maybe some high school friends who are approaching 'management level,' but no established contacts. Why?"

"A couple helped me out indirectly in busting Joey. I don't want Marco to pick up their scent to square things, and I wanted to know his likely troop strength."

"What makes you think Marco would do something?"

I reviewed his general appearance and repeated his comment to me in the courtroom.

"Hmmm. I'd say the Coopers could be in trouble."

I lurched forward in my seat. "I never gave their name to the investigating officer. How did you know it?"

She rummaged through a file and handed me a police report. "Seems the Coopers gave their name to the fire department when they called in the flames, and the fire captain mentioned it to the cop who arrived on the scene."

I read Jesse and Emily's name, address, and telephone number from the last paragraph of the report. "Damn," I said. "I assume the D'Amico lawyer has a copy of this?"

"Got one the first night at the arresting station, as soon as he identified himself as Joey's attorney. Per office procedure."

"Maybe I should have a talk with Marco," I said.

She cleared her throat. "Let me be official, Mr. Cuddy. You go shaking down Marco, and it will weaken you as a witness for the prosecution. I don't want Joey's case riding on old Weeks' 'I hired him' testimony."

"And unofficially?" I asked.

She smiled, using her teeth this time. Nice, even teeth. "Unofficially, mightn't you be giving Marco ideas he hasn't stumbled on himself yet, since he seems to view you as enemy number one-and-only right now?"

I considered it. "I'm not sure you're right, Ms. Meagher. But yours is the better percentage right now." I stood up. "Thanks for lunch."

She stayed seated. "You're from Southie originally, right?"

South Boston is an old Irish/Italian neighborhood of brick and wood three-deckers just past the South Station train terminus. Beth and I both grew up there.

"That's right," I said.

"Me, too," she replied. "In fact, I still live there. On Fourth Street, number 746." She smiled. "Third floor."

I cleared my throat. "I still don't deal with this

gracefully," I said, "but I was married a long time and then widowed. I'm still not . . . well . . . ready. . . ."

Nancy blinked a few times and stood up. "I think that's the most graceful 'Thanks anyway' I've ever heard." She gave my right arm a quick squeeze. "But keep me in mind, O.K.?"

"O.K." I squeezed back and left.

Three

As I sat outside trial courtroom 924, my mind kept skipping from the night of the fire to how much I was looking forward to seeing Nancy Meagher again. We had not met since the bail hearing, although she called me once a few weeks ago to review my version of what happened. Over the telephone, her voice sounded softer than I remembered, and she had advanced to the DA's Superior Court office. She was assisting the head of the homicide division in prosecuting Joey D'Amico, who so far had refused to cop a plea.

I had not seen Joey either, not since the night at the warehouse. I did see Marco two days after the bail hearing, through the lens of my Pentax K1000 as I sat in a rental car outside the D'Amico house on Hanover Street. I brought the photos to the Coopers with the insurance company's final check for their help. I told Jesse and Emily over tea and cookies that they were to call me if they ever saw Marco anywhere around them or their house. They promised they would, but I called them several times in the intervening months just to be sure. No Marco.

A long-fingered freckled hand gave my arm a squeeze as Nancy settled in beside me on the bench.

"What are you in for?" she asked with, I swear, a twinkle in her eye.

"The vice squad caught me doing funny things with turtles."

She laughed, a deep throaty laugh. "Lucky turtles."

I shook my head and turned to business. "How does it look?"

She glanced around to be sure no one she knew was within earshot. "Frankly, it couldn't look better for us. We've got your contact at the insurance company to lead off with the surrounding circumstances, Weeks to describe the 'contract,' you to put Joey in the warehouse with his statements and Craigie alive shortly before, and a lab man who took specimens off the butt of Joey's gun that match Craigie's blood type and color hair."

I considered her summary. "Why no plea?"

Her turn to shake the head. "Makes no sense to me. Speaking professional to professional, Joey's lawyer is a hack. Very little pretrial stuff, at which Joey could have testified to try to suppress his statements to you under any number of theories. With his record, Joey doesn't dare testify at trial because we'd nail him to the cross with his prior convictions."

"Maybe they figure the deal from your side might be better if they push you to the verge of trial?"

"Maybe, but we're not going to be very generous on this one."

I became aware of people shuffling their feet a little distance away from us, and I turned to look at them. The Coopers. In their Sunday best and scared.

I whipped my head back to Nancy. "Did you call them?"

She turned the way I had. "No, who are . . . oh, the Coopers, huh?"

I nodded.

"Must have been D'Amico's lawyer, though what help they'll be . . ."

"I'm going to calm them down. See you inside."

"You've got some time. You're witness number three, right after Weeks."

I went up to the Coopers and took Emily's outstretched hand. She mustered a smile.

"Why are you here?"

Jesse produced a paper from his inside jacket pocket and unfolded it carefully. "We got this. Last night. It was late, so we didn't want to call you."

It was a subpoena. The signature of the issuing notary public was illegible, but it looked to be in proper form.

"A surly man in a porkpie hat brought it," said Emily. "Along with this." She held open an envelope with some currency in it.

"That's your witness fee, Emily," I said. "You can keep that."

Jesse's hands shook as he refolded the subpoena. "What do they want us for?"

"I don't know," I said as the court officer, uniformed and side-armed, boomed, "Trial session, trial session, court coming in."

I guided the Coopers into the courtroom.

We sat on the left-hand side of the middle aisle, halfway back. On our side of the courtroom was the prosecutor's table, near the as-yet empty jury box. Nancy and a tall, fiftyish man with red-gray hair were conferring. The D'Amico family sat on the right-hand side of the aisle, several rows in front of us but still behind the defense table, at which Smolina sat scribbling on a legal pad. Friend of the Bride, Friend of the Groom.

A clerk of court was shuffling papers in front of the bench, and a stenographer was assembling her miniature transcriber to his right. A side door opened, and two court officers brought in a cuffed Joey D'Amico. He wore a dark blue suit, white shirt, and dark tie. He'd had a haircut but looked pale as a ghost after his six months in jail.

The officers led him to the defense table, unshackled him, and took up positions to his right and behind. At least his lawyer had had sense enough to move that his client not be seated in the dock. The dock is a square, isolated, and elevated box which some say gives jurors a pejorative impression of the dangerousness of the defendant whose fate they decide.

The judge was announced and entered from a different side door. I did not recognize him, but he was about sixty, white-haired, and judgelike. D'Amico's case was called by the clerk. Nancy, her compatriot (who did not introduce himself), and Smolina approached the bench and exchanged preliminaries. The judge asked for witness lists. Nancy handed the prosecution's to the clerk. Smolina, looking perplexed, excused himself and scurried back to his table. He began flipping nervously through his file. Joey looked back at Marco, whose head was down and shaking left to right. Smolina closed his file, apologized to the judge, and said that his only witnesses would be several members of the D'Amico family and "Jerry" and "Emma" Cooper. The judge lectured

Smolina on the need for full names and addresses now so they could be read to the jury during selection. Smolina said of course, of course but . . .

At which point Marco stood up and said, "Judge, if it'll help, I can give you everybody's name and address."

The judge was off-balance for a moment, then said, "Who are you?"

"I'm Marco D'Amico, the defendant's brother, and I live at 767 Hanover Street, North End." Marco went on to list his other family and a priest, speaking the names and addresses slowly enough for the clerk to transcribe them. Marco concluded by saying, "And by the way, the first names of the Coopers are Jesse and Emily and they live at 230 Beech Street, Dorchester."

I felt Emily tense and shudder beside me as we all realized Marco had their names and address memorized. When Marco finished, the judge thanked him and told Smolina he should be as prepared as his witnesses. As Marco sat back down, he turned his head toward us and smiled unpleasantly. I could sense Jesse and Emily grasping each other's hands a little harder. I was thinking of Marco's throat.

The trial, or more accurately Smolina's attempted defense, was laughable. The jury was picked within twenty minutes, Smolina forgetting which side got to challenge prospective jurors first. Nancy's superior, whose name was McClean, made an opening statement that persuaded half the jurors without seeming to press them. Smolina waived an opening, and several jurors looked at each other with surprise. McClean presented my contact, who barely arrived in time, and Smolina asked him no questions.

McClean then put on Harvey Weeks, a miserable, flabby man, with a bald head and horn-rimmed glasses. Weeks described his retention of Joey. Smolina objected a few times, unsuccessfully. Then Smolina cross-examined Weeks, with McClean objecting frequently and usually successfully. The judge even began to suggest questions to Smolina ("Mr. Smolina, why don't you ask him . . .") to try to move the case along. Smolina's thrust seemed to be toward getting Weeks to say he'd hired someone other than Joey.

When Weeks left the stand, I was called. I told my story in response to McClean's nicely paced questions. I'd had a year of evening division law school, and I'd been in a lot of courtrooms for Empire, but McClean was the best I'd ever seen. Why he was taking something around forty thousand from the DA instead of four or five times that from a downtown civil litigation firm was beyond me.

When Smolina began his cross-examination, the defense "strategy" began to unfold. He was trying to create the impression that I was the arsonist Weeks had hired, and that D'Amico had been in the neighborhood, seen the open window and gone in to investigate, only to be framed by me. Instead of objecting, McClean let Smolina go on, and I sensed that the jury was nearly as incredulous as I was.

After Smolina finished, McClean on redirect asked me one question. "Have you ever been convicted of a crime, Mr. Cuddy?"

I said, "No."

"Thank you," McClean said, smiling at Smolina, "no further questions."

After I left the stand, the police lab expert testified. As he described the blood-and-hair evidence, I tried to sort out McClean's strategy. I guessed that McClean felt Smolina's version of the arson plot held no hope unless Joey confirmed it. If Joey testified, however, McClean would impeach him with his prior convictions and then argue "Who should you believe" to the jury.

Smolina declined cross-examination of the lab expert and the judge called luncheon recess. The Coopers and I went across the courtyard to a stand-up place. The Coopers wanted only coffee. As I ate a sandwich, I turned the case over and over in my mind. I couldn't see any way out for Joey.

Neither, apparently, could the jury. After lunch, the defense presented only family and priest as character witnesses, no Joey or Coopers. McClean waived cross-examination, and both attorneys made closing arguments. The case actually went to the jury that afternoon, and a guilty verdict was returned within an hour.

After the jury went into deliberation, I offered to drive the Coopers home, but they said they wanted to stay for the verdict, that they felt they should. After the verdict, I offered again, but they resisted because of the traffic I would hit. I insisted, and they still refused. I was half glad they did, because as Emily kissed my cheek and Jesse shook my hand, I wanted to speak with Nancy Meagher.

A courtroom when a judge has left the bench is like a bus stop at a madhouse. Joey had started crying after the verdict and was now nearly hysterical as the two officers recuffed him. Marco was calling Smolina an asshole, and a third officer was telling Marco to take it outside. Joey's mother was wailing into a hankie and rocking back and forth in the embrace of her husband.

I was almost to Nancy Meagher when Marco finished his piece and stormed out of the courtroom. I doubt he noticed me. I decided to follow him, though, to be sure the Coopers had gotten enough of a start. They hadn't.

As I came out of the courtroom door, Marco was near the elevators. He had Jesse by the jacket front, pushing him against the wall and yelling "nigger" at him and "whore" at Emily. Six or eight people were standing around. Marco looked pretty imposing, and nobody helped.

I came up behind Marco and said, "Take your hand off his jacket or I'll take your hand off your arm."

Marco slammed Jesse against the wall and came for me. He swung a roundhouse right at my head. I stepped under and slightly outside of it, whipping my right elbow forward and up into his right-hand rib cage. I stepped again, this time past him, slamming the edge of my right hand just above his right kidney.

He gave a strangled cry and sank to his knees, both hands trying to feel all his right side, front and back, at once.

I figured I had very little time before the authorities would arrive, so I leaned over Marco. I pulled him by his hair up to communion level on his knees, and said between my teeth, "If you so much as look cross-eyed at these folks again, your family loses its other son."

I felt a hand on my arm. It was Nancy. A growing crowd of onlookers began to encircle us. A burly court officer bustled up behind her with his hand on the butt of his still-holstered revolver.

I let go of Marco, and Nancy said over her shoulder, "It's all right, Frank. I saw it. Self-defense." Frank nodded and began gesturing calmly, dispersing the crowd.

I thanked Nancy, who asked Jesse and Emily if they wished to press charges. They didn't. I told the Coopers I was driving them home. They offered no arguments this time.

I saw the Coopers locked up tight at their house. Jesse assured me he had a shotgun and would use it if necessary. Emily said she would be sure to call me if they saw Marco.

I got back into my car, a '73 Fiat 124 sport sedan, my '63 Renault Caravelle finally having blown an unobtainable part. It was only 5:45, and Al had told me 8:30. Between testifying and Marco, my shirt was pitted out, so I drove back to my apartment, getting the first break of the day in the form of a parking space right out front. I walked up to my third floor one-bedroom and checked my telephone tape machine. Three hang-ups, no messages. I stripped and did push-ups, sit-ups, and other exercises for an hour.

I showered and had a hunk of Vienna bread and Gouda cheese to quell my growing appetite. I washed it down with the first of many screwdrivers that night. I listened to a side of Rachmaninoff with another drink. I finally pulled on a blue shirt, burgundy sweater, and gray tweed sports coat with dark gray slacks.

At 8:00 I went downstairs and drove to the Midtown Motor Inn. I circled through the packed parking area and left my car on Huntington Avenue. I walked back to the Inn and spotted a college-aged kid in an ill-fitting, uniformlike orange blazer behind the front desk.

"Good evening, sir. May I help you?"

"Yes. Could you buzz Mr. Sachs' room and tell him Mr. Cuddy is here?"

"Certainly." I thought the "certainly" was from a training manual and that the kid would have been more comfortable with "yeah, sure." In any case, he flipped through a View-dex card holder and picked up the telephone, dialing four digits. He waited ten seconds, then hung up and dialed again. He shook his head, hung up, and came back to me.

"I'm sorry, sir, but he doesn't answer."

I checked my watch. It was 8:20.

"Well," I said, "I'm a little early. Can I get a drink somewhere?"

"Certainly," again and gesturing, "Our lounge is right through there. Would you like me to leave a message for Mr. Sachs to join you?"

"If I could have a piece of paper."

"Certainly." He slid a message pad and Bic pen to me. I wrote, "If I had to wait for you, guess where?" I decided it sounded arch, so I crumpled it and wrote, "I'm in the bar." I folded it and gave it to the kid, who stuck it in a slot with 304 under it. I went past a bank of pay phones with swing-up directories and into the lounge.

It was dark and nearly empty. A pianist was playing gamely in a corner. A fortyish waitress in black mesh tights brought me a screwdriver. Two half-bagged jerks were hitting on a couple of secretaries with adventures centering around the wholesale hardware game in Wichita. Just as I was thinking of buying a newspaper, the barman turned the lights down another notch.

I was nearly finished with my second drink. My watch said 9:10. The secretaries had split, and the salesmen from Wichita began singing their version of "I Gotta Be Me." The piano player looked like he wished he had been born tone-deaf. I drained my glass, paid my check, and walked back to the lobby.

The same kid was on duty. When he saw me coming, he turned to look at the message box.

"I'm sorry, sir, but Mr. Sachs hasn't come back." I asked the kid to ring Al's room again. No answer.

I went to one of the pay phones and called my home number. I took the remote unit for my telephone tape machine from my jacket pocket and waited for my taped outgoing message to start at the other end. When I heard my own voice, I beeped the device once into the speaker of the phone and heard my machine rewind and play back. No messages. I beeped again to reset the machine and hung up.

I walked back to the kid and asked if he had a newspaper I could borrow. He handed me an evening *Globe,* which I read cover to cover while seated in an overly upholstered lobby chair. At 10:15, I got up and returned it to him.

"May I have your pad again, please?"

"Certainly."

I had been composing my message mentally for twenty minutes. "I trust your deal was big enough to justify crushing the spirit of your dearest friend." I signed it, "Your loyal servant, J. F. Cuddy, P.O.," for "pissed off." I wrote "10:15 P.M." under that, folded it, and asked the clerk to substitute it for the message in Al's box.

The clerk said he was sorry. I left the Midtown, gathered my car, drove home, and hit the sack. I didn't bother setting the alarm.

Four

I WOKE UP THE NEXT MORNING WITHOUT A HANGOVER. IT was light outside, and the clock said 9:20. I rolled over, realized I was slept out, and decided to jog the river. I clicked on the all-news radio station to see how many layers of warmth I would need.

". . . Maxwell canning the winning shot with twelve seconds left in regulation. Over to you, Marcie."

"Thank you, Tom. And repeating this morning's top stories, President Reagan warns the Soviets that arms limitation now depends on them, and the nude, mutilated body of an unidentified man is found on Beacon Hill."

She continued on about staying tuned for Greg Somebody and the weather, but I wasn't listening anymore. There was a little lump at the back of my throat and a tug in my stomach. No good reason to think the man was Al, despite the proximity of the body. The statistics were far the other way. But Al was Al, and Al always showed.

Short-circuiting an hour of internal argument, I picked up the telephone and dialed the Boston police.

* * *

Two fifteen-inch sphinxes crouch at the head of the staircase in that Boston City Hospital building. Down the stairs is a tomb of sorts, but not the grand, permanent kind their giant cousins guard in Egypt. No Pharaohs here, only transients.

We went down the stairs. A set of bright-red double doors led to an anteroom. A white-coated clerk behind a desk nodded to my companion, then returned to entering information from a clipboard onto file cards.

The anteroom was chilly, osmosis from the year-round frigidity of the next room beyond a second set of double doors. The wall tiles were a sickly, pastel green, the floor easily swabbed, single-sheet linoleum. I sat in a molded plastic chair. There was a fluorescent light blinking above me and a young homicide detective blinking across from me. His name was Daley, blue-eyed and sandy-haired. My watch said 11:30 A.M., and the eighteen or so hours he had been away from his bed were taking their toll.

We were waiting for Lieutenant Robert J. Murphy, who was in charge, to drive in from his home. I already had asked if I could see the body just for identification purposes, but Daley had said Murphy had left strict orders no one was to see the body without Murphy himself being present. So we waited.

For distraction's sake, I tried to remember why Murphy's name stuck in my mind. It was common enough and I had never met him, yet . . .

The swinging double doors boomed open and a heavyset black man blew through them. He had maybe ten years on me, I maybe two inches on him. "C'mon," he said to the morgue attendant and the two of us as we rose from our chairs.

"Lieutenant Murphy," said Daley to me as we trailed behind.

The body room itself was twenty degrees colder and snow-blind white. The walls were honeycombed with eighty or ninety slightly oversized file cabinet fronts. The attendant checked his clipboard, then approached one of the fronts. Shaking his head, he moved to the next and gripped the handle. He yanked down and out, stepping aside as the slab on its casters snicked smoothly outward at chest level.

I stifled an urge to grab for the drawer before it slid completely out of the wall and spilled its contents at our feet. An unseen brake, however, stopped it abruptly, the whole device vibrating with a soft metallic hum in the otherwise silent room.

Murphy and the attendant were on one side, Daley and I on the other. It was as though a headwaiter had led us to our table and no one wanted to be the first to sit.

Murphy spoke. "Pull the sheet to his knees." The attendant, with a too-often-practiced flourish, whipped the cover down. My eyes didn't quite focus, then they did and my head involuntarily jerked up and away. I realized I had been holding my breath, so I exhaled and forced my eyes downward again.

It was Al. Almost. He had less hair than I remembered, and more stomach, but those weren't the major changes. Whoever had done him had used a cigarette to burn his upper torso. There were burns showing also on his genitals, which had been slashed repeatedly, probably by a straight razor. The burns continued on his throat, lips, ears, and eyes. The eyelids had been burned away almost completely. I looked at his right hand. It seemed untouched. I couldn't see his left hand from where I was standing.

"Recognize him?" grunted Murphy.

I glanced up at him and came around the slab. "Yeah," I said, bumping rudely into him, "just barely."

The attendant backed away and Daley from behind clamped firmly on both my arms. I swung my head around as if to glare at Daley too, but I was mainly interested in Al's left hand. I caught an unmistakable frame of his left pinky finger. It was bent nearly 90 degrees toward the rest of the hand.

I looked back at Murphy. He wore a grim smile.

"Let's go," he said. Murphy wheeled and left the room. Daley released his grip, and we followed. I took an involuntary extra step as the slab slammed shut into the wall behind us. As we walked, I thought very carefully about how to handle Murphy.

When you decide not to tell the whole truth, it is far better to tell nearly the whole truth. It's easy to get tripped up in a series of lies, because sooner or later the interrogator will uncover one of them. So if you have something to hide, simply omit it, and otherwise tell the truth. I remembered that from MP interrogation training.

I also remembered why Murphy's name meant something to me. Some years ago, the word was that a city councilor had vowed never to see a black reach the grade of detective lieutenant. Oh, it was all right to have them in uniform, and strut them on appropriate holidays in the poorer, blacker neighborhoods. But a plain-clothes lieutenant, especially in homicide, never. Well, it seemed that some liberals had enough pull to get Robert J. Murphy's name on the lieutenant's list and to get it, because of the Irish last name, past the councilman's informal, backroom veto. At the promotion ceremony, said councilman hit the roof. He later saw to it that said Murphy was assigned to Beacon Hill, residential area of many liberals and rich folks, where said Murphy could fuck up royally in front of those who thought they knew more than the councilman. As it turned out, however, said Murphy knew his stuff, and said councilman was eventually defeated for reelection for a hundred other reasons.

Said Murphy now sat across from me, or, more accurately, I sat across his desk from him. A female detective named Cross had replaced the exhausted young Daley. Murphy didn't look exhausted, maybe because of his environment. His office was a degree or two colder than the morgue had been.

I repeated for Cross the background information of how I came to know Al Sachs, his phone call to me, and my futile visit to his hotel.

"You realize, Cuddy," said Murphy, "that this has all the characteristics of a gay killing, either a ritual or a psycho." It was not a question.

"I haven't seen Al for years," I replied, "but I am certain he wasn't gay. He had plenty of opportunities in Saigon, including me, and he never hinted at it."

Murphy sighed. "The medical examiner's preliminary actual cause of death, despite the mutilations, was smothering." Murphy flipped open a folder on his desk, scanned for a second, then read, "Probably a pillow impregnated with a chemical, tentatively identified as a men's cologne called Aramis." Murphy closed the folder. "A lot of gay men use Aramis."

I watched Murphy carefully. No hint of discrimination or distaste. Just a fact. Many Beacon Hill residents were gay. Murphy probably grew up in a neighborhood like I had, where a mere allusion toward homosexuality would cost a kid his teeth. Along the way he had learned to change, if not an attitude, at least the appearance of an attitude.

I shook my head. "No, the method of it is just a cover for something else."

"Like what?" said Murphy, quite reasonably.

"I don't know. I'd had only one call from the guy in the last year. I have no idea what reason somebody would have for singling him out."

His phone rang. "Homicide, Lieutenant Murphy speaking." Good telephone manner, an executive evaluator would say.

"Be right over. Nobody in or out. You included."

Murphy told Cross to get her coat. As she left the room, he grabbed his from a worn coat tree of indeterminable wood and said to me, "Uniforms have secured Sachs' hotel room. You wanna come?"

I thanked him and fell in behind him.

The three of us entered the lobby. A uniformed cop was flirting with an attractive blond desk clerk who stood in place of the kid I had dealt with last night.

"Keller," said Murphy, beckoning to the uniform. Keller trotted over to us.

"Yes, Lieutenant?"

"Which room?" asked Murphy.

"Three-oh-four." Keller gave me a once-over. "Mackey's guarding it."

"Come with us."

"Yessir."

"If you can be spared here," Murphy said.

"Yessir," said Keller. I couldn't tell if Keller had caught the sarcasm.

After two corridor turns, we reached Room 304. Another young uniform, a black man with a thin mustache, was standing four rooms down.

"Mackey," barked Murphy. Mackey trotted to us. I had the feeling that a lot of people trotted to Murphy. "What the hell are you doing down the hall?"

"You told us to secure 304, sir. From where I was, I could watch 304 and maybe someone would approach it, thinking I was doing something else."

A smile began on Murphy's lips before he banished it. I figured a small star would go next to Mackey's name in a ledger book somewhere.

"Fill us in," said Murphy to Mackey. Mackey stated they'd received the call from Murphy through the dispatcher to come here, arrived at 12:06 P.M., checked with the desk clerk, had her open the room. They peered inside, saw nothing striking, then relocked the door, Mackey remaining at the door, Keller returning to the desk with the clerk.

"Twelve-oh-six." Murphy turned to Keller. "Was that before or after the maid came?"

Keller swallowed and reddened. "I don't know."

Mackey interceded. "Lieutenant, the maid for this corridor saw me by the door. She said she had opened 304, looked in, and saw it hadn't been slept in, so she moved on."

Murphy nodded. "Cross, you and Keller go back to that clerk. Find out whether anybody else has been in or out of the room, and anything else about the room."

"Lieutenant?" I said.

"Yeah?"

"When I was here last night, a college-age boy was on desk duty. He'd probably started work in the afternoon. That means someone relieved him before the present clerk came on, unless clerks work twelve-hour shifts here. Maybe the names and even home addresses and telephones of all of them would be helpful."

"I would have gotten that information anyway," said Cross, a bit defensively.

"Fine," said Murphy. "Check on rent-a-car, too."

Cross and Keller started off down the hall. "O.K.," said Murphy, "take your shoes off." Mackey and I did so. Murphy pointed to the door, and Mackey keyed the lock and swung the door open. We looked in for maybe twenty seconds before Murphy led us into the room.

We strolled around, looking here and there without touching. Murphy took out a pencil and pushed the accordion doors of the closet open. A battered garment bag hung in there, nothing else.

I went into the bathroom. Toilet articles were spread out on the sink area. Funny how little a man's habits change over the years. I closed my eyes and pictured how our place in Saigon would look. I opened my eyes. Certain items outside of the toilet kit. Right Guard stick instead of Right Guard spray, but the same shaving cream. Twin-bladed floating head instead of the adjustable "track" razor. Toothbrush, toothpaste, mouthwash all the same.

Inside the kit . . . I could peer inside, without touching, because the kit was unzipped. I expect I frowned.

"Notice something?" said Murphy. I looked at me in the mirror as I turned my head left toward him.

"I don't know. Can I ask Mackey a question?"

"Sure. Mackey?"

Mackey's face appeared behind Murphy's.

"Mackey, did the maid say she left the room untouched or just that she didn't bother with the still-made bed?"

Mackey closed his eyes and answered with them shut. "I asked her, 'Had you cleaned the room?' She replied, 'No, the place hadn't been used, so I moved on to 302.' "

Murphy was staring at me. I spoke. "Can you find out if she touched anything in here today?"

Mackey looked at Murphy. Murphy nodded, and Mackey was off.

"Good cop," I said.

"He'll be better when he can repeat an exchange without having to keep his eyes shut. What's up?"

I sighed. "Maybe nothing, but when we lived together, he always kept the toilet kit zipped up."

Murphy looked at it. "When I was in the army, I did too. When I got home, I didn't bother."

"Like I said, maybe nothing."

He turned and went back into the main room. I leaned over the tub and looked up at the vent above the shower. There were some bright nicks around the screws holding it. I decided I would ask the hotel staff about recent maintenance myself.

We carefully opened drawers and looked under the bed. Mackey returned to report that the maid never even entered 304 that morning. Cross and Keller provided us with the names and addresses of the clerks and bellhops on duty. Cross also reported that Al had made the reservation at the Midtown eleven days earlier and had checked in at 11:30 A.M., Monday, the 22nd. The day before yesterday. He had stayed there Monday night, but apparently not Tuesday night. No one had seen him enter or leave on Tuesday. He had placed two long distance calls to Pittsburgh, presumably home and office, and two local calls, me and presumably a customer, early Tuesday morning.

"Was my message to him still in the box?" I asked.

"Yes." Cross handed it to Murphy. He glanced at it and gave it back to her.

Murphy told Mackey to lock and seal the room, Cross remaining to go through it with the lab technicians she had called from the desk.

"C'mon," Murphy said to me. It seemed to be one of his favorite phrases. We walked back through the lobby to his car.

"Unless the lab comes up with something, this one's going down as what it appears to be."

We were stopped at a light. I chose my answering words carefully, the autopsy I had just witnessed still vivid in my mind.

"I still don't see it that way, Lieutenant. Al wasn't gay."

"Maybe he'd gotten a little drunk." The light changed and we eased forward in the traffic that is a constant of Boston driving during all daylight hours. "He gets a little drunk, some guys talk about having a good time, he thinks combat zone bar or hookers, realizes the real scene a little too late. Maybe he gets insulting and somebody gets mad."

"First, Al was too smart and experienced not to recognize something like that. Second—" I was interrupted by Murphy's horn as a bread truck tried to slam us broadside. I started over. "Second, what was done to him is pretty extreme for somebody getting mad."

Murphy swung onto Boylston Street, bobbing his head. "Agreed. So what's your view of it?"

"I think he was tortured, the rest was red herring."

Murphy shot me a glance and nearly creamed a kid on a moped. "Goddamned things shouldn't be allowed in the city!" He snorted once. "You got any idea why a salesman for some outtatown steel outfit would be tortured?"

"None," I said, omitting Al's gambling remark.

We circumnavigated the Public Garden as we talked about notifying Al's wife. Murphy gladly let me take that.

The lieutenant turned down Charles Street to drop me off at my apartment. As we were pulling to a stop, he said, "Could it have anything to do with his left pinkie being broken?"

"His pinkie?" I said.

"Yeah," he said, giving a false, conspiratorial smile, "you know. The hand you were trying to look at when you bumped me with your indignation routine."

"I don't know."

The smile faded. "You just told me a lie, mister. One more lie in a murder investigation, and your license is just a memory. Dig?"

"Yes, sir. Thanks for letting me ride along."

"Be seeing you," said Murphy as I closed his door.

My primary goal had been to confirm for myself that Al's death was not what it seemed. The pinkie and the carefully tossed room did that. My secondary goal had been to give Murphy enough doubts to make him accept my eventual explanation. It was important for him to have only a little doubt now because I didn't want him investigating too deeply. Somehow I didn't think Murphy's and my view of squaring things would be equally extreme.

As I watched him pull away, however, I wondered if he wasn't a step ahead of me in the doubt department.

Five

THE TELEPHONE RANG AT THE OTHER END OF THE LINE. I glanced down at my watch. 4:35 P.M. A time of traffic tie-ups, Sesame Street, and kids' afternoon snacks. A mundane time of day to tell someone she's a widow.

The fourth ring was interrupted by an adult female voice. "Hello?"

"Hello, Martha?"

"Yes, who is this?"

There was a faint scratchiness on the line.

"Martha, it's John Cuddy, Al's friend from the army. From Boston."

"Oh, yes, John, so good to finally talk with you. Al said he was going to be seeing you. Is he with you now?"

"No, he's not." I took a chance. "Al told me you had a very close friend in your neighborhood," I lied, "but I forget her name."

"Oh, you mean Carol. Carol Emmer. I mean, Krause. Emmer was her married name." I could sense her thinking. She gave a little laugh. "John, are we setting up some sort of long-distance blind date?"

I clamped down hard on my jaw to retard the

gagging reflex. "I'm afraid not. Are you alone right now?"

Her pause on the other end told me she thought it was an odd question. "Yes, except for Al Junior, of course. He's napping. I was afraid the phone might have woken him up, but I don't hear him." A darkening. "John, what's the matter?"

"Martha, when I'm finished talking with you, I want you to call Carol right away, and ask her to come stay with you. . . ."

"Why?"

"Martha, Al is dead. Somebody killed him, here in Boston. I was with the police. . . ." But I was talking into a dead line. I hung up and dialed again. Busy. Twice. I called long-distance information.

Pittsburgh directory assistance had eight "C. Krauses" and three "C. Emmers." I explained the situation to the directory assistance operator, who said she could not help, but would switch me to a supervisor. As I waited for the connection, I cursed myself for not pursuing the blind date opening and getting Carol's number from Martha.

"Hello, Supervisor Seven speaking, may I help you?"

I re-explained the situation to Supervisor Seven. "I'm sorry," she replied, "but I cannot provide any information beyond that listed in the directory."

When you face that kind of answer, your options are several but limited. You can blow up and slam down the receiver. You can ask to go above that person's head, with the person usually poisoning his or her superior against you before you get to speak to the superior. Or you can try a different tack.

I decided to tack. "Look," I said, "my best friend from the service was killed here. I'm really concerned for his wife, widow, but I'm not about to send a police car to her home. Can you do this? Can you cross-check the addresses of the "C. Krauses" and "C. Emmers" against the address of "A. Sachs" and tell me which Krause or Emmer lives closest?"

I heard the supervisor speak to someone off the phone. The supervisor came back on. "If this is a test by Internal Operations, I will personally rip your dialing finger off."

I gave a little laugh. I had discovered a human being. "It isn't, and I really appreciate your help."

Twenty seconds or so passed before the supervisor came back on. "We show a C. Krause on the same street as A. Sachs, probably just a few houses away. Here's the number."

I took it down and thanked her again. I called the number and got a pick-up on the fifth ring.

"Hullo." The voice of a small boy.

"Can I speak to your mom?"

"She's at work."

"It's very important that I reach her. Can you give me her telephone number there?"

"No. Mom said never to give out that information." Click.

This time I chose option number one. I slammed down the receiver.

I kept trying Martha's line every fifteen minutes or so. Busy for two and a half hours. I finally got a ring through about eight o'clock.

"Sachs residence." It was a lilting male voice.

"May I speak with Martha Sachs, please?"

"I'm so sorry, but she can't come to the phone just now. Who is this please?"

"John Cuddy. If you're there, I take it you know about Al."

"Yes." There was a catch in his voice. "You're the bastard from Boston who gave her the news sledge-hammer style."

Before I could respond, I heard a brief muttered argument and another male voice came on. "Hello, Mr. Cuddy?"

I sighed. "Yes, who is this?"

"Dale Palmer. Please excuse Larry, we were all close friends and neighbors of Al, and . . ."

"That's all right. Forget it. Is Martha in shape to talk?"

"Ah, yes." He lowered his voice and said, "But I don't . . . When Carol—do you know Carol?"

"Only by name."

"Well, when Carol called from the lounge, she got me. Naturally, I rushed over, leaving a note for Larry. I've been with her, Martha that is, since five, and she hasn't shed a tear. She just keeps writing on a list."

"A list?"

"Yes. A list of things to do. About Al." He stifled a sob. "I tell you, it's like she was morosely planning a vacation. It's breaking my heart."

He sounded sincere, and I found myself clamping my jaw again. "Listen, Dale, I'll take care of claiming the body and transporting it to Pittsburgh. Is there a funeral home there Martha would want to use?"

"I don't know, but I'll find out."

"Good. How can I reach you?"

"Well, one of us, Larry or I, will be here until Carol, who's really Martha's best friend, gets off work. I'll give you our home number and Carol's, since I'll be either here, at Carol's watching her son, Kenny, or at home."

Dale sounded like he had an orderly mind and reeled off the numbers, one of which I already had.

"I'll call you when I have more information," I said.

"Thanks, Mr. Cuddy."

"John."

"John, thanks for your help and . . ."

"Forget it. He was my friend before he was yours."

"Good-bye."

I felt like having a good drink and a good cry. But I had a lot yet to do. I called a college classmate named George who had gone into the funeral business with his father. George said he would take care of the arrangements and call me with the details.

I then bundled up and headed back to the Midtown.

The same kid was behind the desk. Same blazer, same tie, too. I gave him the benefit of the doubt on shirt and underwear. He saw me coming and frowned.

"I wasn't quite straight with you last night, Mr. Bell," I said, using the first name Cross had mentioned. "I'm a detective. I was here this morning with Lieutenant Murphy and Detective Cross." Never tell a direct lie when a misleading truth carries you as far. "I assume she spoke with you today at home?"

"Yeah," he said. "My landlord didn't appreciate cops coming looking for me."

"I'm sorry, but we are talking murder here."

"I know that."

"Listen," I said, "Cross is on kind of a probationary period. I'm supposed to find out if she asked you certain questions. It's like a check-up on her detecting ability. I didn't want to disturb you at home, so I thought I'd drop by here when I figured you wouldn't be too busy."

"Well," he said, buying it, "she asked me a hell of a lot of questions. I sure wouldn't remember all of them."

"Did she ask you how long you were working last night?"

"Yeah."

"And what was your answer?"

"Same as I always work. It's a school-year job. I work four P.M. to twelve, Monday through Thursday."

"Did she ask you if anyone else asked for Mr. Sachs or his room number?"

"Yeah."

"And what was your answer?"

"I told her no." He cocked his head at me. "How come you need my answers, anyways?"

Sharp kid, Bell. "Well, unless I know what answer you gave to Question A, I won't know whether her Question B was a good one."

"You sound like one of my professors." He smiled. "Except you make more sense."

I laughed at his joke. "Thanks."

We continued through everything else I could think of, including whether any maintenance work had been done recently on Room 304 (no) and whether anything else odd had happened that night (no, again).

"Lastly," I said, "did she ask who followed you at midnight?"

"No, she already knew that."

I called back the other name Cross had mentioned yesterday.

"Teevens? Douglas Teevens?"

"Yeah. He'll be in tonight."

"Good," I said. I nodded to the bar. "Let me know when he comes in."

He nodded and said, "Well?"

I looked at him. "Well, what?"

"Well, did she pass?"

"Pass? Oh, Cross, yeah, she did just fine."

"I'm glad," said the kid. "She was angry about something when she talked to me, but I got the impression it wasn't me she was angry at."

"Yeah," I said, and hoped Cross never found out about her probationary check-up.

Bell looked in the cocktail lounge and gestured that Teevens was here. My watch said 12:05 A.M., and I had nursed three screwdrivers for the past three hours. The place had been quiet, the salesmen from Wichita apparently taking their revue on the road.

Teevens was a carbon copy of Bell, though Teevens' jacket fit a little better. Bell was already gone, so I used the same ploy to warm up his successor. It worked again, Teevens allowing me to take him through Cross' interrogation of him.

"Now, did she ask you if anything unusual happened during your shift?"

Teevens frowned a minute. "No, I don't think so. I think she just asked me if anybody asked for Mr. Sachs or Room 304."

I paused. Maybe Cross should still be on probation. "Well," I said, "did anything unusual happen?"

"No . . . unless . . ."

"Yes?"

"Well . . . it wasn't really unusual."

"Why don't you explain it to me."

"O.K. You see, the lounge closes at two, and so around two-thirty, Milt, he's the bartender, usually calls me in to check his dollar count against his cash register tape. It's kind of unnecessary, you know, since the tape is always checked against his cash pouch anyways. But it's a hotel rule, so we do it. It was maybe two-fifteen when a guy comes into the lobby. He smiles at me and goes into the lounge, then comes out again and says the bartender wants to see me. I figured the guy had wanted a drink and saw the lounge was closed. Also, it was an awfully slow night, so I figured that maybe Milt had his count done and wanted to leave early. So I thanked the guy and walked into the bar. I didn't see Milt right away because he was squatting down counting liquor bottles or something. He said he hadn't asked any guy to get me. In fact, he hadn't even seen anybody. I walked back out and the guy was gone. That's it."

I had a sinking feeling but quelled it. "Can you describe this guy?"

He closed his eyes and opened them again. "I didn't pay too much attention, you know. I mean it isn't so unusual for Milt to ask somebody to get me or tell me something. The guy was short, maybe five-six or five-seven, with a hat, glasses, I think."

"Color hair?"

"Don't know with the hat and all."

"And all?"

"Well, he had on a raincoat with the collar up. You really couldn't see much of him."

"Color raincoat?"

"Trenchcoat type, you know."

"Color eyes?"

"Didn't notice."

"Mustache, beard?"

"Don't remember one, but he could have. Honest, I really didn't pay much attention."

I nodded. He continued, "Is this gonna get the woman detective in trouble?"

"No, no," I said, "I doubt if it's related at all to what she was doing." I resurrected my unsettling thought. "One thing, though."

"Yeah?"

"Would this guy have had time, while you were in the bar, to go through anything at the desk here?"

"Actually, I thought of that and checked around. Everything was still here."

"Yes," I said patiently, "but would he have had time to look at the register, that sort of thing?"

"Well, we don't have a register exactly, we use cards and put them in this View-dex thing. But, yeah, he would have had ten or twenty seconds to look at something before I got back. Course he would have had to use some of that to take off."

"Right," I said and thanked him. As I walked out to my car, I kept glancing around. If I had killed the man in 304 earlier that evening, I would have had his hotel key, and I damn well would have wanted to check his room for any trace that could lead the cops to me. I also would have wanted to read the pink message slip in his mail box. You know, the slip with the name "J. F. Cuddy" on it. The slip implying that the man who had to be killed for some reason had spoken with Cuddy earlier that day. Shit and double shit.

Six

I GOT HOME FROM THE MIDTOWN ABOUT 1:15 A.M. I played back the telephone tape machine in case anything had happened in Pittsburgh. Dale Palmer's voice read the name and address of a no-rip-off, nondenominational funeral home to me and then said Carol would be with Martha all night. Next came George's voice, asking me to call him at home or at work for the details on transporting Al's body. Last came Jesse Cooper, asking me to call. I checked my watch. If I called Jesse and Emily at 1:27 A.M., I would scare them more than Marco had. I set my alarm for 7:00 A.M. and fell into bed.

The next morning, I got up with the alarm. Don Kent on WBZ radio said it was 28 degrees. I laced up my running shoes, did ten minutes of warm-ups, and then pulled on a sweater, sweatshirt, and sweatpants. I tugged a black watchcap over my ears and had my hand on the door when I remembered my talk with the second desk clerk the night before. I pulled the left leg of the elastic-ankled sweatpants up over my knee and jerry-rigged a calf-holster for my .38 Smith & Wesson Chief's Special. The butt of the small revolver hung down about ten inches above my ankle. I pulled the sweatpants leg back down, stood straight, and experimented with drawing the gun past the elastic. After about three minutes, I could execute a reasonably good draw, assuming any potential assailant allowed me time to stoop to tie my shoelaces.

I left the apartment and began running slowly toward the river two blocks away. I got barely across the footbridge spanning the multilane highway called Storrow Drive when the pain of the gun butt bonking against my shin got so intense I had to stop. I looked around and saw no one. I bent and drew the weapon, stuffing it in the front double pocket of my sweatshirt. I then did a mile and a half up the river and back, with my hands in my front pocket stabilizing the revolver. I must have looked like a potbellied clown.

I stopped running on the river side of the footbridge. I walked over it and up Cambridge Street a block to disperse the lactic acid that otherwise stiffens the joints. I also bought a paper and six donuts as a reward for running three miles. Home, I stripped, warmed down, showered, and drank a glass of ice water to rehydrate. I then sipped a quart of orange juice with the donuts over the *Globe*.

By 9 A.M., I was ready to face my problems. I called George and gave him the name of the Pittsburgh funeral home. He explained the details of the transport via Delta Airlines. I thanked him and rang off.

I called Delta to arrange my ticket, then called Dale Palmer's number and got Larry. He apologized for being bitchy the night before. I said not to worry about it and asked about Martha. He said he hadn't seen her since just after he spoke to me. I gave him my flight number. Larry said he or Dale would meet the plane and gave me a detailed description of both. I reciprocated and we hung up friendly if not friends.

Lastly, I called Jesse and Emily. He answered with a tentative hello.

"Hi, Jesse."

"Who is this?" he demanded.

"John Cuddy, Jesse. You called me. Last night sometime."

"Oh, John, please excuse me. I . . . that is, we've been a little upset."

I felt my stomach turn maybe 15 degrees.

"What's happened?" I asked.

"Well, yesterday the phone rang and Emily answered. Hold on, John, she's right here, let me put her on so she can tell you."

"John? Hello?" She sounded shaken.

"I'm here, Emily. What's the trouble?"

"Well, yesterday about noontime, the phone rang. I picked it up and said 'Hello' and a man's voice said 'Hi, Emily. How are you?' I said, 'I'm fine.' Before I could ask who it was, the voice said, real smooth and creamy, 'That's good.' Then he hung up."

"Was it Marco's voice?"

Jesse came back on. "We couldn't tell, it was so soft. The man, that is, spoke so softly."

"Did you hear him too, Jesse?"

I heard Jesse cough. "Well, not that time, no, but he's called four times since, and each time he asks me—I won't let Emily answer anymore—he asks me how Emily is and then says 'That's good' or 'That's nice.' Then hangs up. In fact," said Jesse haltingly, "we get so few calls, I figured your call was him calling again."

"Any sign of Marco?"

"We haven't been out of the house since the first call. I looked up and down the street but I can't tell from the window whether he's out there."

"All right," I said. "Here's what I want you to do. Don't answer the telephone unless it rings twice, stops, and rings immediately again. That'll be me. I'm going to call some people. Then I'm going to drive over to you and check out the streets around you. O.K.?"

I heard both of them speak. "Right, O.K., thank you, John."

I hung up. I thumbed through the blue pages of the phone book for the police district station closest to the Coopers. I reached for a pen and realized that I hadn't played back my telephone tape after my run. I rewound it, heard a message in reverse Donald-Duck talk, and replayed it. A short message.

"Hi, John, how are you? Oh, you're fine. That's nice."

Click.

I looked up the Suffolk DA's number.

The secretary who answered Nancy Meagher's phone said Nancy was on pretrials all morning. I thanked her and left a message that I'd appreciate a return call when she was available.

I drummed my fingers on the desk, then called directory assistance for three area codes before I got the number for the Pentagon main switchboard, the last duty station I remembered J.T. having. I went through ten or twelve holds and transfers before I got "Colonel Kivens' office."

"May I speak with him?"

"I'm sorry, but the Colonel is not available." Her

voice sounded as though she was reading instructions, a Stepford secretary.

"Do you know when he'll be back?"

"I'm sorry, I'm not at liberty to say."

"Is the next line in the script 'I'll be happy to take your name and number and ask him to call you'?"

"What?"

At least an honest response. I couldn't very well leave a "your friend is dead" message, though. "Just tell him John Cuddy called and will call again tomorrow."

"Would you kindly spell that last name, please?"

I did. And got a direct dial number back to him. I hung up, donned my coat, and headed outside.

I walked to Park Square and rented a car to drive incognito to Jesse and Emily's neighborhood. Their part of Dorchester had a simple, gridlike street pattern, with cars parked on both sides of each road. I edged the rent-a-car through the neighborhood in ever-decreasing concentric squares. Marco might have been there somewhere, but I couldn't spot him.

I drove down the Coopers' short street and then back up it. I parallel-parked a few doors from their house and watched for fifteen minutes. Still no Marco.

I left and locked the car and knocked on the Coopers' back door. They let me in, Jesse self-consciously cradling the shotgun in his good hand. Emily had been crying.

"Did the telephone ring since I spoke with you?"

Emily said "Twice," sobbed and turned away. Jesse looked at me helplessly.

"Come on," I said moving toward their telephone. They sat in front of me on their couch as I began to dial.

First, I called a friend at New England Telephone's business office and set the wheels in motion for a changed, unlisted number. Jesse looked at Emily, who managed a small smile.

Second, I called the guy at the insurance company that I was working for when I nailed Marco's brother. I gave him a five-minute lecture on the good citizenship of the Coopers and how much money their cooperation had helped his company to save on the claim. I asked him to approve a private security guard for the Coopers. He said he doubted his boss would go for it but he'd try. He said he would call me at home with the answer.

I checked the white pages. There were fifteen D'Amicos in the book, but there was only one on Hanover Street, in the North End. I called the number and got a heavily accented, older voice. I said, "Sorry, wrong number," and hung up.

I looked up at Jesse and Emily. They seemed much brighter. I sighed and told them a close friend from the army had died here in Boston and that I had to go to Pittsburgh.

Jesse nodded gravely, thinking, I expect, of his own outfit from World War II. Emily squeezed his good hand tighter.

I told them to call me again if anything more happened. They said they would and thanked me again for all I had done for them.

All I had done for them.

I got in my car and started toward the North End via the Central Artery. I felt anger toward the elder D'Amicos for no good reason. I decided to cool off a little first with a different kind of visit.

* * *

In February you can't see any sailboats from her hillside. Her first year there, we had an early spring. Then, a few brave souls, probably amateurs, were out by the last week of March.

"This year, I'd bet April 10th at the earliest, Beth."

Before she'd gotten the cancer, or at least before we knew she had it, we would visit Boston's Museum of Fine Arts once every few months. I always preferred paintings, Beth sculpture. Whenever we entered a room of sculpture, she would stand for fifteen minutes in front of one piece, say a smallish Greek statue, while I would wander around the room. Whenever I got back to her, she would be ready to go on to the next room. She always said she preferred studying one piece of work in detail. I never had the patience to stare at one piece of stone for that kind of time.

Until I lost her.

For months after Beth was buried, I would look only at her ground, not the headstone. Now I would notice the slightest additional scratch on her marker. A relative of hers, an old man, advised me at the wake to shy away from polished marble. He said that, despite its hardness, it always showed nicks and after ten months would look like it had been in the graveyard for ten years.

He may have been right. I tried to believe the marks around her name and years were natural aging, caused by cold and rain or windblown branches. More likely, they were the product of carelessly swung rakes or tossed beer bottles. But, she gently reminded me, I wasn't keeping to the point.

"You're right, kid. Al, Al Sachs, is dead. I identified the body this morning. Someone tortured and mutilated him, Beth. The police are treating it as a gay murder, but I don't think so. He called me Tuesday morning and planned a dinner with me. He sounded nervous. No, more than nervous, scared." I thought about that. In Vietnam we'd both been scared often enough, but I could never remember Al sounding scared. That was the edge in his voice that I noticed but didn't recognize yesterday.

"In addition to sounding scared, somebody searched his room. A pro. He left nothing out of order that anyone would especially notice." I left out the part about the guy who might have checked my pink message slip.

"I don't have the slightest idea why it happened, kid. He was living and working out of Pittsburgh for a steel company, and this was the first time he'd been in Boston for years."

She told me it wasn't my fault. Agreeing with her helped only a little. "Anyway, I'm going to be taking him home to Pittsburgh. Our flight is tonight at six-fifty. So I won't be coming by for a while."

The wind rose up, blowing a little sleet in front of it. I turned up my collar and hunkered down on my haunches. I touched her grave with the fingers of my right hand.

"Give Al my best," I said.

Hanover Street is the main drag of the North End. Tourists and people from other parts of the Boston area cruise it, futilely searching for a parking place near the dozens of Italian restaurants which lie along or just off it. Most of the buildings have a commercial first floor, often a bakery or butcher shop. The remaining floors are apartments. In good weather, the women, young, middle-aged, and old, lean out of windows with their elbows on the sills.

On street level, the men, also of all ages, congregate in knots of three to five on the sidewalk. Some sit in folding lawn chairs, most talk in staccato Italian. Few pay much attention to non-neighborhood people walking by. A lot of Bostonians maintain that the North End is the safest neighborhood in the city.

Seven-sixty-seven Hanover had a small insurance agency on the ground floor. I walked to the doorway next to it and pressed the D'Amicos' bell. The door was painted dark gray, with six stained-glass inserts. I waited two minutes and pressed again. Still no answer. The sleet had blown over, and the sun was out. It was nearly forty degrees, and I felt a little warm in my overcoat.

One of four men talking in front of the bakery next door broke off and walked toward me. He was short and stubby, wearing a heavy blue knit sweater over black dress slacks. He appeared to be about my age, and he neither frowned nor smiled.

"Who you lookin' for?" he asked me.

"The D'Amicos," I said.

"Which ones?" he replied.

"Mr. and Mrs. Joey and Marco's parents."

"The D'Amicos," he said. "They had a lotta heartache this week. Maybe they don't wanna see nobody just now, y'know."

"I know, and I can understand it. That's why I want to see them."

He squinted. "You ain't a cop, are ya?"

"No," I said. "If I were a cop, I would have ignored you and kept pressing their button."

He rubbed his nose. Then he leaned in front of me

and gave their button three quick taps. He looked me square in the eye. "My parents and the D'Amicos come over together. The parents are good people. I went to school with Marco. I don't know which of the sons give 'em more trouble, Marco or Joey. Just don't add to it."

"I'm here to prevent trouble for them."

My emissary broke eye contact as the downstairs door opened. Mr. D'Amico poked his red-eyed head outside. He recognized me and snarled something in Italian to my companion that contained Joey's name.

My companion stiffened and started, "Mr. D'Amico says you're—"

"I'm not here about Joey," I interrupted sharply. "I'm here about Marco, and I need to talk with Mr. and Mrs. D'Amico." I lowered my voice. "Please tell him it's important."

Mr. D'Amico spoke. "He don't need to tell me no thing. I understand English. If you about Marco, we will talk. Upstairs."

Mr. D'Amico turned and I stopped the spring-held door as he started up the narrow staircase.

As I stepped across the threshold, my emissary caught my arm. Not hard or threatening, just a firm grip.

"When you come out, nobody up there better be cryin'."

I looked over his shoulder at the knot of men he'd left. They were all staring at us. I looked down as steadily as I could at my emissary, who bobbed his head once and released my arm. I followed D'Amico up the stairway, the closing door darkening the passage.

Their living room was clean, dry, and awfully warm with all the windows closed. The sofa and chairs were overstuffed, with elaborate crocheted doilies on the arms and backs. Religious scenes dotted the walls, and I could make out photos of younger Marcos and Joeys in triptych brass frames standing on the end tables.

D'Amico sat stiffly on the couch. I was in a flower-print chair across from him. He wore an old, narrow-collar white shirt and brown sharkskin pants. I could neither see nor hear Mrs. D'Amico.

"I have no desire to add to your grief, Mr. D'Amico," I began, "but I would like to speak with your wife as well."

D'Amico swallowed twice. He barely unclenched his teeth. "She too upset from the . . . from the trial. You tell me what you want."

I frowned and spread out my hands. "Look, Mr. D'Amico, like I said downstairs, I'm here about Marco, not Joey, but in order for me to do any good here, you have to accept something about Joey. You have to—"

"I don't need to accept no thing," D'Amico cut in tremulously.

"Yes, sir, yes, you do. You have to accept that you've lost Joey. You have to accept that if you want to save Marco."

"Save Marco?" said a little, tired voice from a corridor we'd passed. "What save Marco?"

D'Amico got up with a pained look on his face and walked toward his wife, who stood small and trembling with her hand clutching a black bathrobe at her breast. Her hair, more gray than black, was askew, and the hem of a white nightgown or slip hung out under the robe. Her face looked sunburned. In February.

D'Amico spoke soothingly in Italian but his wife was having none of it, wagging her head and stomping into the room and toward me.

"What save Marco?" she demanded. "What—" Then a flash of recognition. "You. You the one. Joey! Oh, *Madre di Dio!*" She clenched the fist that wasn't holding the robe together and struck herself hard on the chest repeatedly until her husband restrained her.

"Mrs. D'Amico . . ."

She shrieked and shook her head violently. She began to wail. "Why you here? Why you don't leave us alone? Why, why?"

"To try to save Marco for you, Mrs. D'Amico," I said softly. "To try to save your other son."

She was trembling but stopped crying. She glared at me, her nostrils flaring. She gave her husband a short command in Italian. He protested, and she switched to English. "Sit, sit!"

He gave me a murderous look and released her arm. They took the sofa.

"What you mean, save Marco?"

I decided not to repeat my Joey preamble. "Mrs. D'Amico, have you seen Marco since yesterday afternoon?"

She bit her lip. "What you mean, save Marco?"

I thought of the Little Prince, who once he asked a question, would keep asking it until it was answered. I decided to play too.

"Mrs. D'Amico, have you seen him?"

She bit her lip again and moved her head no. I

looked up at her husband, who glared, but showed no as well.

"I have reason to believe Marco is bothering the older couple whose house I used to watch the warehouse."

"The colored and the white woman?" she asked.

"Yes."

"What you mean, bother?" she said.

"Phone calls."

"Look," said Mr. D'Amico, "Marco, he don't live here no more. He don't make no phone calls from here."

"It doesn't matter where he's calling from," I explained. "If he threatens them, he gets in trouble with the police."

"Marco don't make those calls," said Mrs. D'Amico.

"I think he did. He called me, too. It was his voice, Mrs. D'Amico."

"No," she said, then louder, "no!"

"Why you telling us this things," said Mr. D'Amico warily.

"I was hoping you could talk to him, persuade him to stop before he gets in trouble for it."

D'Amico looked helpless. His wife sunk her face into her free hand, and then went to her pocket, tugging out some crumpled Kleenex to stem the next wave of tears.

"He don't listen no more," said the husband. "He almost as old as you. He don't listen."

Mrs. D'Amico was crying again, choking off sobs in her throat.

"The Coopers, the other couple, are a lot like you.

Only they don't have neighbors to look after them, like you do. You can guess why that is. Cooper, the husband, was a marine. He can take care of Marco if he has to. So can I."

"Marco got friends," he said aggressively. "Lotsa friends."

"I know," I said. "I met one downstairs, remember? But his friends won't back him on this sort of thing. This isn't vendetta, Mr. D'Amico. We both know that. Joey set fire to that warehouse and left the watchman to die. I shot Joey because he shot at me. If Marco hurts someone because of that, nobody will stand with him. Nobody will avenge him, and you'll have lost both of your sons."

Mrs. D'Amico let out a confirming wail.

"Out!" snapped D'Amico. "You outta my house!"

I got up and left the apartment. I closed the door gently behind me and descended the staircase. As I stepped out into the sunlight, I looked over at my emissary. He and the group stared back at me. I nodded without smiling and walked back toward my car. I was glad the D'Amicos' closed windows kept her crying from drifting down to street level.

Seven

I DROVE BACK TOWARD MY APARTMENT. I CIRCLED around my block twice, then parked two blocks away and walked to a coffee shop roughly diagonal to my building. I sat and nursed a hot cocoa for half an hour in a bay window, watching. I didn't see anything unusual, like someone parked in a car for an unreasonable period of time.

I paid for my cocoa and crossed the street. I walked quietly down the alley that turned behind my building, and peeked around the corner. Nobody in sight.

I walked behind my building and hopped over the wooden fence separating our minimal patio area from the alley tar. I used my key on the back door and pulled a long-handled, wide-brushed push broom from the utility closet with the broken lock. I went back outside and lifted the wood brush angle to hook and pull down the last ladder flight of the fire escape. I climbed it, carrying the broom.

I reached my floor and thought about using the handle end of the broom to poke around my window sill from a safe distance. Instead I crawled to my window and looked inside. I couldn't see much, but I watched long enough to be fairly certain no one was waiting for me. I took out my penlight and shined it through the glass toward the front entrance. I couldn't see any wires or trips attached to the door.

I didn't think Al's killer would really try anything for two reasons. First, any attempt on my life, once the police knew I was connected with Al, would put the lie to the cover-up he had arranged. Second, he couldn't be sure that Al hadn't somehow identified him to me, resulting in his being put under surveillance by the police. While I believed that either or both of those reasons relieved me of Al's killer, I didn't feel as comfortable about friend Marco. Hence, my caution.

I flicked off the light and was halfway back down the escape when the cruiser came into the alley and stopped. Both uniforms, a man and a woman, came out of their respective doors and drew and pointed their revolvers at me, bracing their gun hands with their free hands.

"All right, leave the broom there and come down real slow," said the woman, who had been driving.

"Is it all right if I just drop the broom over the side?" I said. "It'll save us having to stand on each other's shoulders to pull the flight down to climb back up after it."

The male uniform muttered something to her. Neither took their eyes off me.

She spoke. "Drop the broom. Then cut the shit. Then come down."

I dropped, cut, and came.

They studied my investigator's identification and compared it to the address information in my wallet several times before grudgingly buying my explanation of Marco's dishonorable intentions. It seemed that a woman sitting in her apartment across the alley had spotted me climbing up the fire escape. As they got back into their cruiser, I felt encouraged by neighborhood security and embarrassed by personal ineptitude, with the edge to embarrassment.

I walked around to the front of the building. I keyed open the door and approached my apartment more conventionally.

Once inside I checked my telephone tape. There were two hang-ups and two messages. The first message was:

"John, it's Nancy Meagher returning your call at three-forty P.M. I'll be in my office tomorrow between eight-thirty and nine-thirty."

The second message was a little redundant:

"Hi, John. How are you. Oh, you're fine. That's nice."

I rewound and then levered out the message cassette. I replaced it with a spare and put the tape into a heavy manila envelope. I checked my watch. Four-thirty. I called Nancy's office. She was gone for the day and so was her secretary. I looked for her home phone number in the book, but if I remembered her address correctly, she was unlisted. I penned a quick explanatory note and slipped it in next to the tape. I addressed the envelope to Nancy at the DA's office, stamped it, and left it on a table near the door for mailing.

Then I called Lieutenant Murphy's office. I got Daley, my companion at the morgue. He said Murphy was out of the office, but that Murphy had told him to tell me that Traffic had found Al's rental car on Myrtle Street on Beacon Hill and about five blocks from where Al's body had been dumped. Elapsed mileage exceeded by about fifty miles the business visits they could confirm Al making. None of the business contacts knew where he was going that evening. The final autopsy report confirmed death by smothering, no further information. I thanked Daley and told him I would be in Pittsburgh for a few days and would call in once in a while. I rang off and walked into the front hall.

I went to the closet and pushed most of the garbage aside. I pulled out the old Samsonite three-suiter, even though I would have to pack only one outfit. A dark, somber one.

After I packed, I carried the suitcase to the door and looked down at the envelope. I pocketed it and went downstairs.

I walked to the rental and returned it to the agency. I carried my burdens to the Szechuan Chinese restaurant in the next block. The decor was red leather with faintly illuminating Chinese lanterns. There were few patrons. I was shown to a small booth by a hostess in a cocktail dress, slit discreetly up the side. I ordered a vodka and orange juice.

One screwdriver makes me thirsty for two. Two make me hearty and gregarious. Three make me unnecessarily aware of little things, like the exact shade of a woman's lipstick. Four make me morose.

I stopped at three and ate my dinner. I also decided not to mail the tape envelope. I settled up and stepped out into a howling wind. I hailed a cab, giving Nancy's address in Southie.

The taxi driver had country and western music on the radio. The back seat was black vinyl with little tufts of white, puffy stuffing poking through. I thought of Craigie's body after the fire, then made my mind change the subject.

Her building in South Boston was a three-decker on a clean street, sort of a wooden version of the D'Amicos' place. Like the Italian North End, the Irish and Italian neighborhoods in Southie had been stable, if stubborn, for generations. A Lithuanian section, dating mostly from the end of World War II, straddled Broadway a little farther west.

There were three buzzers arranged vertically on the outside doorjamb. Each would signify a different floor of the three-story house. The bottom and middle name plates said "M. Lynch" and "A. Lynch." The top one said "N. Meagher." I pushed it. Strains from some detestable C&W song reached me through the cabbie's half-open window, something like "I'm breaking my back putting up a front for you."

I heard footsteps tripping down the stairs inside the door, and a light flicked on over my head. No intercom and buzzer systems in this part of town. The door opened on a chain, and I heard her laugh.

"Well, well," she said, slipping the chain and swinging open the door. "A pleasure call, I hope."

She was wearing a gray Red Sox T-shirt and white tennis shorts. A bath towel, draped clumsily, covered her left hand from the wrist down.

I said, "I'm sorry to bother you at home, but I have a plane to catch, and I wanted to talk with you before I left."

She went up on tiptoes and saw the cabbie over my

shoulder. She shivered a bit. "Pay off your cab and come on up. I'll freeze in this doorway, but I'd be glad to drive you to Logan afterwards."

As I turned back toward the cab, I heard her say, "It's okay, Drew." Someone moved on the second landing and a door closed.

I settled with the driver and lugged my suitcase to her stoop. She tapped ahead of me in sandals up the two flights to her apartment.

Her door opened from the staircase into a big kitchen, perhaps fifteen by fifteen. A screened-in but sealed-off porch lay behind the kitchen. Once inside, I dropped my bag on the floor, and we turned left into a corridor that led to the front of the house. She had a cozy living room with a small bay window. There were throw pillows on the floor, and brick-and-board bookcases along both walls. Two low tables and some indirect lighting completed the furnishings.

She laid the towel carefully on one of the tables and asked me if I wanted a drink.

"Ice water?" I said, feeling the dehydration of the Chinese food and the screwdrivers.

"I have stronger," she said.

"Thanks, just water."

She lowered WCOZ just a bit on the stereo under a shelf of mystery paperbacks. "Let me take your coat," she said.

I shrugged out of it, and she left with it for the kitchen. Her bottom looked firm in the shorts, her legs straight and slim beneath them.

She was back in a flash. "One ice water," she said, handing me a tall, expensive-looking glass. "Pull up a pillow."

She collapsed naturally into one near a table with a tumbler of amber liquid on it. I sat down a little less gracefully.

She scooped up her tumbler and mock-toasted. "Welcome to my parlor."

"Said the spider to the fly," I finished.

She smiled and sipped.

"It's nice . . . comfortable," I said. "Even with the security."

She tilted her head in question.

"Drew," I said. "On the landing, short for Andrew, as in 'A. Lynch'?"

She laughed. "Drew's a cop. He and his wife live on the second floor. She's expecting, and he's just sort of protective. His parents—this is their house—they live on the first floor. Do you want to take your jacket off? The Lynches have to keep the heat up because of her mother. She's pushing eighty and needs to have it warm." She ran her nondrink hand down her T-shirt, neck to navel. "That's why I lounge around like this, even in February."

Her nipples were subtly more defined for a moment under the shirt as her hand moved. She took another sip. I downed half my ice water.

"Under the towel," I said, "revolver or automatic?"

Broad smile but sad eyes. "I knew the assistant DA who was shot in his car in Cambridge last year. He was a class ahead of me at New England." She clenched and unclenched her fist. "But, to answer your question, revolver."

I shook my head. "Revolver is a more reliable weapon, but the hammer could get caught in the towel. You should switch to an automatic or change camouflage."

This time she shook her head. "It's a five-shot Bodyguard. With the shrouded hammer. Drew helped me pick it out."

I pictured a revolver with high, thin steel walls enclosing the hammer and a small, scored steel button on top that could be thumbed back but wouldn't get caught on clothing. Or towels. I finished my ice water.

"Where are you off to?" she asked.

I gave her three sentences about Al.

"Boy," she said in a low voice after condolences, "this is not how I was hoping our next meeting would go."

"The next one after this won't," I said.

She wanted to smile but didn't. "Are you here about your friend?"

"No, the Coopers." I summarized the phone calls, both Marco's and mine, and my visit to the D'Amicos. I dug out and handed her the envelope containing the tape.

Nancy swirled her drink but didn't put the glass to her lips. She laid the envelope carefully on the table next to her. If she wore any make-up, it didn't show.

"Joey comes up for sentencing in two weeks," she said. "Smolina may not be telling the parents, but I'm sure Joey'll get life. I bet Marco knows it, too." She sipped now. "Any chance of getting the Coopers out of town for a bit?"

"I don't think so. No family they mentioned. Or friends. Or money to do it with either."

Nancy sighed. "A year ago, I might have told you I'd see they were watched over. But not after Teresa

Alou." She clenched her fist again. "You remember the case?"

"Yes." Tough one to forget after the *Globe* series. The DA had a squeeze on Alou, a young Hispanic who lived in the South End and knew a lot about the drug trade from her brother. The squeeze was her brother, who wouldn't talk and would go to a bad prison if he didn't. Teresa talked for him. To save him. The brother went to a good prison, a farm, a safe one. He lasted three days. First they'd blinded him with some barbed-wire goggles. Then they beat him to death. With rolled up newspapers. It would have taken a long time.

The DA put Teresa under witness protection in a hotel. Just before the permanent relocation funding was approved by the appropriate bureacracy, somebody slipped down a rope and into the hotel room. The somebody bashed the female operative and did Teresa. By the time the guys outside in the hall realized the inside operative should have answered their knock, the somebody was gone. Along with Teresa's eyes, ears, and tongue. He left the rest. Alive, sort of.

"Sixteen," Nancy said, bringing me back. "She was sixteen." She shivered for the second time since I'd come in. Nancy looked up at me. "The Coopers weren't really part of our case, but I'll ask McClean. And Drew, too. But I can't promise."

"I know." I checked my watch. "I better call a cab."

She shook her head vigorously and hopped up. "No way. It'd take forever, and I said I'd drive you. I'll be out in a minute."

She disappeared for more like two and a half minutes. She reappeared in an L. L. Bean parka like one I owned, and jeans and eskimo boots. She handed me her business card, home phone written on the back. She walked over to the towel and slipped the gun out from under it and into the parka's left side pocket.

"The pocket in my parka's too shallow for that," I remarked as she tossed me my coat.

"Mine was too," she said. "Mrs. Lynch slit the interior and resewed it deeper."

I picked up my bag and we clomped downstairs and into the cold clear night.

When we arrived at Logan Airport, Nancy gave me a quick kiss. I said thanks and entered the terminal just as a cop was waving for her to move along. I checked my bag at the passenger ticket counter and asked directions to the cargo area.

It took a little explaining, but I used George's name, and the Delta cargo employee expressed his sympathies and escorted me to the loading platform. His first name was Dario. He was middle-aged and compact. He also looked strong as a bull.

As we approached the platform, there was a young guy uncertainly maneuvering a forklift and pallet toward a canvas-wrapped, coffin-sized container.

"Pat, yo—Pat," said Dario.

The forklift operator stopped and turned around.

"Pat, let me take that one for the gentleman here."

Pat gratefully hopped off, and Dario replaced him. He coaxed and sidled the lift perfectly. Even without the canvas as a buffer, I doubt the casket would have been marred.

Dario carefully, even solemnly, drove the lift across to a weighing machine. After weighing, he completed a multicarbon form and tore off one copy. He gave me the tearsheet.

"I don't think you'll need this in Pittsburgh, but, just in case."

"Thanks, thanks a lot," I said, folding and pocketing the sheet. "What happens now?"

"We put the coffin into a covered, locked cargo cart and get it on the plane before the other baggage."

I glanced down at my watch.

"Not to worry," said Dario. "It'll make the flight. My personal guarantee."

I thanked him, and we shook hands. I went back out and up to the gate for boarding.

There was no one in the aisle or middle seat in my row on the right side of the plane. The stewardess leaned over and asked me if I wanted a drink. After having had dinner, I thought a fourth screwdriver wouldn't depress me. I was wrong. I began thinking of happy things I'd be doing the next day, like calling J. T. and watching Martha try to sit *shivah*.

We arrived in Pittsburgh at 8:45. I decided to pick up my suitcase later and asked directions to the cargo area. When I got there, a guy in a green worker uniform was standing over Al's canvas-draped coffin on a heavy-duty conveyor belt. In front of the coffin was a three-foot square box stenciled "U.S. Steel." Behind it was a wildly shaped package that looked home-wrapped.

I walked up to the man in uniform. He was fortyish with brown hair and a dead cigar in his mouth. He was just pulling off a pair of work gloves.

"Help ya?" he said through the cigar.

"I hope so. I'm with the coffin. I want to see it safely on the hearse."

The man shook his head as he removed the second glove and stuffed them in a back pocket. He pulled out the cigar. "You know which home?"

"You mean funeral home?"

"Yeah."

"Cribbs and Son."

He smiled and replaced the cigar. "You're lucky. Jake Cribbs is the only guy who'll come out, day or night. Matter of pride to 'im."

I breathed a sigh of relief. "Do you have his number?"

"I can call him for ya. No charge." He dropped his smile and nodded toward Al. "Family?"

I shook my head. "Friend. From the army."

He put the dead cigar in his shirt pocket and wiped his hand. He extended it to shake. "Good a' you to see him through." We shook and exchanged names. His was Stasky.

"I was navy. Just before Vietnam. You there?"

"Yes."

"Him too?"

"Uh-huh."

Stasky pointed to a chair and table with a coffee urn and some mugs in a corner.

"Make yourself comfortable and have some. I'll call Cribbs."

I abstained from the coffee. Stasky returned shortly. "Old man Cribbs'll be here in twenny minutes. He'll give you a lift into town if you need it."

"Thanks, but someone's meeting me."

He left me at the table while he tended to the freight.

Half an hour later, Stasky helped me and Cribbs, a wiry older man in a black stadium coat and commissar's hat, to maneuver the coffin on the folding high stretcher into the back of the hearse. The air was dry and cold. Stasky said near zero.

Cribbs said that Mr. Palmer had taken care of scheduling arrangements at the home. I thanked him, and he said he'd see me tomorrow. I watched him enter the driver's side and pull away.

I tromped back into the terminal, my exhaled breath remaining a visible cloud about a heartbeat longer than in comparatively balmy Boston. I followed signs for the passenger area and the baggage carrousels. The stores along the corridor were the usual collection of coffee shops, shoeshine parlors, silly little bars, and Steeler memorabilia stands. Only the bars were open, the rest locked with chromed gratings in front of them.

I got to the baggage area. My three-suiter wasn't on the nearly empty and stationary carrousel. I looked around the room. A short, chunky man with a toupee stood up from one of the plastic seats. My suitcase was on the chair next to him. He waved to me, and I walked over to him. He didn't match Larry's description of either of them.

"Mr. Cuddy?" he asked.

I recognized his voice and extended my hand. "John, please, remember? You're Dale Palmer?"

He smiled confirmation and shook.

"When I didn't see you," he said, "I thought I'd better grab your bag."

"Thanks. I was with . . . the undertaker."

The smile dropped. "Ah, yes. Well, my car is just out front and to the right." He turned.

I hefted my suitcase and followed him.

Eight

"If you didn't know her, you'd think she was doing pretty well." We'd driven about five miles in his small Pontiac from the airport toward downtown. So far, we had determined my accommodations for the night, me insisting on a motel, him insisting that Larry and he already had made up their guestroom, me not wanting to put them out, him assuring me that it would make logistics easier tomorrow and Saturday. I relented. We had finally gotten around to Martha.

"I've never met her."

"I know. That is, she told us. After the . . . ah, call."

I rubbed my eyes with my right hand. "I'm truly sorry about that."

"Listen. It wasn't your fault." His right hand started to leave the gearshift knob and come toward me. He stopped it abruptly and brought it back to the steering wheel instead.

"I appreciate your concern," I said. "And all you've done for Martha."

He swallowed once, hard. "Martha was our friend. I mean from before they were married. We persuaded them to move into the neighborhood." He paused. "Al was a good friend, too."

I let out a long breath. I was too tired. And depressed. I shut up the rest of the trip.

As we drew toward the city, Dale began speaking again. He gave a sort of nervous, pointing geographic orientation of the U of Pittsburgh, Carnegie-Mellon, downtown, Three Rivers Stadium and half a dozen residential neighborhoods whose names meant nothing to me. Dale identified the bookstore where Larry worked. Dale taught piano at home.

We pulled into an older, seedier neighborhood of party-wall townhouses, some with two stories, some with three. Most were old brick, few had bay or bow-front windows. One block had ten beautiful, restored houses, another ten burned-out shells.

Dale explained this area was called Mexican War, each of the streets named after an event or personage in the 1840s conflict. He slowed and parked in front of a picture-perfect two-story and cut his engine.

"Home at last," he said with false cheer. "This is our place. Carol is directly across the street"—gesturing and twisting—"Martha's the ash-toned one, two doors down from her." He dropped the merriment. "How do you want to handle this?"

I glanced at my watch. Ten-twenty-five. "Too late to see Martha?" I asked.

"Oh, no," he said. "I'm sure she'll still be up. That's part of the problem."

"Maybe if I could drop my suitcase at your place and then we could go over?"

"Perfect," he said. We left the car and climbed his three steps. He let me in and sensed the Cook's Tour of the house could wait. He showed me to my room and signaled toward the bathroom. I popped my suitcase and hung up my suit for the next day. Then we both sucked in a little courage and walked over to Martha's house.

The three concrete steps leading up to Martha's door were chipped and cracked. The heavy door and jamb were painted, but the overhead light betrayed it as gray primer futilely waiting for a top coat. There was no doorbell and only a residual outline and a screw hole where the brass knocker might have been. Dale drew one ungloved hand from his pocket and tapped lightly with two knuckles. The air was painfully cold. Dale tapped again, harder.

The door swung halfway open. "In! Come on, come on. In quickly, before we lose heat!"

Dale scooted ahead of me with a short laugh. I hopped over the sill. Our greeter, a slim, boyish man in a Beatle haircut and a tight ski sweater, closed the door with an extra push needed at the end. He threw the deadbolt and turned to us without a smile.

"Larry Estleman," said Dale. "John Cuddy."

I extended my hand. Larry's features sagged and he shook my hand. "Again, I'm sorry . . . about . . ."

"I'm sorry, too," I said. "It was a bad time all around."

Larry said, "Yeah," and dropped my hand.

"Where's Martha?" asked Dale.

"In the kitchen," said Larry. "With Carol. We have the oven on."

Dale nudged Larry to precede us. I took off my coat. We walked through a small living room; I tossed my coat on a chair. The walls needed repainting, the ceiling replastering, and the furniture replacing. It didn't feel much warmer inside than it had on the stoop.

Dale whispered to me. "They hadn't paid their oil bills, so . . ."

I nodded to stop him, but he continued.

"The stove's electric, and Larry put an old space heater of ours in Al Junior's room. I called the oilman, he'll deliver tomorrow and add it to our bill."

I nodded again as we entered the kitchen.

The two women sitting at the table looked up. One was blond and a little prim. She looked calm and one hand held a pencil hovering just over a grocery pad. The other resembled Audrey Hepburn in her early thirties, short black hair and a thin, tired face. Both had sweaters and coffee cups.

Larry leaned against the refrigerator and stuck his hands into his pants pockets. Dale spoke to the blonde. "Martha? This is John Cuddy."

She smiled and got up. I awkwardly waved her to stay down, but she came over and gave me a peck on the cheek and a polite hug. "Oh, John, welcome to our house. Al told me so much about you." She spoke in a falsely buoyant tone.

Her head inclined to the woman still sitting, Martha spoke again. "And this is Carol Krause."

I looked at Carol, she riveted angrily on me.

"Why don't we move into the living room?" said Martha. "We'll be more comfortable."

"I felt a little chill in there, Mart," said Carol. She had the smooth, even voice of a TV anchor. Or a hostess in an expensive lounge. "Couldn't we all just stay in here?"

Martha blinked then smiled. "But chairs . . . we wouldn't all—"

"That's okay, Martha," said Larry quickly. "I ought to go up and check on the boys anyway."

"Good, good," said Martha, moving her head a little too vigorously. He slipped out of the room, and the rest of us went to sit down.

Martha was halfway into her chair when she popped back up. "Oh, I'm so sorry, John. After the trip, you and . . . You must want some coffee?"

"No, no, thank you," I said. "Martha—"

"Oh, tea then? Beer?" She stepped to the refrigerator and pulled open the door. The little light didn't come on, but even without it the shelves didn't look too full. "Soda? We have plenty, really."

"Not just now, thanks."

"None for me, either," said Dale.

I was aware of Carol twisting and untwisting her fingers. I glanced around the room. The tile around the sink was loose in its mortar, the wallpaper was twenty years old and curling, and only one bulb shone through the three-bulb plastic fixture over the table. Martha's list was at right angles to me, with entries, crossouts, and connecting arrows all over it.

Martha closed the door and came back to us. She suddenly looked up and to the right, closing her eyes for a second, then she sat down, said, "Excuse me," and wrote something more on the list, drawing another arrow from it to an earlier line.

"John," said Carol in a barely civil voice, "could I see you in the living room for a minute?"

"Sure," I said, Martha giving no indication of noticing Carol's change of heart toward that part of the house.

Dale cocked his head at us as we left, her in the lead.

From the rear, she was perhaps five-five, with a slim torso but wide hips. The hips would move in a sexual sway no matter how stiffly she carried herself.

As soon as we were in the living room, she turned on me, her crossed arms hugging herself against the cold.

"Where the hell have you been?"

"Could we sit—"

She pigeoned her head forward. "She's been waiting up for you. She said she couldn't go to bed without meeting you. The man who told her her husband was dead. On the phone. Like calling in a mail order . . ."

I considered slapping her, but she wasn't hysterical, just mad, and I was a convenient target.

"So where have you been?" she hissed.

"In airports and on a plane. With the cold body of an old friend."

She lost a little height and weight, sinking into herself. She walked over to the couch and sat, leaning forward to conserve her heat. I got my coat, put it around her shoulders. She tugged on the lapels to tighten it around her.

"What a stupid . . . lousy . . ."

"Look, I didn't—"

"No, no," she said, sighing. "Not you. Al's death. No reason for it. The papers here, and some cop from Boston on the phone—"

"Murphy?" I said.

"Huh?" She looked up.

"Murphy. Was the cop's name Murphy?"

"Oh, I don't know." She released a lapel long

enough to wipe her eyes. She had on heavy lid-liner and lipstick. The eye makeup smeared a little.

"I didn't take the call," she said. "Dale did. Larry was too upset to help much. I was still at work. She reached me—" Carol broke off what she realized was irrelevant. "It was the way they . . . the way it was done. . . ."

"About Martha," I said.

Carol blew out through her lips, making them flutter without any accompanying noise. "I don't know. We've been friends, all of us for a long time. Like pioneers, you know. We sort of settled this block when, well, it was after my divorce, and things weren't too fashionable here, despite all the renovations since." She looked around the room.

"How hard up is Martha for money?" I said. "Bottom line."

She shrugged. "You've got eyes. Most of us on the street had to do a little bit at a time. You seen Dale and Larry's place yet?"

"Just a walkthrough."

"Well, Dale got a chunk of money from an aunt who died, so they did their place a little faster than most, but all of us were trying, including Martha and Al. But somewhere, I dunno, the steel glut, the recession, something must have happened. I didn't know about the oil, when Kenny—he's my son, he's upstairs asleep with Al Junior—when Kenny and I walked in here, it was freezing cold. I hadn't even worn a coat, just rushed over and . . . I don't know how they . . . I mean this is Pittsburgh, you know, *February?*"

"What are you two doing in here?" said Martha,

coming in, her coffee cup chattering a little against the saucer she carried under it. Dale followed.

"Just getting acquainted, Mart," Carol replied.

"Good, good," said Martha.

I heard Larry padding down the stairs. He appeared with his coat over his arm. Dale, as if on cue, retrieved his from the chair and tugged it on.

"Oh, Dale, Larry," said Martha in a hostess voice, "do you have to go already?"

Larry stifled a yawn. Dale gave his short laugh. "Yes, yes. Larry has half the early shift at the bookstore, and my first lesson is at eight o'clock." He turned to me with a smile. "A lawyer who wants to learn how to play. To surprise his wife." He winced as soon as he said it. Martha seemed to notice nothing, neither the gaffe nor the wince.

"Thanks for the ride in. Ah," I said remembering my suitcase but not feeling I could leave yet.

Dale, anticipating me, covered his faux pas by fumbling out a house key and pressing it into my palm as we shook. "This'll get you past the front door. No alarms. Just be sure to put on the deadbolt and leave on the front light."

"Thanks. I'll try not to—"

Dale waved me off. Larry was already on the doorknob. Dale walked to the door, turned with a serious look. "We'll see you here at one-thirty tomorrow."

We all nodded and they left.

"Well, now, John," said Martha. "How was your flight?"

"Fine," I said, "clear weather, no delays."

"Al hated flying, you know. Ever since the war. He always preferred taking trains, so he could read, you know."

"Al liked to read."

"Were there trains in Vietnam?" Martha asked.

I glanced at Carol, but she was focused on Martha.

"Yes," I said. "There were a few. Mostly Vietnamese used them. They would be crowded, unpleasant. We never rode them."

"Funny," said Martha. "Al preferred trains."

"Martha, has anyone—"

"Oh," she interjected, standing, "your coffee. It must still be in the kitchen. I'll just—"

"No, Martha," I said, trying to keep the protest out of my voice. "I don't take coffee."

"Oh," she said, still standing, "how about tea then? Soda? We have plenty of everything, really."

Her repetition of hospitality sounded so brittle I thought she would break.

"No, really," I said, motioning for her to sit down. "Martha, we have to talk about things here. Have you—"

"Things here," she said with a smile. "I have a list already. I'll just be a minute."

She bustled off into the kitchen.

I looked at Carol. "How long has she . . ."

"Since your phone call."

I rested my chin on my chest. Dale had already told me that. I must be more tired than I thought.

"One of us should stay with her," I said.

"I went back home and got a bag. Kenny and I will sleep here tonight."

I stood up. Carol started to push my coat off her shoulders. "Keep it," I said. "I'm just going across the street."

"Macho man." She frowned. "It's probably five below outside."

"I'll keep my hands in my pockets."

Martha came back into the room, list and pencil in hand. "Oh, John, are you going already? Are you sure I can't get you anything? Tea . . ."

"No, thank you. Martha, I'm fine. I'll see you tomorrow."

"Right," she said, coming over and giving me the same aloha peck and hug. "See you tomorrow. Sweet dreams."

Carol followed me to the door, insisting I take the coat. I saw slivers of china out of the corner of my eye before I registered the breaking sound and Martha's voice.

"Damn you!" she yelled, "damn you to hell." She had followed through like a major league pitcher after smashing her cup against the wall. She was yelling at the stain running down the wall. "How could you, Al, how *could* you? After all the scrimping and saving. All the . . . pain and sacrifice and . . . no vacations and no clothes and no . . . Oh God, oh my God, oh God, God." She sank down to her knees, then sat back on her ankles rocking and clutching her arms around her. "Oh God, the stain, the coffee."

Carol ran over to her and threw my coat around her. She kneeled down and hugged her, rocking with her.

I quick stepped to the kitchen and wet a towel. I

came back in and cleaned up the wall. I could hear kids crying upstairs. I spelled Carol while she went upstairs to quiet them.

After Carol came back down, we moved Martha to the couch. We took turns holding and rocking with her through the night.

Nine

I FELT A STIRRING AGAINST MY RIGHT SHOULDER. I opened my eyes.

There was a lamp still on. A full head of blond hair was nestled into my shoulder. It looked as though it had been there awhile. Martha.

Then I noticed the kids. They were squatting Indian-style on the floor, in front of us on the couch. They were both wearing pajamas, the ones on the younger boy a bit small for him.

"W-w-who are you?" said the older one. He sounded scared.

I lifted my free left hand to my lips in a silent shush. The older boy noticed. My watch said 6:30 A.M.

I raised my chin so I could turn my head to the right without nudging Martha. My neck was awfully stiff. Carol lay partially across Martha, sharing my coat with her. One arm disappeared behind Martha and probably belonged to the hand whose knuckles were pressed into my right side. Carol's other arm was across Martha's stomach. Martha's forearms and hands lay limply along my thigh. We were like three puppies, huddled against the cold.

Puppies? Cold?

I exhaled and could see my breath. I looked down at the boys. The older one hadn't been scared, he was shivering from the cold. So was the little one.

I couldn't see any way to help them without moving from under Martha. I started to slide out from under her. The little one said, "M-M-Momma. Mom-maa!"

Martha's head flicked up instantly. She blinked and looked around wildly. "It's okay, Martha," I said. "We're just—"

She looked at me terrified. "Who are . . . where . . . oh, oh, yes." She blinked and leaned forward, rubbing her eyes.

Carol's arm fell behind her, and Carol slid down and toward me, wakening with a start.

"Mom?" said the older boy.

I caught and steadied Carol. Martha spoke. "Kenny, Al. You must be freezing. Come up here both of you."

They scrambled up and climbed onto the couch in that stiff mincing way kids move when they're cold. They cuddled with their mothers under my coat.

"Kenny," said Carol, rubbing his back vigorously, "how long were you sitting down there?"

"I-I-I . . . d-don't . . . know," he said, stammering now more from the rubbing than from the cold.

"Well," said Martha. "We'll have to get you guys some breakfast. How does hot oatmeal sound?"

"I want some," said Kenny.

"Me too," said Al Junior.

"Me three," said me.

Martha and Carol laughed and got up with the kids. Martha seemed O.K. Carol flashed me a real smile, a mixture of friendship and relief.

Over breakfast in the kitchen, I found myself

watching Al Junior. I hadn't known his father at his age, of course, but you could see the big, brown vulnerable eyes and the curly hair, light brownish thanks to some genetic factor from Martha. He ate thoroughly and slowly, as if he wanted to do it right. I suppressed the thought that maybe he hadn't had much practice of late. The kitchen was toasty warm, the more so since we'd left the oven on last night before slumping on the couch.

Al Junior finished his last mouthful.

"Would you like some more?" said Martha at the stove and over her shoulder.

He shook his head. "Where's Daddy?"

Martha's shoulders went up and down once. Carol said, "Daddy's on a trip, remember?"

Al Junior smiled and said, "Oh, yup." He looked at me and frowned. "Who's he?"

I figured I could handle that one. "I'm a friend of your Daddy's, from the army."

Kenny said, "From 'Nam?"

The abbreviation had a hollow ring coming from his young body. "Yes," I said.

"Did you—"

"Kenny," said Carol sharply.

Kenny shut up and went back to his food. We all ate breakfast a little faster after that.

I excused myself, saying I wanted to go over to Dale and Larry's to clean up. Carol followed me into the living room.

I turned to her and she helped me on with my coat. "You were real good with her last night, you know."

"It would have been a disaster without you there."

She closed her eyes. "It's still going to be one. She's got nothing now. No way to go."

I gave her a false wink. "I'll talk to his boss at the wake. Don't worry."

She crossed her arms and followed me to the door, locking it behind me.

The morning was clear, the air brutally cold, a torrent against the face. I ached everywhere from unnaturally held sitting positions. I tried to walk it off into the wind. A solitary jogger in a ski mask and Gore-Tex suit passed me. I got a block and a half before I had to turn back. With the wind behind me, the walking was almost pleasant, the cold piercing only the pants below my coat's hem.

I reached Dale and Larry's doorway. My watch said 7:15. I keyed the lock quietly and slipped in.

Their foyer was warm. Larry appeared in a restored wooden archway to the right. He wore lilac designer sweat pants cinched at his waist, no shirt. His upper body was spare and taut, like a junior high athlete.

"How's Martha?"

"Tough night, but she's holding up. I thought I'd flop upstairs for a while."

He nodded, wary. "Want some breakfast?"

"Had some already, thanks."

He nodded again and disappeared back through the arch.

I trudged up the stairs.

I recognized the light tapping.

"Dale?" I asked.

"Yes," he said outside the door. "Larry said you looked pretty beat but it's almost twelve noon and I thought . . ."

I sat bolt upright in the guestroom bed. My watch agreed with Dale.

". . . you might like some lunch before . . . beforehand, that is."

"I need a shave and a shower first."

"All yours," he said, a little quickly. "Take your time. Cold lunch. No rush."

"See you soon."

"Right," he said.

As I unpacked my suitcase, I began to appreciate the extent of the restoration in the house. In my bedroom, the furniture was perfect: mahogany four-poster, dry sink, and night table; powder blue wing chair with matching hassock; one hurricane lamp. Only the window was modern, double glazed and aluminum. Everything else seemed original equipment. Brass wall sconces, glass doorknobs, wainscoting naturally woodstained (which undoubtedly meant laborious stripping and prestaining). The floors were wide-board hardwood, probably sanded and polyurethaned. I had friends in Boston who had undertaken similar projects on one-bedroom condos. Redoing an entire townhouse would register near the top of the sweat-equity scale.

The bathroom contained a large tub with raised claw feet and a massage-style showerhead. Brass rings on the wall held dark blue towels, contrasting nicely with the light blue tiles and paint. A home that would be a pleasure to live in.

I was dressed and downstairs by twelve-thirty. Larry and Dale were sitting at a table in the dining room, which was just through the archway I'd seen on my way into the house. Larry, back from the bookstore, had changed to a continental-style, gray pinstriped suit, and was laconically turning the pages of a magazine. Dale was in the trousers and vest of a solid gray suit, a small bulge of shirt-covered belly visible above the belt buckle. The table was set but no food served.

"We can offer smoked breast of chicken with lettuce and tomatoes on homemade bread," said Dale rising and smiling broadly.

"Sounds terrific," I said. He moved quickly into the kitchen ignoring my proffered help.

I sat down across from Larry. It was silent for an awkward twenty seconds.

"The house looks super," I said. "You must have poured a lot of time into it."

Larry gave an ironic smile and held his place with a finger. "Look," he said, "I'm not being rude, but I just don't think you and I mix well. The Better Homes and Gardens routine is Dale's bag, not mine. He'll really appreciate the compliments, honest. Me, I just don't feel much like talking, O.K.?"

"O.K." I said. He returned to his magazine. Dale appeared a long two minutes later with a tray of sandwiches and a magnum of white wine.

"I think you'll like the chicken," he said. "A farmer friend of ours raises and smokes them himself." He hefted the wine. "I also think we all could use a brace for this afternoon."

"This house is magnificent, Dale," I said as I reached and took half a sandwich.

"Oh, thank you," he said, pouring my wine. "It was a ton of work. We should have time for a little tour after lunch."

We ate in one-sided silence, Larry's only contribution being, "Good wine, Dale." Dale beamed and continued the I-love-Pittsburgh theme begun on our ride in from the airport. I was mildly interested in the information and deeply grateful for his filling the air.

Larry insisted on clearing the table so that Dale could show me the house. The living room was tasteful in old rose and powder blue, with a matching-background Oriental rug and a functioning fireplace with Italian cherub tile. Beyond the dining room and alongside the kitchen was a back parlor with a baby grand piano and a southeastern exposure. The rear wall was glass, overlooking a twenty-by-twenty back garden. Many plants, all cacti in pots, hung by monofilament inside the glass. Dale explained that the piano couldn't tolerate a lot of humidity, so the interior flora selections thus were limited.

We skipped the basement ("a small wine cellar, some herbs and mushrooms under grow lights") and took in the second story. The master bedroom was a macro-version of the guestroom and occupied the front half of the floor, with a private bath and a huge walk-in closet under an eave. We climbed an attic pull-down ladder in the closet and up through a hatchway. The snow shook down deeper onto a redwood deck.

"I got the idea from two friends in New York. You don't see many roof decks in Pittsburgh, but there's nothing better for really enjoying the sun without all the sand and catcalls—" he broke off.

"I agree with you," I said. "Sundecks have it all over the beach."

He followed me back down the ladder, securing the hatchway above him.

I picked up my coat and we went downstairs. The

three of us saddled up and, insufficiently braced by the wine, crossed over to Martha's house.

Carol let us in. She and Martha were dressed and ready. Neither could get a sitter until Carol's regular one came on at four. Larry enthusiastically volunteered to stay behind and watch Al Junior and wait for Kenny to come home from school. He said he would join us thereafter. The four of us easily fit into Dale's Pontiac, the two women in the back. It was a quiet ride to J. Cribbs and Son.

The funeral home was a renovated Victorian on a commercial street three miles away. It was white with black shutters behind a sidewalk and semicircular drive more manicured than shoveled of the dirty snow around it. There was plenty of parking behind the house. We walked in pairs as we had ridden, silently, exhaling frosty breath into the wintry overcast.

Cribbs the Son met us at the front door, dressed in his profession's uniform and speaking in low, comforting tones. We introduced ourselves and were guided into a parlor with a dark blue decor and cushioned chairs arranged as if to hear a speech. Cribbs the Father was standing respectfully with hands folded, in front of Al's closed coffin. We said hello again, and he cued his son, who left the room. The father took Martha's coat and showed her to a front row, center aisle chair. The rest of us shucked overcoats and arranged ourselves around her. We took turns moving haltingly to the coffin and saying our first good-byes to Al.

When my turn came, I had to fight my dipping reflex, there being no kneelers at the coffin as in Catholic establishments. I pictured Al as I knew him in the service, sitting in an old French easy chair in his room in Saigon, reading or listening to symphonic music on the stereo set he had bought at the PX. I skipped back to him clouting the Virginian in the brawl at the BOQ. I skipped forward to Martha and Al Junior in the rundown townhouse with little food and less heat. Then I thought about *13 Rue Madeleine* and Al on the slab, and somebody, the somebody, who was going to pay for all that. Then I said good-bye and returned to my seat.

The rest of the afternoon took a lot longer to pass than it does to describe. The outside door kept opening and closing, but the hushed voices and occasional sobs gravitated toward another room and someone else's sorrow. At three o'clock, the older Cribbs came in and, perhaps embarrassed at the turn-out, stayed with us for a bit. Dale bravely tried to start a few conversations, but not even Carol was contributing so he stopped. I excused myself and got Cribbs' permission to use his office phone.

I wanted to call my number first, to check my telephone tape machine. I took out my Ma Bell credit card. I tapped my jacket pocket for my remote beeper, but it wasn't there. I closed my eyes and could picture me putting it on the desk at home, then forgetting to pack it in the suitcase. Terrific. Really professional.

I tried J.T. at the Pentagon instead. Same receptionist, same response. No one else there could help me. I chanced leaving Al's name and Dale's number with her. I spelled the names and repeated the numbers twice.

I tried Nancy second. Not in, but I left both Dale's and Martha's home numbers with her secretary.

Next I tried my friend at the company that had covered the torched warehouse. He was not in and was not expected back. I asked his secretary to please follow through on the security request for the Coopers. She said she would do her best, but "it's three-thirty on a Friday afternoon, after all."

Next I called and reached my friend at the telephone company in Boston. He gave me the Coopers' new, unlisted telephone number. It rang five times before I got Jesse's tentative hello. Relieved it was me, he said mine was the first call on their new line, and they had neither heard from nor seen Marco. I told him that was certainly good news. Jesse and Emily (who had come on the line) both thanked me profusely. Emily asked about Al's family, and I told a few lies to make them feel better. As I rang off, they insisted I come over for dinner as soon as I got home. I agreed.

Lastly, I dialed Lieutenant Murphy. This time I drew Cross. She confirmed Daley's conversation with me, said she had spoken personally with Al's two business appointments, neither of whom were going to order anything from him or knew anything more about him. Murphy's investigatory approach was comprehensive and professional, but I could hear the "case closed but unsolved" tone creeping determinedly into Cross' voice. I told her I would check back with her on Monday and hung up.

I got up, thanked Cribbs' secretary, and went back downstairs. The crowd had not filled in since I'd left.

At 4:20, though, Larry joined us. Dale nudged him in the ribs, and Larry went up to the coffin and stood there for fifteen seconds or so, head bowed. When he turned and came back, I was surprised to see he was crying. He sat back down and began sobbing into Dale's shoulder. Carol clenched her teeth, the tears welling within her but not pouring from her. I blinked a lot and twice went to my eyes with the edge of my index finger. Martha simply sat, stoically staring at the coffin.

At five o'clock, a young heavyset girl of perhaps nineteen came in. She looked at us and began sniffling. She fumbled in her bag for some Kleenex and got to it just as the tide broke. I got up and guided her to a chair.

Her name was Trudy Murcher, and she was the secretary for the salesmen at Straun Steel. She saw the newspaper story and was so shocked, and had tried to call Martha at home, and got Larry, and felt she had to . . .

She lasted seven minutes and then had to leave.

At 5:40, a dumpy guy with a blue polyester sports jacket and polyester houndstooth pants came in. He introduced himself as Norm Denver and had been a salesman with Al. Norm apologized for coming so late and having to leave so soon, but he'd just come from an all-day meeting and had to get home. He had Scotch on his breath and a stain on his tie. The stain dated from the late seventies.

He wished Martha luck, stood uneasily in front of the coffin for a couple of seconds, and then turned to go. I caught him in the foyer as he was buttoning up and an after-work rush was heading into another wake.

"Mr. Denver," I said, "can I speak with you for a moment?"

"Jeez," he said, looking down and fumbling with

his second button, "I'm late now. Gloria'll kill me if I don't get home to see the brats into bed."

I waited until he looked up at me. I said evenly, "I need to speak with someone about Al."

He exhaled. I wondered how he could smell like an exhaust fan at a Seagram's factory and not show it.

"O.K.," he said, abandoning the button, "but honest, just a couple of minutes, O.K.?"

"Thank you," I said, and we edged into a corner of the foyer where there was no table or chair.

"I need to speak with whoever is in charge of benefits at Straun."

He looked a little furtive. "Benefits?"

"Yes. Like life insurance, survivors' health care, that kind of thing."

He swallowed and began again with buttons. "Maybe you better call the company."

I slapped his hand away.

"Hey," he said, rubbing the slapped hand with his other. "What's the idea?"

"The idea is you tell me who to contact at Straun. Is there something wrong with that?"

"You can't reach anybody until Monday, anyways. Look," he said, lowering his voice, "I don't want no trouble. I got a job, and I do O.K., and that's a lot more'n most have in this town right now, O.K.?"

"Go ahead."

"Straun—old man Straun, there's a son too, a lawyer, but he works for the company—old man Straun hired Al because he heard Jews were supposed to be good at sellin' stuff, you know. Now, Al, he wasn't. He was an O.K. guy, but he didn't wanna do the stuff you gotta do to close sales with the customers. You know anything about steel?"

"Not much."

"Well, the big boys, the heavy steel and sheet producers, are gettin' murdered by the Japs and all dumping in our markets. Dumping in the sense of sellin' steel in our markets below our cost, I mean American companies' cost, to make the stuff. When the big boys hurt, we hurt, 'cuz our best way of gettin' sales is by piggybacking the reps of the big boys into the customer. To do that, you gotta, well, sort of compensate the reps, you know?"

"I'm getting the picture."

"O.K. So Al doesn't like to do that stuff. So Al thinks that after Straun's been in business somethin' like fifty-three years—the company was started by old man Straun's father in the twennies—and survived depressions *and* a war with Straun's fuckin' cousins, Al thinks he can do it different. Al thinks he can go in cold and sell to the generals—the guys who build the buildings that use our stuff—direct, by personal contact. Well, he thinks wrong. He couldn't do it, you couldn't do it. Nobody could do it."

"All of which adds up to what?"

Norm stole a look at his watch and grimaced. "All of which adds up to he wasn't making his draw, follow? He wasn't closing the sales to cover his pay. He was overdrawn like at the bank."

I felt a cold wave but nobody had opened the door.

"His insurance?"

"Buddy, I gotta guess that Al lost all that months ago. The only thing keepin' him on was old man Straun's stubbornness. He'd made the decision to hire him, and that meant he couldn't admit he was wrong by firin' him. But stubborn don't mean stupid, and it sure don't mean generous. Straun wouldn't carry a puppy to its mother."

"Where can I find Straun?"

He went back to his buttons. "In the office on Monday."

"Tomorrow is Saturday," I said. "Where do I find him tomorrow?"

"Look, buddy, you gotta understand. There are ten guys in this town, maybe twenny guys, who'd kill for my job. If old man . . ."

"He won't find out you told me."

"But if . . ."

"Where will he be?"

He buttoned the last button. "Till the last couple of years, he'd be in the office. Catchin' up on paperwork. Then he realized he could sit home and have his kid the lawyer bring the paperwork to him. He'll be at his house."

"Address?"

"Aw, come on . . ."

"I don't know the city. All I know is your name and where you work. Now what's the address?"

"Forrester Drive. One Hundred Forrester. He's real proud of that, sounds impressive, don't it. Number One Hundred. It's like a mansion, big red brick and white columns."

"Thanks," I said. "Sorry about the slap."

He became the salesman again. "Hey, no problem. You're upset. We all are. Hey, tell Martha again I'm sorry I couldn't stay." He stole another look at his watch. "Jeez, Gloria's gonna kill me."

I walked back into the room. Dale suggested dinner, but Martha said she'd rather stay through till nine, so we all did. No one else came to say good-bye.

We stopped on the way home and picked up a deli spread that Dale had had the foresight to order.

Ten

It had been decided, because of the delay with Al's body in Boston, to have the funeral on Saturday at 1 P.M., after only one day of wake. In view of Friday's turnout, it looked like a good decision.

I had a quick and simple breakfast with Dale, Larry having gone off on his own somewhere. Dale had a full morning of lessons, but he insisted I borrow his car and gave me detailed directions to Forrester Drive.

Number One Hundred was as Norm described it objectively, but not subjectively. It was made of red brick, but the brick looked dyed. The columns were too short, and the grounds more lotlike than estate-like. There was a cast-iron lackey in black-face at the ornate lamppost and two Cadillacs, one silver, the other blue, in the driveway. The overall impression was nouveau tacky.

I parked on the street and caught a chill walking to the house. I pressed the doorbell and got no immediate response. The cold made me press the button again, a little sooner than was necessary. The door opened. It was a young man with thinning hair and a narrow nose. He wore black, horn-rimmed glasses with small frames, like the kind the army would issue you for free. He asked what I wanted. As he spoke, the glasses slid halfway down his nose.

"I need to speak with your father," I guessed. "About Al Sachs."

The man swallowed and pushed his glasses up with his middle finger. "I'm sorry, but we're busy on other matters. Please call my office on Monday—"

I stepped one foot over the threshold before he thought to close the door. "I won't be here on Monday."

"Now look, fella—" he said, glasses slipping again and being righted again.

An authoritative voice from inside the house yelled, "Buzz, who the hell is it?"

Buzz. I immediately felt deeply sorry for anyone who looked like this and was nicknamed "Buzz."

"It's a man who wants to talk about Mr. Sachs."

"Get rid of him."

Buzz looked down at my foot. His glasses slid again. "He won't leave," said Buzz for me.

A disgusted guttural sound from inside the house. "Well, then, bring him in before you let every fuckin' degree of heat outta here."

Buzz showed me in.

We turned left into a large living room. There was a fire in the hearth. The furniture was expensive but ill-matched. A man in his late fifties sat on the couch, papers spread on a coffee table in front of him. He had a gray crew-cut, stolid features, and would probably have been stocky if he'd stood to greet me. He didn't bother.

"Who are you and what do you want?" he said.

Papa Straun wore black horn-rimmed glasses too. They and the last name appeared to be the only things father and son had in common.

I took one chair and Buzz took another. "My name is John Cuddy. I want to know what Al Sachs has coming to his family."

Straun snorted. Buzz said, "Are you an attorney, Mr. Cuddy?"

"No. Al was a friend from the army."

Buzz seemed to fill out a bit, perhaps relieved that he was the only lawyer in the room. "My father and I are in the process of reviewing Mr. Sachs' file, and we intend to provide Mrs. Sachs with a detailed memo of—"

"Cut the shit, Buzz," said Straun. "You an MP too?"

"Yes."

"I was Armor. With Patton. Didn't have to go. They had deferments then for guys in steel. Defense plant priorities, that kind of stuff. But I went anyway." He gestured toward the papers spread on the table. "Sachs said in his interview that he was an MP. Weren't many Jews in my outfit."

I made no comment.

"Aren't a hell of a lot of Jews in the city. Some people think I hired Sachs because he was a Jew and could sell. That's bullshit. I hired him because he was from New York, and we thought we could get some orders back there by usin' a guy from there. But he wouldn't play the game, you know."

I made no comment again.

"He had ideas about how to do things different. So I gave him a chance. But he sucked." Buzz flinched, and Straun dug out a ledger sheet. "He made his draw three months outta the last twelve. I shoulda sacked him in August." Straun tossed the sheet in a spinning motion so it ended up on my side of the table. "See for yourself."

I didn't look down at the paper.

Straun worked his mouth a little without speaking. Buzz was fidgeting. I broke the silence.

"He left a wife and a child. What do they have coming?"

"Nothing," said Straun.

"You see, Mr. Cuddy," said Buzz, "Mr. Sachs exercised his option to convert what insurance was provided to cash as a credit against his draw. It's all here in detail in a draft memo—"

"Buzz," snapped Straun, pushing a mug toward him, "get me some more coffee."

Buzz looked from me to him then back to me.

"Mr. Cuddy," he said, crestfallen, "would you like . . ."

I shook my head. Buzz picked up the mug and stepped from the room.

"You ever read Dr. Spock, Straun?"

"What?" he said.

"Skip it. In plain English, where does Al's family stand?"

"The kid's right," said Straun defensively. "Law school, Harvard Law School, can you imagine. He goes through Harvard and he's like a rabbit, you couldn't trust him to run a pony ride and do it right. But he writes a hell of a memo, that boy. He's dead right about Sachs. The guy gave up every kinda benefit we give to keep covering his draw. He was gettin' the heave-ho this week. Then he got killed." Straun's face changed a little, almost human. "Funny, you know the papers had how he was done in. I never figured him for a queer."

I tried to remind myself that guys like me aren't supposed to hit people older and smaller without physical provocation. "Did Al know he was going to be fired?"

Straun blinked at me. "Yeah, he knew. I told him two weeks ago. Two weeks ago today. The state says you gotta give 'em two weeks' notice, so that's what he got."

Buzz came back in, clutching the coffee mug in both hands. His hands trembled and some spilled onto his top fingers. He winced, but kept silent and kept coming.

"Anything else?" said Straun, taking the mug in his left hand.

"Yes," I said. "The funeral's at one. Today."

Straun slurped some coffee. "Don't wait for us," he said, motioning Buzz to the paperwork.

I leaned across the table and grabbed Straun's left wrist. I thought about twisting it toward me, spilling the coffee onto the papers, but I figured that would only inconvenience Buzz. So I twisted away, toward Straun's ample lap. He jumped up screaming.

"What the fuck was that?" he shrieked, grabbing his crotch and jumping from one leg to another.

"A small gesture," I said.

Buzz ran to get some towels and ice while I let myself out.

When Beth died, Joe Mirelli, a priest and friend, said her funeral mass. I remember him delaying the beginning of the service so that the latecomers could be parked outside and seated inside. I'm sure Jake

Cribbs often made the same suggestion. But not that day.

Martha and Carol, Dale and Larry, and me. The kids were at Carol's house with her sitter. The elder Cribbs and the younger Cribbs. All told, one man short on pall bearers.

We stood in the same room as yesterday. Jake Cribbs checked his watch at the stroke of one and bade us be seated. After Martha sat down, Cribbs walked over to her, bent at the waist and held her right hand with both of his. He said something, and she nodded. Then he walked graduation step to the slim podium next to Al's coffin at the front of the room.

He spoke for perhaps four minutes. Al's birth, schooling, military service. Meeting Martha, marriage, life in Pittsburgh. No mention of work, means of death, or thinness of crowd. Acknowledged each in the audience by first name, correctly assigning us to one or another part of his or Martha's life. Then a pause, then a moment of silence for Al. I recalled Beth's hour-long high mass and eulogy. Religion be damned, tradition be damned, when my time comes, let there be a quiet, sincere professional like the elder Cribbs. To recount briefly and acknowledge accurately. No incense, no ritual, no organ music.

Cribbs asked us to stand. We did so. Martha was seated immediately in front of me. Her shoulders rose and fell a bit more frequently than normal breathing would require, but no sound, no tears.

Cribbs gestured toward Al. Larry, Dale, the younger Cribbs, and I positioned ourselves two on a side at the coffin. The younger Cribbs tugged and pushed the stretcherlike contraption upon which the coffin rested, and we wheeled it down the aisle. It was a symbolic journey only, the coffin stopping at the door. We mourners filed out of the room and the home, leaving Al with the professionals for maneuvering the coffin into the hearse.

We had come from Martha's house in Carol's ten-year-old Buick four-door, but a liveried driver awaited us in the driveway. He stood at parade rest rather than lean against the black Cadillac limousine. We squeezed in, sitting close and salon-style in the facing seats. We pulled away from the funeral home, the hearse sliding behind us, headlights ablaze. Not even Dale attempted conversation for the next fifteen minutes.

The cemetery had a graveyard's gateway and ground plan. Given all the hills around Pittsburgh, the terrain was surprisingly, even disappointingly, level. I couldn't help comparing Beth's sloping view of the harbor to Al's blind, bleak valley, even though I knew her site was more comfort to me than to her.

The driver pulled to a stop at a landmark I couldn't distinguish. He got out and yanked open our door. The comfortable if claustrophobic interior of the limo had insulated us from the winter outside. An icy blade of wind plowed through the salon, giving us the shivers. All exited, we males repeating our superfluous escort of Al's coffin as we wended between already occupied plots to the open gash he would fill. I wondered what machinery was necessary to dig holes in this weather and how simpler generations managed in the old days.

Two cemetery employees materialized at the grave. I paid not much attention to the details of what came next. I was watching Martha as we arranged ourselves, buffeted by the wind and cold, on one short end of the grave.

The ceremony consisted of a neutral reading by Cribbs and the slow, steady lowering of the coffin by the cemetery staff using strong sashes which were recovered as the coffin reached bottom. The younger Cribbs produced, magicianlike, a small bouquet of roses. Beginning with Carol, we each in turn broke a blossom off its stem, bent over the grave and tossed underhand the blossom onto the coffin. Martha was last. As she edged to the opening, I edged near her. When she let go her blossom, her eyes rolled back up into her head and her right leg started to slide forward, like a driver's foot applying brake pressure in slow motion.

Carol cried out, and Dale and Larry snapped their heads up. I caught Martha at the shoulders just as she unconsciously, and perhaps subconsciously, began her slide down toward Al.

"She's still asleep. The boys too."

The television showed a boxing match silently progressing. The fighters were lightweights, neither seeing his tenth professional fight yet. But at five-fifteen on a Saturday afternoon in February, beggars couldn't be choosers. I had turned the sound off during the first round to avoid some local 'caster who modeled himself on Howard Cosell.

Before she went upstairs to check on Martha and the kids, Carol had been in the kitchen, counting leftovers from last night's deli spread. Before that, she'd been curled up in one of the two chairs in the room, thumbing through a magazine while I killed three vodka/rocks. Now she took the other end of the couch. Within touching range.

"That Ruthie is a *great* babysitter," she said. "She wears Kenny *out.* All I have to do is feed him and forget him."

She gave me a big smile. I smiled back.

"And those pills. I'll have to remember the name of them. They knocked Martha clean out."

"You'd need a prescription for them," I said.

"Easy enough. I meet a lot of doctors at the club. Doctors, lawyers, bankers, you name it."

We had gotten Martha from the cemetery to a local emergency room, where Dale and I cooled our heels in the waiting room for a few hours while Larry and Carol rode back with Cribbs to pick up her car and rejoin us. The doctor, when we finally saw her, prescribed some tranquilizer/sleeping pills, which we filled on the way home. Carol changed at her place while dismissing supersitter Ruthie, then got Martha and the boys bedded down back at the Sachs residence. She was wearing designer jeans that made a little too much of her little too ample rump. She also wore a lamb's-wool V-neck sweater and no apparent breast supporter.

"Not many private eyes, though."

"I'm sorry?" I said.

"Not many private detectives at the club. Lawyers and doctors and such, but not many detectives."

"Tough way to make a living. Most of us don't."

"I'll bet you're pretty good at it. Can you tell me about some of your cases?"

I closed my eyes and leaned my head back. Carol was exhibiting what I call the post-mortem high. When you witness your first few deaths and burials, particularly in your age group, you feel so relieved to be quit of the depressing rituals, not to mention so relieved that you're still alive, that you adopt a partylike attitude. Gregarious, flirtatious, boisterous. Different people adopt different attitudes. But they all point in the same direction, toward life and away from death.

The only problem, I have found, is that after enough deaths, especially close ones, you wait at the departure point long after your fellow mourners have begun moving toward the destination. You remain a wet blanket at the party.

"Well, can you talk about your cases?" she said, trying to fill the clumsy silence I was creating.

"Not much," I said. "Professional confidentiality."

"Uh-*huh,*" she said terminally. "Well, I guess I'll go check on supper again." She stood up. "What do you want?"

I suddenly found I couldn't swallow too easily. Carol really did look a lot like Audrey Hepburn, a little harder in the eyes and softer in the hips, but a lot.

"John? What do you want?"

"I want," I started thickly, then forced a swallow. "I want you to sit next to me, and hug me until I fall asleep."

She blinked three or four times, then came over and knelt down on the couch next to me. She buried her face in my shoulder and clamped her arms around my neck. We started crying at about the same time, crying with each other and for each other and for all the slights and hurts and tragedies that had piled up since the last time either of us had an other to hug.

Eleven

I AWAKENED AT 9:30 P.M. CAROL WASN'T THERE BUT A jackhammer headache was, partly from the straight vodka itself and partly from the dehydration it causes. I ran my tongue over my front teeth. They felt furry. I heard cutlery clatter coming from the kitchen. My stomach growled in reaction. I could feel the death gloom sliding away, eroded by soothing sleep and growing hunger.

I was stretching and thinking about searching for aspirin when I heard a faint tapping at the front door. I crossed the room and opened it.

Dale blew in, borne by an arctic blast. "Christ, what a climate," I said.

"Oh," he said, pushing back his parka hood, "you get used to it." He dropped his voice. "How's Martha doing? We were afraid the telephone might wake her up."

"I think she's fine. I just woke up myself."

"John," said Carol from the kitchen, "who is it?"

Dale looked from the kitchen to me and cleared his throat. I guessed my hair and clothes looked like I *had* just awakened and, possibly, not alone.

Carol came out. "Oh, hi, Dale, we're just about to attack your food again. Join us?"

Dale relaxed a little. "That would be fine. An old friend of Larry's from college is in town and they're out . . . having dinner."

"Terrific," said Carol, pirouetting and heading back to the kitchen. "Martha and the boys—"

She was interrupted by a plaintive "Mommieeeee" from upstairs. She was by me like a punt returner and halfway up the steps. "Get started," she said. "I'll be right down."

Dale laid his parka on a chair, and he and I went into the kitchen. Carol had laid out the now-smaller spread in an appetizing fan around the table.

"Dale," I said, "do you have any idea where Martha would keep her aspirin? I got a little drunk after we got home, and I was just recovering from passing out when you knocked."

My explanation was a bit elaborate for a mere aspirin request, but the dismissing of my and Carol's shadow relationship seemed to relax Dale even more.

"Nooo, but"—he dug into the pockets of his pants and came up with a one-dozen tin—"I'm never without these."

He popped the tin, and I thanked him for the two I took from it. I had washed them down with tap water, and Dale was halfway through his migraine tales when Carol reappeared in the doorway.

"Bad news, fellas," she said, sagging her shoulder into the doorjamb. "Kenny's sick. Fever and sore throat. The last thing Martha needs now is a sick Al Junior, so I'm gonna take Kenny home right away."

"No problem," I said. "I'll stay here tonight and keep an eye on Martha."

Carol nodded. "I just looked in on her. She's dead to the . . . she's sound asleep. Little Al, too."

Dale insisted on making her a sandwich to take back, and Carol went upstairs to bundle Kenny up. When she came back down, I walked her to the door.

"Here's your sandwich," I said, sliding it into her coat pocket. Kenny was completely concealed in a blanket. "Would you like some help with him?" I said.

"No, thanks," she said. "Lean down, though, will you?"

I leaned down toward her, and she gave me a quick but a shade-more-than-friendly kiss on the lips. "If you get lonely and want to talk, give me a call. I'm in the book. K-r-a-u-s-e."

"I remember," I said. "Thanks."

I opened the tundra turnstile, and she scooted outside.

When I got back to the kitchen, the vodka bottle was three fingers lower than I'd remembered leaving it. Dale sucked liberally from a tumbler with just ice and clear liquid in it. My vodka memories being too recent and still powerful, I chose a beer.

"I don't know. I just don't know. . . ."

It was nearly eleven o'clock. Dale and I had polished off two sandwiches each. I was only on my second beer. The vodka tide was ebbing inexorably from the bottle and toward Dale. At first I thought he was suffering a post-funeral low. Then the conversation turned to Larry.

"I just don't know," said Dale for the third time. He had put in a tough couple of days, too, so I kept up my part of the conversation.

"Know what?"

"Oh"—Dale blinked and sucked up another mouthful of vodka—"life. The 'where-is-it-all-leading' problem. I'm forty-six years old. Larry's twenty-nine. I love teaching and tutoring music, but if it weren't for some family money, I'd . . . we'd . . . never have been able to afford the house. As it is, I don't know what I'd do if I needed to buy a new car. I had a German car, a VW Bug, until three years ago. But after, you know, the recession, I couldn't, I *couldn't* stand not buying an American car with American steel. It's not such a great car, but whenever I complain about what I've got or where I am, all I have to do is click on the TV or walk down the street. Do you know what this city's unemployment rate is?"

"No," I said. "I don't."

Dale grimaced and took another gulp of booze.

"The official rate is fifteen, sixteen percent. Unofficially, counting the people who've been out of work so long they're probably not in the computers anymore, the real rate now must be almost twenty-five percent. Walk down the streets, you'll see them. Big, strong men in bowling jackets and baseball caps just standing on corners. Or waiting in line for *any* kind of job that's listed. Their jobs, the industries that made their jobs *real,* are gone. Some gone to other countries, some just gone for good. A man who used to make steel can't feed his family, but I can make a living teaching piano. You figure it out."

"It is out of whack, a little."

Dale sighed and seemed to run out of steam. Which was just as well, because I needed some answers before he slid into a different kind of trance.

"Dale—"

"No, not Dale," he said. "Stanislaw. That's my real name. Stanislaw Ptarski. I grew up in a little town fifteen miles from here. My father was in steel. God"—he laughed—*"God,* he would have cracked me good for saying that. That he was 'in steel,' like he was 'in stocks' or 'in banking.' He was a steelworker, pure and simple. Thirty-six years. He'd tell me about the Depression, how people pulled together. I'm glad he never had to see what's happened now. Or hear the name change. After he died, I found that people didn't want piano lessons from a portly gay named Stosh Ptarski. I don't know, maybe it hit a little too close to home, with the ethnic name and all. So I changed it, and people were much more comfortable with a portly gay named Dale Palmer, like I had been imported from somewhere else, like I hadn't grown up with them here and still turned out . . ." He seized up for a minute.

"Dale . . ."

"Do you know," he said blinking, "do you know how I picked the names, 'Dale' and 'Palmer'?"

"No."

"Well, when I was younger, and TV arrived, my favorite cartoon characters were Chip 'n Dale, you know, the Disney chipmunks. And just after Dad died, this baseball pitcher, terrifically handsome guy named Jim Palmer, had a great season and was all over the papers. I was in Baltimore once and even went to see him play. And I can't stand baseball, to me it's like watching golf, you know, all tension and no real release. Not like football, where you get to take out . . . no, no, that's how I named myself, after a chipmunk and a jock."

Dale closed his eyes and leaned back in the chair.

"Dale . . ."

"Yes," he said quietly.

"I need to know some things. To help Martha."

"Yes?" he said, opening his eyes.

"I can see for myself that this place hasn't been brought along at all. There are things that have to be done that haven't been done."

Dale's expression changed from philosophical to sad. "Nobody likes to meddle in another family's problems. But pretty clearly things weren't going too well for Al at his job. I assume they told you that this morning."

"Yes."

"Well, most of us around here, Al and Martha included, bought under a special mortgage program. Even if I weren't half drunk, it would take a lawyer to explain it to you. But basically, because of some federal/state deal, we got low-interest mortgages to come in and try to revive this area. The catch is that renovations have to be mostly done by a certain deadline, something like two years after you move in. You also have to complete the work by something like a year later. Larry and I finished ours way ahead. Carol was just under the wire. Al and Martha had already been inspected—the state sends somebody to walk through your house—and the inspector failed them. I mean, you see the fixtures and all, he had no choice. With the economy around here, speculators are hovering like vultures over properties like this. Two families on the next block already lost their places. I never asked Al about it, but—" Dale moved his hands in a shrugging gesture that rattled the cubes in the glass he was holding but couldn't hurt the long-departed vodka.

"You mean unless the renovations are done pretty damn quick, Martha loses the place?"

Dale nodded slowly. "The renovations are the big thing. The monthly mortgage, property taxes . . . they could be manageable . . . look"—Dale leaned forward, put his glass down on the table and wiped his hands on his pants—"I've never told Martha, but Al borrowed money from all of us. Me, Carol, and I'm sure others, though from the funeral, perhaps not. Al was in desperate financial shape. I honestly don't know how he thought he'd pull even."

I got that sick-stomach feeling again, the one I'd gotten when I heard the radio announcer in Boston describe Al's body being found. I was beginning to realize how Al thought he could pull even.

"How much?" I said. "How much for the renovations?"

Dale inhaled deeply and exhaled slowly. "I would guess twenty thousand."

I did a quick room-by-room allocation. "That doesn't sound like enough," I said.

Dale pinched his nose. "One Sunday last fall, I'd gotten two free tickets to a Steelers home game. I asked Al, but Martha and Al Junior were both sick, so he had to stay home. I dragged Larry along. He's not much for football, but he came anyway so I'd have someone to go with. Anyway, about midway through the second half, three guys a few rows behind us started saying . . . things. About my toupee, about Larry, who had worn some, well, tight jeans to the game, and so on. They were drunk and really obnoxious, and we left just before the end of the game. On our way up the aisle, Larry said something to one of them, and that one tried to come after us, but we moved pretty quickly and lost him in the crowd.

"It was still nice weather so we had walked to Three Rivers stadium and were walking home. Just as we turned onto our street, I heard a car roar up behind and then slam on its brakes as it pulled even with us. It was the three guys from the game. I don't know how they found us. There are a lot of bars down in the square, maybe they were headed for one of them, maybe it was just a wild coincidence. Anyway, the guy Larry had said something to at the game got out of the car and came running up to us. We were across the street from our place, perhaps five doors down from this place. The other two guys came up too. The first guy grabbed Larry—he was at least two hundred pounds—and slammed Larry against the car, screaming the usual 'homo' stuff at him. I said to let him go, and he didn't, I said it loud and he still didn't so I punched him hard, just above the kidney. You know what I mean?"

I thought back to Marco at the courthouse elevator and said, "Yes, I do."

"Well," said Dale, "that was a really stupid thing for me to do. Maybe the guy would have been satisfied to just push Larry around and scream some more. But once I punched him, and he sank to the ground, the other two guys jumped on me. One pinned my arms, the other began punching me in the stomach. The second punch really hurt, and I cried out. Larry kicked the guy who punched me, and that guy turned and punched Larry hard in the face. Larry went backwards onto the hood of the car, blood everywhere. I was struggling, but weakly because of my stomach hurting so much. The guy I had hit staggered up. He and the guy Larry had kicked then started punching and kicking Larry, hard, viciously. I think I started screaming.

"I never even saw Al approaching us. I found out later he'd heard some yelling and looked out his front window. The next thing I knew, Al was behind the two guys who were hitting Larry. Al kicked one of them hard behind the knee cap, and he just went down. The other guy, the one I had punched, turned and swung at Al. Al just let the man's fist go by his head, then jabbed at the guy's throat, just quickly and lightly"—Dale demonstrated—"like a snake striking. This guy started coughing and dropped to his knees. The other guy, the one on the ground, was just writhing, yelling about cramps.

"I realized the guy holding me had let go. He was watching Al and backing away. I ran over to Larry. He was conscious but in a lot of pain.

"Al ignored the third guy, instead he bent down and yanked the wallets of both of the men he'd hit. He flipped through them, reading, and then pulled out money from each.

" 'Hey,' said the third guy, 'what the hell . . .'

" 'Just squaring things,' said Al, just like that. 'Just squaring things.' "

Dale and I looked at each other for a moment.

"Then Al asked the third guy if he was the driver. The guy said no, Al said, 'You are now,' and with that Al pulled open the rear door and tossed, and I mean just picked them up and threw, the two guys into the back seat. He flung their wallets in on top of them. By this time, the third guy was getting in on the driver's side. I got Larry's arm around my shoulder and pulled him off the hood. The keys must have been in the ignition because the third guy started it up right away. Al leaned into the passenger's side and said, 'I know who you two are and where you live. You guys and us are square now. Debt owed and paid. You give my friends any more trouble, I pay you guys a house call. Now get out of here!' "

"The third guy put the car in gear and took off, tires squealing. Al pushed the money into my pocket and drove us to the hospital. Larry needed some stitches in his lip and we were both black and blue for a time, but without Al, we'd have been . . . And then for Al to die . . . the way . . . the papers said."

Dale stopped and bowed his head. It was so quiet in the house that I could hear the refrigerator motor clicking and whirring.

"No," resumed Dale, head still bowed. "I have a few friends in the trades who owe me favors, too. To square things, twenty thousand would be plenty."

Dale left a few minutes later. It is eerie to be alone in a strange house when you can't make much noise. At the same time, it was the first time I had been on my own, and conscious, since getting on the plane in Boston. I wasn't really sleepy after my nap earlier, but I was afraid calling Carol might strengthen a wrong impression.

I tried to discharge my night-nurse duties toward Al Junior and Martha. Shortly after closing the door behind Dale, I tiptoed upstairs and looked in on them. Both seemed sound asleep in their respective rooms. I came back downstairs and found a science fiction paperback by Larry Niven and let my thoughts drift with his. I finished the book at 2:30 A.M. and tried to tote up what I knew so far about Al's death.

Murphy's investigation confirmed that Al had come to Boston on business legitimately. Al had called me, seen his customers, albeit fruitlessly, and had one other appointment. He hadn't told me he was in money trouble. He had told me he'd made a bet on the Bruins the night before and won. I couldn't remember Al ever talking hockey before, and he had never been a gambler. Of course, a man in a money squeeze might try a lot of new ways to ease the pressure. Still, Al would have been too smart to trust some guy in a strange city to pay him off the next night. And I couldn't quite picture a bookie killing Al by mutilation and passing it off as some ritualistic slaying to deflect attention.

In fact, when you thought about it, what could have been worth what Al's killer had gone through? I had to admit that a secret appointment suggested blackmail. Assuming the killer was Al's secret appointment, why keep the appointment at all? Why not just run? Identities can be changed, passage and even sanctuary bought pretty easily. The killer must have had something more to protect than just his own skin. Maybe some illiquid asset or business operation. That would explain the pass-off method of killing. It would also explain the torture, the tossing of Al's room, and the gander at my message. The visit to the motel room and desk were both risks, small risks to be sure, but nevertheless risks of being spotted, identified, and connected with Al and therefore with Al's death. The killer would have run that risk only if his identity were subordinated to protecting something else. He preferred to risk being spotted in order to be sure something that tied him to Boston was secure.

And about Al's being so oblique with me on the telephone? He had to let me know he was trying something so the something wouldn't be gone forever. But he also couldn't drag me into it beforehand and therefore perhaps unnecessarily. No matter how pressed for money Al was, he would never have asked me to help him with something shady. He would have had to handle the someone alone.

A someone who was good enough to take Al, who only a few months before was himself still good enough to cool a couple of stadium toughies. I didn't think Al would have met someone like that selling steel gizmos to distributors or general contractors. But we had both met a lot of people like that somewhere else. I moved J.T.'s name up near the top of my list of tomorrow's phone calls.

Twelve

I BLINKED. THE DIM SUNLIGHT OF A FEBRUARY MORNING in Pittsburgh slanted through the front window. I was lying on the couch. My teeth felt as though they would fall out if I didn't brush them soon. I sat up, and my kidneys ached all the way to my shoulder blades. A full night's sleep on a horizontal and firm mattress would do me a world of good.

From the kitchen came some quiet tinkling of tableware and the scuffing sound of slippered feet. I walked into the kitchen.

Martha was at the sink, her back to me, carefully stacking glasses on the dish rack. She had pulled on a turtleneck sweater with a hole in the left elbow. Her hair was drawn back into a bobbed ponytail. The clock above her head said 10:20 A.M.

"Good morning," I said softly.

She jumped but recovered nicely, reaching for a towel to dry her hands. "Good morning, John. I wish we had a better place for you. How did you sleep?"

"Fine." Her voice sounded steady and strong, with none of the false bravado high, or grief. "You?"

"Uh," she giggled, embarrassed, "those pills must really be something. I remember Carol making me take two. I'd hate to think what more of them would . . ."

The possibility darkened her face like a small cloud crossing the sun. It passed quickly, and the sun shone again.

"I'm afraid I haven't been too steady the last few days. I do want to thank you for all you've . . ."

I slowly put my hand in a stop sign. She stopped, broadening her smile. She came over to me, and we hugged as brother and sister might.

"He tried so hard," she whispered past my shoulder.

"He always did, Martha."

We broke apart. She returned to the sink.

"I'm sorry I didn't get to those last night," I said.

She shook her head over the sink. "Don't be silly. There's coffee on. Help yourself."

"I don't take it," I reminded her.

"Oh, right. I'm sorry. I forgot. Help yourself to anything else."

"Thanks, but I think I'll hop over to Dale's and clean up instead. Anyplace nearby where I can get a newspaper?"

"The Pittsburgh papers are in a couple of stores in the square. If you want the *New York Times,* go to the drugstore." She looked up at the clock. "Tell them you're staying with us, Al always . . . they save one for us."

"Right," I said. "How's Al Junior?"

"Fine. He was up at seven pounding on me to play with him."

"Carol had said Kenny was a little sick last night. She took him home."

"Carol's a wonderful girl. Really a heart of gold.

Always watching out like an older sister." Martha stopped, then added quickly. "She's not really *older*, you know. I mean, she's maybe a year or so older than I am. I mean she just seems more, well mature."

"Hard times can do that," I said, and immediately regretted it.

Martha's silence confirmed that she was just thinking about that herself. I said I would see her later and left.

I used my key at Dale's front door. I closed it quietly behind me. There was some soft symphonic music playing through the living room stereo speaker.

"Larry. Lar—" Dale stopped when he saw me. He was standing in the archway to the dining room. He was wearing a black kimono with orange dragons. It looked like silk from across the living room. He recovered by saying, "Oh, John! You know, I had forgotten all about you. I was too soused to have heard you come in last night, anyway."

"I stayed at Martha's as sentinel. Carol had to go home with Kenny."

Dale struck his forehead with a mock fist. "Oh, of course. The beauty of vodka is it doesn't leave me with a hangover no matter how many brain cells it kills." He looked back into the dining room. "Sundays are pretty casual around here. Join me for brunch?"

I'm not too good at guessing whether truly courteous people are being sincere or just being courteous. I gambled on sincere. "Sounds terrific."

I won my gamble because he brightened considerably.

"Dale, do I have time to brush my teeth?"

"Sure thing," he said. "And shower and shave too if you want." He frowned. "I don't mean you have to, I just mean . . ."

"I'd rather shave and shower as long as it won't wreck anything."

"Oh no, no, please do. Since I didn't know when . . . I planned everything flexibly today." He scratched the back of his neck, to distract him, more than me, from his thoughts.

"I'll be down in twenty minutes."

"Perfect," he said.

As I trotted up the stairs, I thought, with the haughtiness of a true Boston liberal, that Larry was screwing up a pretty good man.

Brunch was apple fritters, country sausage, fresh pineapple, and corn muffins. Neither of us had learned our lesson the night before, so we washed it down with fresh-squeezed orange juice laced with vodka. We had a pleasant talk, I assuring him that I would be flying out in the afternoon, he assuring me that I could stay as long as I cared to, me declining politely. I turned the conversation gently back to Martha and her progress, then toward Al's house before asking him again.

"Last night you said twenty thousand dollars of renovation would satisfy the inspector."

"Twenty thousand will do it." Dale fixed me solidly. "But I can't believe that Al left anywhere near that."

"Maybe he had some insurance."

"Through Straun?"

I shook my head.

Dale tilted his quizzically. "Through the army?"

"Maybe. In a manner of speaking."

Dale squinted at me. "What do you mean?"

I rapped my knuckles lightly on the tabletop. "I'm not sure."

The sun kept the cold wind at the invigorating level. There were a number of couples out walking arm in arm, here and there two men or two women, not arm in arm. I hit the square in three blocks and turned into the drugstore.

There were maybe ten or fifteen people shopping, dressed up from church, some with bakery or small grocery bags in their hands. Three or four kids squealed. Somebody's mother told them to be quiet. I walked to the newspaper stand and hefted a thick *Pittsburgh Press*. I didn't see any *New York Times*.

I made my way to the counter. Two burly guys about my age in sweat outfits and workboots were thumbing through a *Penthouse*. They smelled pretty ripe, and I had a feeling they wouldn't be buying it. They had their backs to me when I asked the older man behind the counter for a *Times*.

"Sorry," he said, "sold out."

"Maybe you're saving one. I'm staying with the Sachses."

He smiled just as one of the guys said, "Sachs! That's the fuckin' faggot who got killed. Remember, you asked me and I couldn't remember his name. Sachs, yeh."

The old man dropped his smile and got sad and angry at the same time. The two still hadn't turned around. "Hey! This ain't no library. Buy somethin' or get out."

It became quiet around the counter. Still without turning, one guy gave the old man the finger while the other very deliberately dropped the *Penthouse* on the floor and picked up a *Oui* and began thumbing through it.

I glanced around. Most of the men were middle-aged or young and "professional" looking. I didn't believe the guys knew that I was the one who had mentioned Al's name.

I set my paper on the counter and cut off the old man's next comment as I turned to face the backs of the two browsers.

"Take it back," I said in a deeper than conversational tone.

One guy stiffened a little, the other turned around easily, smiling meanly.

"Ya say somethin'?" asked the relaxed one.

"Yes. I said take it back."

The stiffer one spoke. "Take what back?"

"What your friend here just said about my friend."

"Your friend?" said the relaxed one, stiffening a little now himself. "Whaddaya mean, *your* friend?"

"Sachs. Al Sachs. We went through the service together. I just buried him, and you just insulted him. Now take it back."

There was a little buzz behind me. The counterman started to say something, but stopped when I held up my hand.

"I ain't takin' nothin' back," said the formerly relaxed one. His partner stole a quick look at the entrance to the store.

I looked at the partner. "Long ways away, that door." I looked back at the speaker. "Now, take it back."

"Fuck you," he said, growing less relaxed by the minute. "My brother-in-law's a cop."

"Take it back or you'll wish he was a plastic surgeon."

Speaker wet his lips with his tongue. He searched around for support from behind me. I was pretty sure he wouldn't find any. His eyes told me he hadn't.

"I ain't takin' nothin' back."

"This is like the schoolyard, boyo. You said something I didn't like. All you have to do is take it back. But you have to do that."

"You can't hold us here," said partner, eyeing the door again. "That's like kidnappin' or somethin'."

"In a minute," I said, "it's gonna be like atrocious assault and battery or somethin'." I could feel my blood rising for the fight. It showed in my voice. "Now, take it back."

Speaker wet his lips again. He glanced around the crowd futilely a final time. He dropped his eyes and mumbled something.

"Louder," I said.

"I take it back! I take it back! Awright, awright, ya satisfied now?"

"Yeah," I exhaled. "I'm satisfied."

Speaker flew by partner who dropped the *Oui* and followed him outside. A few people talked quietly but nobody laughed. I bent over and replaced their magazines on the rack. I took the shaking *Times* the man extended to me. I dropped four dollars on the counter, scooped up my Pittsburgh paper, too, and left.

As I walked back to Dale's, my spirit was down again. I tried to persuade myself that my macho show was a reaction to the derogatory word speaker had used. Rather than a reaction, you see, to the underlying implication. And the resulting association that I still found insulting and threatening. Yeah, sure.

Dale and I polished off the remaining screwdrivers while exchanging sections of the *Times*. He tried to camouflage his glances toward the clock, but as they became more frequent, I had the impression that my presence was increasing rather than lightening his embarrassment over Larry's continuing absence. I asked if I could use his phone, and he directed me to the one in the upstairs hall. I asked him if he had heard from a J. T. Kivens. He said no, but, with being out, literally and figuratively . . .

I went upstairs. I started with the airlines. USAir had a flight to D.C. that night and two the next morning, but both the Monday A.M. flights were full. I chose the 7:30 P.M. flight, which gave me five hours till I had to check in. I remembered Marriott had a hotel at the Key Bridge, and I used their 800 number to book a room for that night and Monday.

I had directory assistance scour the listings for D.C. and every surrounding suburb I could think of, but no "Kivens." J.T. might be unlisted, or he might live farther out from the District. I called the Pentagon direct dial number for J.T. No answer. I tried the Pentagon main number. The duty officer who answered was about as helpful as a 1963 calendar. He would not confirm that a Colonel Kivens was still at the Pentagon and certainly could not divulge any "data" about anyone's home address or telephone. He suggested that I try again on Monday morning.

Next I used the operator to call the Coopers. The

voice at the other end was familiar, but chilling. "I'm sorry, but the number you have dialed is not in service. Please—"

It was their new, unlisted number, but it had rung all right on Friday.

I hung up immediately and called Nancy Meagher's home number. No answer.

I hung up and tried District C, the police division in Dorchester. "Boston Police Emergency—Sergeant Jenkins—you are being tape-recorded. Go ahead, please."

"My name is John Cuddy. I'm a private detective in Boston, but I'm calling from Pittsburgh. A couple who helped me catch a guy were threatened by his brother, and I get a number-not-in-service when I try to reach them. Can you send a car to check it?"

An exasperated grunt. "Look, buddy, this is an emergency line and—"

"The guy who threatened them is the brother of the torch who tied up and left an old watchman to die in a warehouse last—"

"Oh, shit, I'm sorry. Damn, that'll be on the tape. I'll have it checked. What's their name and address?"

"Cooper. Jesse and Emily. Two-thirty Beech Street."

"Cooper. What was that address again?"

I repeated it for him.

"Got it. I'll—hey, wait a minute. Hold on."

I could hear some clattering, more like clipboards than computer keys.

"Mr., ah, Curry, was it?" He sounded subdued.

"Cuddy. My name is Cuddy. Their name is Cooper."

His tone grew quieter. "Mr. Cuddy. I'm sorry. Here's Detective Mooney."

"Mr. Cuddy?"

"Yes."

"Detective Dan Mooney. I'm afraid you're too late. Somebody blew up the Coopers' place. Call came in at two-oh-four A.M. I just got back. The place cooled down enough to go in. They were in a back room. In bed together. Both burned to death. Are you a relative?"

"No," somebody said.

"Can you tell us who might have—"

"Do you know Nancy Meagher?" the somebody continued.

"Assistant DA?"

"Yeah."

"Yeah, I know her."

"Talk to her. The killer's name is Marco. Marco D'Amico. His parents live on Hanover Street."

"In the North End?"

"Yeah," replied the somebody.

"Mr. Cuddy, can you tell us—"

The somebody on my end hung up the telephone.

Thirteen

I WALKED INTO THE GUEST BEDROOM AND SWUNG MY suitcase up on the bed. I could fly on to Washington or back to Boston. I snapped the latches and opened it up. If I fly on to Washington, I could probably see J.T. sooner about Al. I twisted the bars that held the suit compartment closed and bent back the barrier. If I fly back to Boston, I could probably see Marco sooner about Jesse and Emily.

I packed very slowly, very deliberately. I could *call* J.T. as easily from Boston as Washington. One sock. On the other hand, Marco by then could be in custody. One pair of briefs. Of course, he might make bail. A tie. No, his brother hadn't, and it was Sunday. A crumpled shirt, the funeral-day one. Of course, it would all depend on the judge at the bail hearing, and how high he set . . .

Shit, I wanted somebody to beat, to really cream. I wanted Marco, or the guys in the drugstore, or—best of all—the shadow who killed Al.

I slumped down on the bed, then slid off and down onto my knees. I leaned over, so the top edge of the mattress pressed deeply and firmly against my tense solar plexus. Then I buried my face in my hands and prayed.

After fifteen minutes or so, I surfaced. It was stupid to go back to Boston tonight. I couldn't find Marco at my leisure last week, with his family at least approachable. I'd never find him on a Sunday night with the D'Amicos and their neighbors buttoning up the fortress. Planning Jesse and Emily's funeral would be simple enough, since neither had any family. All I had to do was call George, the friend who had helped me with the arrangements for Al. If I could reach Nancy by telephone, she could put things on hold till Tuesday night, by which time I'd be back in Boston. I was also pretty sure that whatever J.T. could give me would lead back to Boston. So, Washington it was.

I finished packing and went downstairs. Dale was scraping one-third of brunch for three into the garbage. He renewed his insistence on driving me to the airport. We confirmed six o'clock.

I left the house to cross the street. I debated between Carol's house and Martha's. The biting February wind encouraged me to make up my mind quickly. I chose Carol's.

She answered on the second ring and gave me a throw-your-head-back laugh. "John, you look *blue*. Come in, come in."

I moved past her into the hall. What I could see of her house was similar in floor plan to Martha's, and somewhere between Martha's and Dale's in decor.

She took my hand and tugged me into the living room. "Your hand's like ice, Detective," she said, leading us to her couch. "You've got to learn to wear a coat in this town."

We sat down. She had on a mesh sweater and the same jeans. She didn't seem to be wearing anything under the sweater. Again. Women seemed to be doing that a lot lately.

"What can I get you? Ask for what you want. If I don't have it, I won't be embarrassed."

"Vodka. Maybe orange juice."

"Comin' up." She squeezed my hand and went to the kitchen.

I looked around the room. Two chairs, the couch, a coffee table. Dark brown rug and fireplace. Picture frames standing on the mantel and some of the shelves. Photographs of Carol, of Kenny, of Carol and Kenny together. One or two of Martha and Al, Dale and Larry. Homey. But none of any other man. Like a man for Carol. Not so homey.

She came back into the room juggling a tray with a bottle of Gordon's vodka, a plastic decanter through which orange juice showed, and two glasses with ice.

"For a waitress, you don't look too steady."

"Thanks," she said sarcastically, "but I'm used to six-ounce glasses, not thirty-two-ounce bottles."

"They're metric now."

"Huh?"

"Metric. The booze bottles. It's not quart anymore, or fifth. Now it's point-seven-five or one liter."

"Oh," she said, examining the bottle as if it were a recently discovered artifact. "You're right. I never noticed before. Huh." She smiled. "So, how many whatevers do you want with your juice?"

"One finger would be fine."

She smiled. "Glad to see some things don't change." She fixed my drink and stirred it with a spoon on the tray, then repeated for herself.

She handed me my glass. "Cheers," she said, clinking.

"Cheers," I said and sipped. She wasn't breaking eye contact.

"So," she said, running her index finger around the rim of her glass. "Did you sleep well last night?" She smiling, eyes glittering naughtily.

I took another sip. "Fine," I said. "Carol, look, I'm sorry to change gears on you, but I just got some bad news. Some people I know, a couple who helped me in Boston, are dead. They were—" I stopped. Carol had dropped her smile, and I realized I was just taking a coward's way out, using Jesse and Emily as my way.

"John," she said putting down her drink, "I'm so sorry. I . . . can I do anything?"

I shook my head. "No, the police are on it, and there's—"

"The police?" she said. "You mean they were . . . killed?"

"Yes," I said.

"Oh, God." She twisted her hands in her lap. "God, this doesn't have anything to do with . . . with Al's . . ."

"Oh, oh, no," I said, and just stopped a smile of relief in time. "No, they were helping me on an arson case and, well, I won't be sure till I get back there, but I'm betting the brother of the guy—" I stopped again and frowned.

"What's the matter, John?"

I took a long swallow from my drink and set it down. "Carol, I'm kind of a jerk. My wife died and, well, whenever I'm with someone who, well—I—I tend to . . ."

She was looking at me a little strangely. "You tend to what?"

I sighed. "I tend to fend her off because I'm still not ready. I start to use some story or whatever to deflect—"

She put her index and middle finger on my lips, but made no move to kiss.

"You're a nice man, John. And while I took the . . . uh, the hugging and crying to be more than . . ." She put her hand back to her lap. "Look, I got divorced, you know, almost four years ago. For eight years I'd been straight as an arrow with Charley . . . that was my husband's name. He was a halfback in high school who slid into a slob working at Big Dorothy. That's a steel furnace over to Duquesne. I didn't work. He wouldn't let me. Pride, you know. Well, steel went bad, and he had no seniority, and he got laid off. I mean, no-hope time. So I went to work as a cocktail waitress, in one of those places where the tips are big because the costumes are small? And I was still straight with Charley. I had plenty of offers, even some that I would have liked but I stayed straight and—"

"Carol, I didn't mean—"

"Now be quiet and let me finish. You didn't know what you wanted to say and I know what I want to say, O.K.?"

"O.K.," I said.

"O.K. Anyways, I had the offers, and I turned them down. For Kenny's sake as much as Charley's or mine. Well, one day I was sick as a dog, I went to work anyways and, well, Charley because of the pride and the lay-off and all, wasn't *functioning* too good. At least, that's what I thought. So I leave work sick and come home early, and the bastard, the unbelievable bastard, is in our bed, with some bimbo *he'd* picked up in his bar, where him and his laid-off buddies went. Can you imagine? I'll spare you the rest of the scene, but I got a lawyer, and filed for divorce and Charley got nothing, and basically instead of Charley and me sharing the equity in the house, the lawyer and me—he was a customer at the club—the lawyer and me sold the house and "shared" it. Oh, I was really mad at Charley, and this lawyer was real smooth, tall, distinguished, and it wasn't until maybe six months later that I realized the lawyer was taking me worse than Charley had. So I broke off with him and got this place and worked three jobs to persuade this banker—who was also a customer at the club, but not a, well, you know, not like the lawyer—so I got the house and worked myself into the ground to pay for it, while Martha or Dale or Ruthie babysat Kenny. The point—" She stopped to take a breath and a slug of screwdriver. She also calmed down a little. "The point of all this is that after the lawyer, I wanted no part of anybody, maybe for all the wrong reasons, but I didn't. And it seems to me that what you're saying is that you don't want, or aren't ready to want, but it seems to me, for all the right reasons. So"—she picked up my glass and handed it to me—"here's to friends, O.K.?"

I could feel the tide rising in my eyes, and saw it reflected in hers. "Here's to friends."

We clinked and drank.

"So tell me," Carol said, "you got any relatives, male and unattached and ready, like you in Pittsburgh?"

We laughed, and the laughter made the few tears seem natural.

"Carol, before I leave—"

She was wiping her eyes but interrupted me. "Oh, John, you don't have to, we—"

"No, no," I said, holding up my hand. "I mean, before I leave for Washington tonight. I have to . . . I need to tell someone here."

"O.K."

"And I don't want to upset Martha anymore, and Dale seems a bit shaky right now, and—"

"John, just what the hell is it?"

"Carol, promise me that you won't tell anyone anything about what I'm going to say unless I tell you to."

She gave me a hard stare and frown. "But why—"

"Please, promise first."

She sighed. "I'm a sucker for promises. But I guess you can tell that already." She inhaled. "O.K., I promise."

"Carol, I don't think Al was killed by some sexual psychopath."

"Oh, but the paper said—"

"I know, I know, that's how even the police have it figured. But I roomed with Al and you've known him for years."

"Yes, but John, at the club, you see guys get drunk, and with all the pressure on Al, he could have . . ."

"I know, I know." She looked frustrated. "Look, I'm sorry I keep saying that but I heard you out, now you hear me, O.K.?"

She nodded. She didn't like it, but she let me continue.

"I don't think Al got drunk and was drawn into

anything. I think Al was pretty desperate for money, and he knew Straun was about to fire him. I also know that when Al called me in Boston, there was an edge in his voice. I was half asleep, and I can't remember every word he said, but there was something in his voice I'd never heard before. Fear. I can't say it wasn't fear over money, but the point is that I think Al was killed for something he set up."

"Set up?" Carol said. "What do you mean, set up?"

"Basically, I mean blackmail."

She nearly swung, but decided to stand up and stamp around instead. She crossed her arms against her chest. "Blackmail," she snorted. "Why, John, that's crazy. Ridiculous. Al Sachs was the most honest guy I ever met."

"Al was honest, Carol, but he had a funny twist. You ever hear him talk about squaring things?"

"What?"

"Squaring things. Like paying off a debt."

She closed her eyes for a minute. "Once. Just a comment. Somebody . . . what the hell was it. Oh, I was at their house, and Kenny and Al were watching a Steelers game and there was some commotion on the field and Kenny asked Al what happened and Al said something like, 'The Eagle hit the Steeler quarterback late, so the Steelers went after theirs. Squaring things.' I remember I told Al I would just as soon that he didn't explain things that way to my son. Al shrugged and that was it."

"Yeah, well, he signed off his telephone conversation with me like that and"—I thought of Al's broken pinkie and decided conclusions were better than details—"I'm convinced someone killed him, someone Al felt had a debt to repay. So for Al, the set-up wasn't blackmail, it was like squaring things. Paying the debt."

Carol sat down next to me again, arms still crossed. "John, I could be wrong, but I don't remember Al even mentioning he knew anyone in Boston. Not even you."

"That's why I'm going to Washington. I don't think Al would have met anybody in the steel business who would have . . . gone to such lengths to cover a killing. With luck, I may find something in the files from when he and I were in Vietnam."

Carol looked dazed. "Al's death was bad enough. But this . . . blackmail, murder. I don't know."

"Carol," I said softly, "snap back to me, please."

She looked at me, blinked a few times, then busied herself with the vodka bottle. "I'm sorry, another drink?"

"Yes, a light one." She fixed one more for each of us. No toasting, no clinking, just a couple of long draws.

"The reason I told you," I said, "is that I was wondering if you knew anybody on the local police force?"

"Police force?" she said. "Well, yeah, a couple of guys. Why?"

"I'm not trying to start a panic, and I have no reason to think anybody is interested in Martha or—"

"Oh, Jesus Christ!" Carol burst out. She slammed her drink down on the table. "This isn't funny, John. I don't want to hear—"

I set my drink down and took both her hands in mine. "I'm sorry to put it on your shoulders, kid, but you're the most solid person in the group. Just keep an eye out for anyone out of the ordinary. If you see something, like an unfamiliar car on the block for a long time, or guys in doorways, or even workmen in a vaguely painted utility truck, I want you to call your friends on the cops, and I want you to call me, and if you can't reach me, a lieutenant on the Boston force named Murphy. I'll write out names and numbers for you. But I need your promise to watch over things. O.K.?"

She slipped her hands from my grip and dropped her head down. She wrapped her arms around my neck and pulled herself into my chest, her face nestled in the hollow of my right shoulder.

"O.K.," she said softly.

"You're one of the good ones, Carol."

"Oh, yeah," she said, not leaving my shoulder. "So how come the good ones like me always find the wrong ones like you?"

I had no answer for that.

Carol released me a minute later. We exchanged a familial kiss at her door before I snowshoed down to Martha's. She answered my second series of knocks, and we walked into the living room. She had finally given up on offering me coffee, so we just sat down, her on the couch, me in a chair.

"Martha, I'll be leaving tonight."

"I really appreciate everything you've done." She ran her hand back through her hair. "John, I don't know what to say. I . . ."

"I'm going to Washington to speak to some people in the army. I'm expecting there will be some benefits coming to you."

"Benefits?"

"Yes," I lied, or almost. "As a result of Al's service."

She squinted at me. "Al let his GI insurance lapse." She gave half a laugh. "Al let lots of things lapse."

"Well," I said, "you never know. He saw some combat, and well, that's why I'm going to find out."

She looked skeptical. "Wouldn't the local Veterans Administration be able to answer that kind of question?"

"Maybe."

"Then why go to Washington?"

"Best to start at the top."

She crossed her arms and tapped her foot. "John, what is it?"

"What?"

"What you're not telling me. What's going on?"

"Nothing," I said, smiling and raising my hand. "Scout's honor."

"Does it have . . ." She swallowed hard and tears peeked over her bottom eyelids. "Is it because of the way Al died?"

I swallowed too. "Partly. I really can't tell you any more."

"For my own protection?"

I shook my head.

"I'll bet," she said. "For God's sake, John, are we in danger? Tell me!"

"Martha, I don't believe you're in any danger. If I did, I wouldn't leave you and Al Junior alone. But there is something that I can't identify or describe to you that's wrong with Al's death. Also, I just got word that some friends . . . an older couple I'd come to know in Boston, were killed in a fire this morning."

"Oh, John," Martha said, distracted, as are most decent people, from her own tragedy by news of another's. "I'm so sorry. Can I help or . . .?"

"No, no, it's all being taken care of. It's just that—" I broke a weak smile. "It's just that I'm not my usual Gaelic happy-go-lucky self."

She laughed and the tension was gone for a moment. "John," she said, "please be careful. Nothing can bring Al back, and if I thought that you—"

"Not to worry," I said. "I'm just going to see a couple of bureaucrats, that's all."

Fourteen

"You know, as long as the snow isn't falling, I think I like Pittsburgh best at this time of year."

The Pontiac bounced over a freeze-thaw pothole and Dale had to wrestle the car back into our lane. A limo with windows tinted black honked an arrogant, unnecessary warning as it blew by us on the left.

"Bastard," said Dale with gusto. He turned to me. "It did no good, but it had to be said."

"Yeah." I was running low on small talk. I had already thanked him for driving me to the airport, told him a little about Jesse and Emily, and avoided the subject of the still-AWOL Larry.

"I like it—winter, I mean—best because it's the cleanest and the purest season. Pittsburgh used to have a terrible pollution problem. Air pollution, I mean. Fifteen years ago, you couldn't wear something white outdoors unless you wanted the air to embroider a soot pattern on it. Then the town fathers with, I'm sure, some prodding from Washington, began cleaning things up. In the summer, of course, it's hot and uncomfortable anywhere. But in the winter, with so little pollution and the cold, clear snap of the arctic and sunshine like we had today, well," he said, winding down, "it's just my favorite time."

He made me think back.

"My wife and I used to go to the beach in the winter."

"Caribbean?"

"Oh, yeah, sometimes. But I meant the beach in Massachusetts. North of Boston maybe forty miles is a town called Newburyport. East of the town is an island, a peninsula really, called Plum Island Reserve. The feds run it as a bird sanctuary, and it's still pretty wild, in the picturesque sense. She'd pack a light lunch and a flask of brandy. We'd bundle up against the cold and walk like Eskimos along the shoreline. You don't get much surf in New England generally, but in the winter, on a windy day, you'll see three- or four-foot rollers slamming in on the rocks, scattering sea gulls and jerks like us who'd crept too close looking for tide treasures."

"Sounds delightful," said Dale sincerely, then uncertainly. "Have you been divorced long?"

He caught me off-balance. "No. She died."

"Oh, John, I'm sorry . . ."

"Some time ago."

"It's just that you're so young, I never—"

"Dale," I said, "skip it. No offense meant, no offense taken. It was a natural enough question. I just didn't . . . see it coming."

Dale bobbed his head. "Here's our exit." No gusto left.

Dale insisted on coming in with me because he was sure he knew the USAir customer service rep who would be on duty. He did, and got me the best seat on the plane, aisle for leg room, just forward of the wings for ride comfort and ease of exit.

The service rep swung my bag onto the belt behind him while I crushed my ticket folder into my inside breast pocket. Dale and I walked toward the gate.

I stopped and spoke. "You know, there's no sense in your waiting with me for the boarding call."

"I know," he said, then with a quick Groucho imitation, "more's the pity."

I laughed and so did he. I gave him a quick bear hug, and he returned it, slapping my back at a shoulder blade with the flat of his hand.

"Take care of Martha," I said.

"We will."

We broke. He sort of waved. I waved back, turned, and walked away.

The airport was virtually empty. At a newsstand, I found a *Time* magazine behind some "Steel Curtain" and "Love Ya, Steelers" T-shirts. I skimmed it absently at the gate until the flight attendant called us for boarding.

The plane was proportionately as empty as the airport had been. We arrived later than expected at Washington's National Airport. I picked up my Samsonite, grabbed a cab, and got to the Marriott Key Bridge by 9 P.M.

I checked in and was shown by the elevator operator to my room. I bounced on the bed, then picked up the telephone. I called Nancy's number in Boston.

"Hello?"

"Nancy, it's John Cuddy."

"Oh, John, I'm so sorry."

"Yeah, I know."

"No, please. I asked Drew Lynch to call his friend at District C and the friend went by the Coopers' house every two hours. He's the one who called in the fire. There'll be a thorough investigation."

"Thanks, Ms. DA."

A little moan on her end. "You're right. You told me in my apartment that they didn't have any family?"

"Not that they mentioned. Jesse was in the marines, Second World War. Emily taught at some private school. There must be records somewhere." I gave her George's name for the funeral arrangements.

"Well, tomorrow I'll also call a friend who's a public administrator for Suffolk County. Do you know what—"

"A lawyer who administers estates of people without relatives?"

"Yes, basically. He'll do everything necessary, assuming there's no will around."

"Probably no will." I punched out a breath.

"You sound really beat."

"Battered but unbowed."

"Is there anything else I can do?"

One frame of a happy, future home-movie flickered through my head. "No, thanks. If you can just follow through on the Coopers personally, maybe postpone the funeral, I'll be back tomorrow night or Tuesday. Oh, and keep the cops on Marco's trail."

"Please call me when you get back."

"I will."

"Bye, John."

"Good-bye, Nancy."

I hung up, looked at the comatose TV and the predictable, bland wall-hangings. The view of the Potomac out of the window was postcard quality, but not an evening's worth.

I was tired but not sleepy. I hadn't brought any running or exercise clothes, but their health club and pool would be closed by now anyway. Instead, I changed shirts, got a cab, and headed into Georgetown for some life. Or at least some noise.

I left the cab at M and Wisconsin. I found a saloon that I think said "Clyde's" on it and had a hamburger plate with a couple of Beck's drafts. Most of the life was coming from the Sunday Night Movie over one end of the bar. Unfortunately, most of the noise was coming from three assholes from Akron who asked the bartender every five minutes where the action was.

I gritted my teeth and asked for one more Beck's draft and the check. The bartender took the time to lift away my dinner plate and swab down the bar in front of me. He even replaced my cardboard coaster with a new one to accompany the next Beck's in a fresh glass.

The Akron contingent downed their drinks, one sucking on his ice and then spitting it back into the glass. They clumsily got on their coats and stumbled out, reinforcing each other's clamoring for action.

I put a twenty down on my check. The bartender took it, cashed me in, and returned my change.

"I'll bet you just love the tourist trade in here," I said.

He smiled. "Some more than others." He was about twenty-three, maybe a high school pulling guard who had lowered his sights over the last five years.

"Look," I said, "is there anyplace around here where there'll be some activity? I'm not"—inclining my head toward the departed trio's end of the bar—"looking to join those three. I just attended the funeral of a good friend, and I'd like to go to a place where there are people talking, dancing, and maybe laughing."

He dropped the smile and looked at me hard. Satisfied that I wasn't just a variation of the Akron syndrome, he spoke. "Two places. One's diagonally across the street. Called the Library. Disco atmosphere, rock and soul music. Young professionals and a lotta foreign nationals, like students and fringe diplos, you know. The other place is called Déjà Vu. It's about fifteen blocks up M, take the left fork at the end of the business district." He glanced at his watch. "Probably okay to walk there now, but get a cab to go home. Older crowd, sixties music and swing. Lotta couples."

I thanked him, left thirty percent of the tab as a tip and got up.

"Hey, man," he said, the smile back, "the information's free. I'm a tourist bureau, you know."

I winked at him. "The extra's for the fresh glasses, new coasters, workin' the wipe cloth, you know."

"Have a good evening."

"You, too."

Since it was closer, I first walked across the street to the Library. A bouncer who had about thirty pounds on my bartender greeted me with a smile and opened the door for me. I walked down the flight of stairs in front of me and turned right into the place. It had an elliptical bar on my level and a postage-stamp dance floor a few steps beyond and below the far end of the bar. The ceiling was low. The walls were lined with bookshelves, and, to the casual eye, real books. A rock song came on the stereo system, and twenty or so people got up to dance.

All the men in the place wore jackets. A lot of males were black, wearing continental three-piece suits. Many others were Asian, pencil-thin in dark two-piece gray or brown suits. The women were mainly American, black and white, in their twenties and secretarial in their clothes. I sat at the bar and ordered a screwdriver.

A slim, light-skinned black woman on my right started a conversation with me. Not pick-up, just pleasant. Unfortunately for her, I wanted to be just a spectator and, fortunately for me, she got asked to dance. I found myself thinking how much this place reminded me of other singles bars in New York and Boston. There were nice people, and noise and dancing, but the smiles were like the ones you flashed for a wedding photographer and the laughs like the ones you trotted out at job interviews. I downed my screwdriver and left.

It took me about twenty-five minutes to reach Déjà Vu. It looked like a greenhouse someone had tacked onto the Sheraton Hotel it abutted. A clone of the bouncer at the Library welcomed me in, asked if I wished food, drinks, or drinks and dancing, and gave me directions accordingly. I walked through an interior garden, overhung with huge plants of both the flowering and merely multicolored leaf varieties. I could hear swing music coming from around the corner. Benny Goodman plays the Amazonian rain forest.

I turned the corner. The main room was like an airplane hangar. There were twenty or so couples twirling on a huge dance floor. There was a long bar on the right side of the dance area, tables on two other sides, and a wall with a grand piano and sound system on the fourth side. People of all ages, skin tones, and dress codes were arrayed around the outer ring of the floor. If I were twenty years older, I think I would have said the joint was jumping.

The swing song ended, people applauded, and the Rolling Stones' "Satisfaction" came on. There was a whoop from the bar area to my right, and the world changed over, from 1943 to 1965. Probably two-thirds of the swingers left the floor, and their spaces were swallowed up by four-fifths rockers. A college-looking girl asked me to dance. I declined, a guy about my age next to me said he would, and they went stomping out there. I ordered a vodka and orange from a harried but cheerful waitress, and zigzagged into another room to check my overcoat. I came back to the dance room. I stood and watched and listened as the Stones turned to the Temptations, then to the Beach Boys, then back, as my screwdriver arrived, to I think Glenn Miller and Harry James for one each.

As nearly as I could tell, the generation gaps in the place were more apparent than real, and everybody was having a ball. I saw my waitress again, and ordered two more drinks to save her a trip. A thirtyish woman maybe five-nine came up and said I looked like I wanted to dance. I told her she was clairvoyant. We danced three rock tunes when a slow one came on. I told her thank you and turned away. I found my waitress and got the screwdrivers.

I danced three or four more times and touched up my waitress maybe twice more for two-handers. I know I grew only dimly aware that the crowd was thinning out and that I was no longer being asked to dance. I also know I had a little trouble finding the men's room, a little more retrieving my coat, and still a little more finding the front door as the house lights came up to "the-party's-over" level of brightness. I remember the bouncer asking me if I wanted a cab, but the cold air felt good again, and I waved him off, not quite completing whatever sentence I was saying. Within a few blocks, my eyes grew a little big for their sockets, the sidewalk a tad slippery from the absence of snow or ice. That struck me funny. That's why I was having trouble walking. In Boston, there was so much ice and snow on our never-shoveled sidewalks that I was so used to allowing for it that I just couldn't make the adjustment back to good old unadulterated concrete . . .

I bounced my head off the concrete before I realized I had been hit. I remember only two of them, but later I was told there were three. I was lying on my left side. The first one I saw was the guy who bent down and sent the left jab at my right eye. I twisted my face left and back and took a glancing shot off my right cheekbone. I sent my right hand cupped, fingers stiff, up into his throat, and he pulled away, gagging and coughing.

I levered up on my left elbow and got a wicked kick

from behind, just to the left of my spinal column and barely missing my left kidney. The pain approached the paralyzing level. I reached my right hand back and got kicked in my forearm. I forced myself to roll away from the kicker and got my forearms crossed in front of my face just as he delivered his third shot with his right foot. The crotch formed by my forearms absorbed most of the force, but the toe area of his boot caught me just under the chin. I locked my hands around his calf and put my head just outside his right knee. Then I lunged up onto my knees and forward, driving my shoulder below his knee and pulling his foot into my body to dislocate the knee joint. I slipped a little, though, and as he and I went down, I felt his ankle and knee just twist funny. He yelled in pain. I took a couple of kicks to my left thigh from somebody else, which didn't help the cause. Somebody, maybe the new kicker, put an amateurish forearm lock around my throat from behind. I got back onto my knees, and the first kicker rolled and crawled away from me. I whipped my left fist up into the forearm's groin area but missed the target, him just releasing and running. I realized a car was pulling up, high beams on and horn honking loud and long. I also realized that I was alone on the sidewalk with my wallet intact but my clothes and me less so.

"Y'know, ya coulda been dead by now."

I pulled the handkerchief away, and inspected the bloodstain. I licked a reasonably clean corner of the cloth and began dabbing.

"I appreciate your stopping."

The cabbie, beefy, bald, and fiftyish, glanced up at me in his inside rear mirror. "You're just lucky those three wasn't good at this yet. No knives. If they'd had knives, they woulda used 'em, and a fuckin' medical convention couldn't a helped you then."

"You're probably right," I said, looking down at the holes in the knees of my pants.

"You bet I am. I spotted those kids. Maybe an hour ago. They was hangin' around the edge of the retail strip. I knew they was lookin' for a mark, but the fuckin' cops can't do nothing. Used to be the cops would arrest the fuckers or at least roust them. Now, not only won't the arrest hold up, but the fuckin' Soo-preem Court'll let the kids sue the cops. For civil rights violations. You figure it out."

"I can't help you there," I said. My cheek hurt, my chin and knees burned, and my lower back and thigh ached. Worst of all, the adrenaline had sobered me up.

"Ya sure ya don't wanna go to the hospital?" asked the cabbie.

"I'm sure, but thanks."

"Hey, citizens gotta stick together. Ya know, lotsa guys, cabbies I mean, woulda seen you get jumped and turned right around. Mebbe two or three I know woulda radioed the dispatcher to send the cops, but that's it. Me, I think you gotta help. It's no good to complain about things if you don't, y'know. Then we're like animals." He pulled into the Marriott Key Bridge's drop-off area and a doorman, just inside the door, reluctantly put down a magazine and started out toward us.

"Animals," continued the cabbie. "Just like those fuckin' kids that jumped you."

I handed him a twenty. "Thanks, my friend."

"Thanks, buddy," replied the cabbie.

I turned, waved off the blinking doorman, and limped into the hotel lobby.

Fifteen

In the movies or on TV, you always see the hero leap up after a brawl and be unmarked and unrestricted the next time he appears. In real life, it doesn't work that way. Where I grew up in Southie, a lot of the kids went into amateur and then club boxing. Not as many as in the white sections of Dorchester, or almost-all-black Roxbury, but a lot. I remember the kid who lived next door. He was only eighteen years old, but after a particularly tough three-rounder, he would walk, sit, eat, and talk funny for three or four days. You take it easy, use ice, and chew carefully. You rarely call Gidget to go surfing.

I had put ice on my cheek and thigh when I got in the night before. When I woke up, though, my right rib cage hurt like hell. I couldn't remember getting hit there, but I showed a fist-sized bruise to match the two on my left thigh. My back ached just enough to tell me there was substantial, but not serious, damage. I did not try to touch my toes. I moved slowly to the bathroom. No blood in the urine. I turned to the sink. My right cheek, reversed as my left in the mirror, was dull red and purple, not the brighter, almost glossy red and purple you get when you don't ice it. My chin was scraped and scabby like that of a nine-year-old who had fallen while running during recess. I realized that the ribs must have been the first hit, the one that put me down, because I had only a little swelling on the left side of my head from the bounce off the sidewalk. I thought about the cabbie's remark on knives, and I suddenly had to use the toilet again.

I took a long, hot bath and shaved very delicately. I ordered breakfast via room service, no orange juice. The bellboy bringing in the tray did not indicate by word or look that he thought I had been hit by a car. I tipped him a princely sum.

I chewed breakfast on the left side of my mouth and reached for the telephone.

Amazingly, I got J.T. right after Ms. Lost-In-Space.

"Colonel Kivens speaking, sir."

"Sir?" I said. "How often do people above colonel call you?"

"Who is this, please?"

"Christ, J.T., you sound a lot more—" I stopped. Cold. Al and I had had such a similar conversation when he called me.

"Who is this?" said J.T., a bit more aggressively.

"J.T., it's John Cuddy. I'm sorry to—"

"John, how are you? Wait a minute, *where* are you?"

"I'm here. In D.C., I mean. I just came in from Pittsburgh. J.T., Al—"

"I know," he said quietly. "There was a blurb about it in the *Post.* I'm really sorry."

"Yeah," I said. "Listen, I need some information. I need to know some things about what Al was doing in Vietnam. I'm convinced he wasn't killed by any—"

"Listen," he said knowingly. "Everybody goes

there. If I were you though, the one thing I wouldn't miss is the Smithsonian Air and Space Museum. I think it's the best."

"If I meet you there, can we talk in the clear?"

"That's right," he said cheerfully.

"Twelve noon today?"

"That's fine. Be sure to see the Spirit of St. Louis. Enjoy your stay now."

"I'll be the one with the red carnation."

He gave a forced chuckle and rang off.

Terrific. Either J.T. was worried about somebody overhearing what I would say to him about Al or what he would say to me about Al. Or what he would say to anyone about anything. Just terrific.

I hung up and called the Suffolk County DA's office. I asked for Nancy Meagher. A secretary came on and said Nancy was out for the morning. I told her to tell Nancy that Mr. Cuddy had called and would call back later. She thanked me and hung up.

I propped up some pillows and lay back on them. I thought about calling my "friend" at the insurance company who was supposed to get a guard to watch over Jesse and Emily. My ribs hurt every time I inhaled and only a little less as I exhaled. I thought about calling the D'Amicos and complimenting them on the depth of their son's loyalty to his brother. I noticed that my thigh didn't ache when I was lying down. Instead of those calls, or calling Martha and commiserating, or Carol and misleading, or Straun and cursing, I put on the pay-TV channel and watched Clint Eastwood do to about a hundred guys in sequence what I should have done to my three the night before.

* * *

The taxi left me about two hundred feet from the steps of the building. My thigh spasmed every time my left leg hit the ground, but I knew the more I walked on it, the sooner it would loosen up. My back and rib cage would ache for a few days.

It was a clear, bright day, somewhere in the high 40s, which was good, since the seams under both arms on my topcoat were split and hence being repaired back at the hotel or some subcontractor thereof. I had junked my pants, so I was wearing the funeral suit. Gingerly, I climbed the stairs.

I walked into the crowded lobby. Somehow I'm reluctant to use "museum" to describe a place that has things in it that I remember as current events. The huge Apollo space capsule exhibit was off to the right. A number of airships, from World War I bi-planes to post-Korea jet fighters, were hanging from the ceiling, fifty or sixty feet above my head and suspended in eternal flight. I spotted J.T., in uniform but strolling unmilitarily around the base of the Apollo exhibit while the *turistas* streamed along a walkway over his head to see into the spacecraft. I edged over to and under Lindbergh's plane, staring up at it like a little kid in church. Lindbergh was well before my time, and I didn't mind thinking of his plane being in a museum.

"A brave man," said a familiar voice from behind me.

"Who gave a lot to his country," I replied.

J.T. stepped even with me.

"Sorry about the telephone."

"I assumed you had your reasons."

He was frowning. "I did. And do. How is Al's family taking it?"

"Wife's O.K., son is too young. Everybody else is dead."

I must have sounded pretty despondent, because J.T. didn't reply right away.

"What is it you need?"

"Al was killed by somebody who knew what he was doing."

"The paper, uh, implied that—"

"Yeah, I know. But his room at the hotel in Boston was tossed professionally, after he was taken and maybe even before he was killed. Also, Al called me to set up dinner after some meeting he was going to have. He'd have had no reason to go looking—"

"Hey, John. Take it easy. *I* wasn't implying anything. I just meant the paper—"

"Yeah," I said, shaking my head. "I know, I know. Let's walk a little."

"I noticed your limp. And your face isn't exactly yearbook material."

"Last night I had a little brush with Washington's version of the Welcome Wagon."

J.T. smiled. "Drunk?"

I smiled back. "Me, not them." My cheek hurt a lot when I smiled.

"So, how can I help you?"

"The way Al was done, I'm convinced it had to be somebody from Vietnam, somebody he was going to blackmail or something. I think he—"

"John, that was, what, over thirteen years ago, anyway? Why would Al wait so long . . ."

I shook my head again as we walked in the shadow of an incongruously small but nevertheless lifesized DC-3. "I think it was something that just happened or just suggested itself to him when he hit Boston. He was in desperate financial shape, about to lose his job and probably his house, and I think it was somebody out of the past. I can't believe that he ran into anybody like that in the steel industry selling widgets, and anyway, I've talked to everybody, wife, friends, business associates, not a whiff until he got to Boston."

"So you figure that something or someone he saw or knew in Saigon touches him off thirteen years later to blackmail somebody who kills him?"

I clicked my tongue off the roof of my mouth. "I agree that when you put it that way, it sounds crazy. But I don't have any other place to start."

"Place to start?"

"Yeah, why I called you. I want to go back into all the records that someone must have at the Pentagon somewhere, the records of all of Al's time there. Maybe I can make the same connection Al did."

J.T. frowned. "A lot of that stuff gets asked for by writers, researchers, and so forth to make us look worse than they already did back then. We've kept a lot of it away from them, even with the Freedom of Information Act, on the grounds that the records are still part of an ongoing investigation. If I let you, an outsider, a civilian, see them, and the researchers found out, they'd scream bloody murder and it'd be my career."

I regarded J.T. very carefully. "Are there still ongoing investigations, J.T.?"

He opened his eyes a little too widely and quickly, then grinned. "John, it was all over, basically, ten years ago. Most of the statutes of limitations have run out by now."

"Are there still open investigations?"

"Oh, John," said J.T., doing a half turn to his right. "You know the army, there are *always* investigations of some kind going on."

"J.T., look. Al and you and I were friends. We looked out for each other, saved each other's butts a couple of times. Somebody killed Al, horribly, after torturing him, like the Vietnamese. You're nobody's fucking fool and not, even after all this time and a pension so close you can smell it, such a stiff that it doesn't get to you. Somebody killed our friend. Somebody has to pay for that."

J.T. looked grave and sounded stern. "*You* look, John. This isn't Saigon, and it isn't wartime. You can't get away with things here, and neither can the guy who killed Al, whoever he was. He'll be discovered eventually and—"

"Bullshit," I said, a little too loudly, causing an elderly couple in front of us to jump. I lowered my voice. "The police in Boston have chalked this up as a category crime, and the guy who did it was neat and careful enough so you can't even blame them. I want at those records. If I find something, I'll check it before I bring in the cops. But that's all. If this guy could take Al, he can take me, and I'm only looking to even up the ledger. No blood feud, just let justice take its course."

J.T. didn't believe me, but he said, "I'll have to think it over. I'll be back in my office by thirteen hundred." He pulled out a card with his name and a different direct dial number on it. "Call me around thirteen-fifteen."

He turned and drifted off toward the door, stopping to read a plaque. I sought out a uniformed employee and was directed to the nearest spot for lunch. Soft ice cream and milk.

I called J.T. at 1:10. He answered.

"J.T., it's John."

"It's set. Be here by fourteen hundred hours. Use your name, my name, and the following three-digit number. The security guard at the first public barrier you come to will call for an escort who'll bring you in."

"Thanks, J.T."

"See you at fourteen hundred."

I hung up and looked again at my watch. Time for a couple of quick drinks but I decided against it. I was about to do something that two drinks, two dozen drinks, wouldn't ease for me. Something I never thought I'd do. Ever.

I was going back to Vietnam.

My escort was a young MP, slim, female, and black. She had smiled when her counterpart at the barrier had checked my ID and confirmed me to her. She introduced herself as PFC Waller, and off we went.

She threaded us through seemingly endless hallways, small pockets of humanity appearing in various civilian and military uniforms. We took half-left turns at indistinguishable corridors and subcorridors. In less than three minutes, I was hopelessly lost.

"Should I be dropping a trail of pebbles?" I said, then dodged a navy officer whose head was buried in a file he was carrying, choirboy style.

Waller laughed graciously. "You get used to it after a while, sir."

"How long have you been in?"

"A little over a year now."

"Planning on making it a career?"

She gave me a cautious sidelong glance to be sure I was serious. "Probably not, sir. I'm more interested in data processing."

"I see." Whenever someone brings up computers, I tend to acknowledge the topic and then cease all conversation. My reticence was covered by her abrupt stop at a door bearing only a room number. She knobbed it open.

We entered a small suite of offices. A woman, probably my telephone partner, barely glanced at us as we walked past her toward a desk occupied by a youngish, male staff sergeant who looked tall sitting down. He had reddish brown hair, close-cropped. As we approached, he rose. And rose.

I seemed to recall a six-foot-six maximum height, with a waiver for up to two additional inches. I guessed he needed the waiver. His name tag said "Casey." "The Colonel will see you, Mr. Cuddy." He winked at Waller. "Thank you, Waller."

Waller nodded, said "Sir" to me as a good-bye, and left us.

Casey knocked on an office door to his left. He waited for an affirmation from inside before he opened it. "Sir, Mr. Cuddy."

"John! Good to see you!" I entered the room. J.T. sprang up and came forward as though we were brothers reunited after twenty years of separation. "Thank you, Sergeant," said J.T.

"Yessir." Casey backed out and closed the door as J.T. pumped my hand a few times for effect and then motioned to one of several steel, green-cushioned government office chairs in front of his desk. We sat.

"Well," he said. "This hasn't been easy."

"Especially on such short notice."

"Right. I had to pull strings and call in favors." J.T. looked a bit distracted, checked a desk calendar. "I have a meeting at fifteen hundred across the District, so I've got to rush. I have all the files from a month before Al and I got to Saigon to a month after he left. That's roughly September '67 to December '68. The files are chronological."

"I remember."

J.T. frowned and sank a little lower.

"I suppose you wondered how come I didn't make the funeral."

I shook my head. "Actually, no, not until you told me you'd read about it. I just assumed it wouldn't be enough publicized for you to be aware of it."

"We've been busy, John. Pressure-cooker busy down here. I just didn't have time to come, or even return your calls."

I held up my hand. "You don't owe me any explanations. Or apologies."

"But I owe . . . owed Al. Like you said. Everybody did. He was a great guy."

"Yeah, he was."

There was an awkward silence as J.T. stared past me.

"Your meeting?" I said.

"Huh?"

"Your crosstown meeting. At three o'clock?"

"Oh, damn! Yes, thanks." He tapped a buzzer on his phone, and Casey's head was in the partially opened door before the buzzer sound had died away.

"Sir?"

"I'll get Mr. Cuddy set up next door. You get the car and pull 'round to Bravo Seven. I'll see you there in five minutes."

"Yessir."

"And Case?"

"Yessir?"

"Get Ricker to relieve you on the desk."

"Yessir." Casey's head was gone.

J.T. got up and moved toward the door. I did likewise.

J.T. said, "Everything's in the next room, kind of a conference room. You can take notes, but no photocopying, understood?"

"Understood."

We walked out his door and into the next room. "I'll be gone the rest of the day with Casey and," he dropped his voice, "the receptionist is an airhead. But if you have any questions, Sergeant Ricker can field them. Be sure Ricker leads you out when you're finished."

"How late can I stay?"

"Eighteen hundred. I'm sorry, but no later."

"I appreciate it, J.T."

"Yeah." He gave me a quick smile and handshake. "Just keep the door closed, O.K.?"

"O.K. I'll call you tomorrow."

"Right." He sighed and swung his head around the room. "I hope it's here," he said and left.

I closed the door behind him. I tugged off my suit jacket, undid my collar button, and pulled down my tie.

The room measured about ten by fifteen. There was a slate-green rectangular table with a half dozen pencils, two pads, and some ice water and paper cups. There were five chairs. The space for a sixth chair was occupied by an olive-drab file cabinet with five drawers. It would contain fifteen months of operational paperwork for our MP unit in Saigon. Somewhere in there was Al's killer. Maybe.

I rolled up my sleeves and yanked open the top drawer. The files were packed in tightly. I levered ten out and sat down with them. I poured and drank one cup of ice water. Then I opened the first file and stepped back fourteen years and as many thousand miles.

Sixteen

AT FIRST IT WAS ALMOST AS IF I WEREN'T READING THE reports but translating them from army jargon and abbreviations to real English. I went slowly through the first files, refreshing myself with designations and geography. Then, like the return of a foreign language, it came back to me in the clear, my brain automatically decoding the cryptic report texts.

I riffled through the simpler, ordinary stuff of traffic accidents, drug overdoses, fights, and petty thefts that happened just before Al got to Saigon. I lingered over two reports.

In the first, a quartermaster staff sergeant named Kevearson was killed shooting it out with MPs raiding a heroin refinery. He turned out to be the entrepreneur. The MP in charge was a Captain David L. Bonner. I remembered Al mentioning him once. I wrote down Kevearson, Ronald B., then Bonner's name.

In the second report, an MP sergeant named DeLong had siphoned seized heroin from an evidence locker, replacing it with flour. Al later testified at the court-martial, but I couldn't recall why. DeLong, Alvin B.

I reached the point chronologically when Al and J.T. had hit Saigon. There were dozens of major crimes in the files for the eight weeks before I arrived. Several had Al's name on them.

One was the shooting of a pace trooper named Brewer by a bar girl. He apparently wanted things a bit kinkier than she tolerated. The report suggested he had lived. Brewer, Delvin J. I remembered his name for some reason, so I wrote it down.

J.T. and Al both covered a second lieutenant in the infantry who went AWOL. Brought him in from the boonies, living with a Vietnamese woman outside a formerly French plantation. How the hell he had avoided being killed by Charlie in the three nights out there was beyond me. There was a photo in the file of the lieutenant. He looked miserable. Court-martialed, imprisoned back in the States. Named Ralser, Lionel P. Write it down. A guy who would risk living in the bush was capable of anything.

A staff sergeant named Crowley, Matthew M., got his head blown off by a Eurasian drug merchant named René Bouvier. There was a photo in the file of a short, black-haired sergeant with two or three other staff-looking noncoms around him. Everyone was smiling, and the flip side of the photo said the short guy was Crowley. The Eurasian was never found. Al and a technician CID named Clay Belker investigated the killing, Belker signing on the body's fingerprints. Belker I remembered, a gangly, surly white guy from Alabama. Al always thought that Belker was O.K., God knows why.

I reached November 1967, when I arrived in Saigon. The next file involved Al directly.

An MP was knifed and died when he stumbled on

two GIs buying heroin from a Vietnamese. On his way down, the MP winged one GI named Curtis D. Chandler, who was caught six blocks away, bleeding freely. Al interrogated Chandler, who refused to give the name of his partner. I wrote down the full name of Chandler and the word "partner?" There was no further mention of partner except that "further interrogation proved unsuccessful." Involuntarily, a picture of a different kind of interrogation came to mind and decided to stay awhile.

The hallway was in the damp basement of the South Vietnamese National Police substation three blocks from our headquarters. To the basement were brought confirmed or suspected VC (Viet Cong). The hall was dim, one 25-watt bulb on a wire about halfway down the corridor. The place stank more from disinfectant than puke, urine, or feces, but not by much. The atmosphere of successful interrogation, National Police style. Rumored but not seen. Well, not often seen.

Sometimes they did it with switches of split bamboo, swacking the stick against a prisoner's bare feet or palms until the screaming gave way to the short-lived relief of unconsciousness. A little slapping about the face, and the questioning proceeded. A slow mode and strenuous.

A second method was cigarettes. No, not as bribes. Lit ones. Applied to earlobes, lips, eyelids. Like the killer had done with Al. Some noise and smell, agony extreme but intermittent. Effective and less strenuous, but still time-consuming.

For quickest results, a crank telephone box and a

couple of wires were employed. The interrogator's aide would crank the box, the current thus produced transmitted by the wires connected to the prisoner's genitalia, male or female. The aide's muscle tone and endurance weren't much limitation on the pace and the duration of the questioning here.

I was to be present at an interrogation because the prisoner, doubly damned as VC as well as black marketeer, supposedly spoke good English. He therefore would be able to give me names of American servicemen providing products from the PXs, either through the front door (by discount purchase) or through the back door (the ultimate discount). My National Police guide escorted me down into the basement to the interrogation section.

You've heard sitcom laughtracks? Well, if the producers of a horror movie ever wanted a screamtrack, they really missed their chance back then. Name your scream and the NP would provide it, on cue. A seventy-year-old woman's long, piercing wail. A thirty-five-year-old father's gasping outbursts of anguish as he realized he would be fathering no more. Perhaps a sixteen-year-old girl for whom permanent disfigurement must have seemed a vague and distant concern compared to the cause of her shrieking and gagging hoarseness.

"This room," said my escort, smiling brightly. "Please?"

He swung open the door. The smell of disinfectant was very strong. There were three NP men in the room. One was seated at a table taking down machine-gun sentences in Vietnamese. The speaker was a fiftyish man in dark red prisoner pajamas who sat across from him. The pajamas seemed three sizes too large. The prisoner was speaking so fast the seated NP could not transcribe it. The NP standing next to the prisoner clouted him on the cheek with a backhand and spat a Vietnamese word. The prisoner slowed down.

The third NP spoke to my escort quickly in Vietnamese, then addressed me in English. My escort fetched a chair.

"Welcome. I am Captain Ngo." He inclined his head. "You will please to sit?"

"Thank you," I said, sitting and tugging a pad and ballpoint pen from my shirt pocket. "I'm Lieutenant Cuddy. I understand this man speaks English?"

"Oh, yes. We will . . ."

He shot a terse question in Vietnamese to my escort.

"Sus-pend," said my escort.

"Ah, yes. We will sus-pend now and you will question him. The traitor's name is Can Gai Trinh. He has much to tell you."

Captain Ngo barked something at Trinh and the guard who was about to clock him again. I heard a scrabbling sound from the room next door. I hoped it was a rat. If not, it was probably a child.

Trinh stopped talking to the NP transcriber and looked at me.

"Yessir," he said.

"Your full name and address," I asked.

He told me.

"How long have you been here?"

"Whole life."

I shook my head. "No," I said. The guard took this as a request to strike Trinh.

I looked at Ngo. "Tell him to stop hitting the prisoner."

Ngo spoke, and the guard backed off a step.

"I mean, how long have you been in this building?"

"Oh, maybe full day."

"How old are you?"

"T'irty-one."

I looked at him. He flitted his eyes around the room, fearful he'd sparked more retribution. He still looked fiftyish. The pajamas covered everything but his head, weak hands, and bare feet. There were no marks on those parts. Probably used the crank box.

"Tell me the GIs who work with you in the black market. Names, outfits."

I got a stream of people. Twelve or thirteen, from PFCs to a master sergeant.

I took it all down, got some functional details and some future dates to mark.

I looked up at Captain Ngo. "Who knows he's here?"

"Nobody. We catch him clean. Behind a building. Nobody see."

I inclined my head toward the prisoner. "I may need him at the trial of the bad Americans," I said. Trinh's face lit up, the hope, however, tempered by experience.

I locked Ngo with my best stare. "Will he be alive then?"

Ngo frowned, disappointed. "If you like," he relented.

I shook off the interrogation memory and waded through about twenty more reports. Names, faces, places. The absurdities of a big city at the edge of an unnatural war. I went through December of '67 into January of '68. I dreaded reaching the end of that month, so I got up and took a stretch-break. My interlude with the muggers was taking its toll in stiffness and soreness. I finished the ice water and took the pitcher to the door. I opened it.

The receptionist was gone, but a master sergeant swiveled around in the seat Casey had occupied hours ago. He stood up and smiled.

"Help you, sir?"

"Yes. Are you Sergeant Ricker?"

"That's right, sir. What can I do for you?"

He was about six feet tall. Maybe one-eighty in shape, two hundred with his pot. I was tired, and he had that vaguely familiar look of many middle-aged noncoms. Bald, forty-five or so, with a Southwest twang in his voice.

"Just some cold water, if you can."

I extended the pitcher as he said, "Sure thing, sir."

I looked up at the clock. It said 16:45. He noticed me and shook the pitcher at me.

"Now, don't you worry none about that clock, sir. Casey, Sergeant Casey, he told me you was here on something important, and I already called the missus. I'll be here jest as long as you need. I got me a book and everything."

There was a Louis L'Amour novel spread open face down on his desk.

"Thanks, Sergeant. I really appreciate it."

"Would you like some coffee, sir? It's no trouble."

"No, thanks."

"Jest be a minute."

He was gone perhaps thirty seconds.

"Here you are, sir."

"Thanks, Sergeant."

"You jest take your time." He smiled. "There ain't nothing goin' on over in the old D. of C. on a cold Monday night in March anyways."

I went back in, closed the door and sat back down. Mid-January 1968 became January 20, then January 25, then finally January 30. The dawn of the Year of the Monkey, the lunar New Year holiday all of Vietnam celebrated.

They called it "Tet."

Some military historians trace the strategic beginning of the Tet Offensive back to September 1967, in terms of North Vietnamese and Viet Cong planning and stockpiling in and around the cities of South Vietnam. Tet was really the first time the cities were hit, the VC up till then being a nearly invisible enemy, indistinguishable citizens by day, raiders in rural villages and an occasional town by dark. One North Vietnamese general suggested much later that since the offensive did not result in widespread, spontaneous uprisings by the people of South Vietnam, it was, in effect, a military defeat for Charlie. Americans who were there that night might disagree with him.

The Viet Cong caught the whole country sleeping. They attacked air bases, corps headquarters, National Police substations, even our Embassy, which squatted like a concrete sewage plant in a neighborhood of French villas on Thong Nhut. Al and I were sacked out in our BOQ when the first explosions awakened us. We got dressed and raced downstairs, the pop and crack of small-arms fire filling the air between the louder blasts of rockets and sappers' satchel charges.

We leaped with eight or ten others into a deuce-and-a-half-ton truck that barreled the mile or so to our headquarters.

The doorway to our station looked like the entrance to an anthill. MPs were scurrying in and out, passing, tossing, dropping equipment. Jeeps and deuce-and-a-halfs were pulling up and pulling out with a lot of noise but little pattern. The harried captain on duty split us up, Al drawing a barricade reinforcement north of the headquarters and me a recon by jeep toward the red-light district on Tu Do Street. Al was wounded almost as soon as he left the station, so I figured I would just skim the reports from the start of the attack onward. There was no reason for me to relive my memories. Still, the nightmare images from that night flashed back no matter how quickly I flipped the pages.

Two MPs, a young blond PFC and an older black sergeant, lying dead next to an overturned, burning jeep at a street corner. Both still held their .45s, jacked open and empty. Nine Viet Cong, some with automatic weapons, sprawled in a staggered attack formation in front of them. An incredible stand.

Four National Police officers stopping a vegetable truck. They pulled the driver out and shot him to death, rumor being that the VC had infiltrated their weapons and explosives for Tet in such vehicles.

A farmer, elderly with arthritic, stained fingers and a few long strands of chin beard. He wore a broad, peaked coolie hat and clutched a copy of *Chinh Luan*, the Vietnamese-language newspaper. He was sitting motionless in a corner of a blown-out building, staring at another corner. God knows how he came to be there or what happened to him afterwards.

A red-haired trooper, who had spent the entire night of the attack with a B-girl, being dragged between two MPs into the station. He looked so young, a ninth-grader being taken to the principal's office for detention.

Viet Cong prisoners, the men in cheap white dress shirts, the women wearing white kerchiefs. All kneeling in gaggles of five or six, arms bound behind them. The National Police would snug the rope just above the elbows, tugging back so hard that the elbows nearly touched, creating an image of supplicant, unisexual Venus de Milos.

Two of my men, hit by an AK-47 in the hands of a skinny Vietnamese hiding in a dark doorway. They went down all akimbo, as if they were marionettes and someone had cut their strings. I fired three rounds into the shooter, who spun and belly-whopped on the pavement. A shadow in the next doorway moved, and I fired three more times at it. The shadow slammed back against the door, landing so that the feet were in the light. A child's feet.

An American nurse, blond and thin with terrible acne, stroking the face of a head-bandaged sergeant and assuring him that his eyes weren't gone forever.

A GI, screaming in Spanish and shooing a scrawny cat away from a dead body. The cat had been going after the corpse's eyes. The GI started throwing up.

A mother lying face down in the street, her eyes open, snot and blood and broken teeth all around her. Her daughter, maybe four years old, howling and beating her fists bloody on the pavement while two National Policemen stripped and looted the Viet Cong bodies in the alleyway.

Standing in a gutter, I look down and see an arm. A

black left arm. With a faded gold high school ring on the fourth finger. A blue stone.

Two B-girls, still in their slit-sided hostess dresses, crucified on a side wall of a Tu Do Street bar for fraternizing with us, the enemy. They had been raped and slashed repeatedly. One was still alive when my sergeant put a bullet through her head. If you had seen her, you wouldn't be asking yourself that question right now.

An explosion that ripped through a convent school. Intentionally set, no mistaken bomb dropped randomly from above. Thirty-nine girls, aged seven through eleven, blown into a thousand once-human fragments.

Tet. The joyous lunar new year. *Auld lang syne.*

I rubbed my eyes. I got up and opened the conference room door. Ricker swiveled around and stood. It was 18:10. Christ, where had the time gone?

"More water, sir?" he asked.

"No thanks, Sergeant. Just stretching."

"Yessir. Anything else I can get for you?"

"Yeah, a new set of memories."

He laughed respectfully. I closed the door and went back to my reading.

Al was in the hospital until mid-February. I slowed down when I saw his name reappearing prominently.

Al and a Sergeant Kearns brought in an acid freak named Farrell who had fragged his platoon leader. Farrell swore he would get Al, swore to God, Timothy Leary, and his mother. Farrell, Wiley N. I remembered him. One more for the list.

Al busted a French national named Giles LeClerc

who was drawing young GIs into a homosexual prostitution ring. LeClerc had a Vietnamese boyfriend and partner named Tran Dai Dinh who hadn't been caught. The method was consistent, but a long way and a long time for a lover's vengeance. I wrote LeClerc and Dinh down anyway.

Al turned in an American captain of intelligence who had taken too enthusiastically to NP methods of interrogation. Bradley D. Collier. Disgraced, court-martialed, convicted, and sentenced. I fingered a photo of him. Sullen, a look of betrayal. A strong contender.

I stumbled on a reference to one of Al's combat assignments. When the infantry came up short on platoon leaders, the combat colonels would dip into the MP officer pool for fresh blood.

I remembered vividly one combat mission with Al. It was a three-day, company-strength sweep maneuver skirting the jungle. The company commander was a gung-ho jerk, with a Kit Carson scout (a "reformed" North Vietnamese regular) leading the way. I hated the jungle. I preferred anything, even the rice paddies, to it.

The first day was uneventful. Instead of returning to base camp, of course, we bivouaced in the bush. The second day was as quiet as the first. The second night, one of my perimeter guards led Al up to my foxhole.

"Boy," said Al, hunkering down when the sentry left us, "have I got a great deal set up."

I looked up at him blearily. "A deal?"

Al checked right and left, then whispered, "A tiger hunt!"

"A what?" I said, well above a whisper.

"Shush." He looked around again. "A tiger hunt. No shit, John. There used to be a lot of them around here before the war."

"Al," I said, "there has always been a war in this country."

"No, no. I mean a long time ago. Before the Second World War. But there are still some tigers. And an old guy in that last village said he was a guide. I was there when the scout was questioning him. Honest."

"So?" I said.

"So," said Al, looking crafty, "for fifty dollars American, we can get ourselves a shot at a tiger."

I closed my eyes and hung my head. "Why," I said to the ground, "in the name of God, do you want to shoot a tiger?"

"Aw, c'mon, John. When are you ever gonna get another chance like this. A big game safari for fifty bucks!"

"Al, we are pulling out at zero-five-thirty hours tomorrow."

"Tonight, John, tonight. We'll be gone and back by midnight."

"Man, do you have any idea how much a tiger weighs, or do you already have bearers signed up to carry it out?"

He sulked. "Ah, c'mon John. We'll probably never even see a tiger. It's the thrill. A once in a lifetime chance to have some sport in this godforsaken stink-hole of a country."

I held up my hand. "Al, I am not going stalking through a jungle at night after a tiger."

"But that's the beauty of it, John. The guide'll take

care of that. He knows a watering hole that the cats use. It's close by. He'll lead us there, then bring a goat and stake it out for us. It'll be like sitting in your living room."

"Then why do you need me?"

Al sighed. "Because I'm not about to go after a tiger with just a scout and an old man as back-up. I want a friend I can rely on."

I thought back to the BOQ brawl when Al jumped in to help me. "O.K.," I said.

Al clenched his fist, shook it into the air. He rose up and danced a little jig.

Al convinced the company commander that Al and I wanted the experience of setting up a night ambush with the scout. The commander thought our attitude was "outstanding." We slipped through our perimeter, advising the guards of our likely direction and return time.

In the bright moonlight, we moved quickly back up the trail to the village, a little less than a kilometer. The scout, whose name was Van, connected us with the guide, who was called *Chúa te'*, or simply "master" in Vietnamese. Master had a scraggly, dung-encrusted goat on a rope. I didn't catch the goat's name.

Through Van, Master asked us for his money. I always carried real cash, not MPC (Military Payment Certificates), in the boonies. I once heard that a Finance Corps lieutenant was killed when he tried to buy his way out of a tight situation with MPC. The locals wanted real currency, not monopoly money.

After the exchange of cash, Master produced two large-bore antique rifles. He demonstrated how the breech-loading mechanism functioned, then doled out four bullets each to Al and me. I gave Al a murderous glare. He pretended not to notice. There were the sounds of a dog barking and a child crying from somewhere in the village as we struck off.

The path was narrow, but well worn. I asked the scout about it. Master explained in Vietnamese, translated by Van, that the villagers occasionally used the watering hole in daylight hours. We continued on in silence.

After perhaps two hundred meters, we started downhill and quickly reached a pool of stagnant, bug-covered water, a quarter acre at most in size. Master looped the goat's lead around a branch, chattering in Vietnamese and gesturing at a large tree. Through the moonlight I could make out a crude platform in a limb crotch halfway up the trunk. I thought about asking why, if I could see the blind, the tiger couldn't also. However, Master was already up the tree, and Al on his way, so I didn't bother. I followed the first two climbers. After Van handed heavenward all our gear, he joined us.

The blind, sturdy enough in a hand-hewn way, faced the pond. There were some newer branches and fronds camouflaging the front. Master explained through Van how the tigers would appear at the far side of the pond, and where to aim, and so forth. Al was to have the first shot.

Master scrambled back down the tree and led the goat around the pond to a point directly across from us, perhaps forty meters line-of-sight. He tied the goat's lead to a downed limb and then lightly stepped back around to us. The goat, who I assume by now was getting the general drift of what was happening, began to bleat. Incessantly.

Master returned to our platform, a big smile on his face. He said something to Van, and Van said, "Master say we wait now."

It took nearly an hour for the goat to cry itself hoarse, straining against the leash. It took another hour for me to lose a pint of blood to the mosquitoes. Nothing moved in the bush.

I started to say something humorous. Master hissed and Van said, "All quiet now."

Another half an hour of nothing. I closed my eyes and thought of back home: summer Sundays on Carson's Beach in Southie or Crane Beach in Ipswich, the Yankees against the Red Sox at Fenway Park, the (back-then-realistic) rivalry between Boston College and Holy Cross in football.

A stand of high grass rustled off to our right. Four heads whipped over there, five counting the goat's. The bait had no more voice, but resumed hopping and tugging against the lead for all it was worth.

"Cop," whispered Master. No need for translation now. Tiger.

More rustling, then a pause, then more rustling, then a pause. The unseen creature moved around the perimeter of the pond. Al tensed and eyed his weapon. I was to have the second shot, but I had no intention of firing unless the cat was coming straight at . . .

A stumble and crunch in the bush as the creature neared the virtually hysterical goat. Al seated the rifle butt against his shoulder. The creature cried out, not a roar, not a growl, just a simple word.

A seven- or eight-year-old girl, yelping what was probably the goat's name, rushed up to it and began hugging it.

Master cursed. Van said, "That is the girl from father that Master buy goat." I remembered the child's voice crying back at the village. The girl started trying to untie the goat's lead.

Al said, "Jesus," and lowered his rifle. Master, still muttering curses, drew a knife and put it between his teeth. He started down the trunk.

"Van," I said. "Tell Master that if he touches the girl I will kill him."

Master, who had probably heard the English word "kill" often enough, nodded vigorously as if to confirm that was the goat's, and possibly the girl's, immediate destiny.

Al said, "John . . ."

"Tell him," I snapped at Van.

Master had started around the pond. Van spoke to him in Vietnamese. Master stopped, turned, and protested. Van said to me, "American pay for tiger hunt, American get tiger hunt."

I said, "Tell Master he can keep the money. The girl keeps her goat, and the Americans go back. Now."

Van translated. Master shrugged, sheathed his knife.

I said, "Now tell the girl. Call to her. Tell her the Americans give her back her goat."

Al said, "John, for chrissakes, there may be VC within earshot."

"Tell her," I repeated.

Van called over to the girl. She succeeded in untying the goat, then bowed down to us as she led it off around the way she came.

She got maybe five meters when a mine exploded. The top half of her somersaulted through the air toward us. Head, arms, trunk to her waist. It splashed into the pond, scattering a roomful of insects. A few branches and clumps of grass and goat followed her trajectory into the water.

Al bit his lower lip, then lowered and shook his head. Van showed a tear. Master, who had hit the deck at the explosion, was standing up, brushing himself off.

"Let's go," I said, and climbed down out of the treehouse.

As we walked back to our perimeter, I wondered what kind of funeral the little girl would have. Not a military one. No flag-covered coffin, surely, the Stars and Stripes whipped down and tucked securely around the base.

The first time I remember seeing an American flag around a coffin was President Kennedy's funeral. On television. A cold, blustery November Saturday. The riderless black horse, John-John saluting, the older males in the family walking solemnly uphill in mourning coats, their path lined by Green Berets with weapons at "present arms," bagpipes skirling.

My strongest memories, however, are of other military funerals. Or wakes, if you will; I guess the funerals took place back home. The wakes were in Vietnam, though. Three filthy, stinking GIs, standing over a sealed green body bag at some impromptu

Graves Registration Point, alternately dragging on a joint and saying, "Shit, man."

It is, I think, the greatest irony of our time, at least of my time. A President I thought I understood and would have died for dropped us into a war in a country which none of us understood and where nobody should have died.

Seventeen

I REACHED THE POINT WHERE AL SHIPPED HOME. WE had a short-timer's party for him at the Officers' Club, and I could barely walk for two days afterward. Al promised he would stay in touch. And he had.

I closed the last file. I tossed down the last of the ice water and reviewed my list.

Twenty-three names. Most Americans, some French and Vietnamese. Maybe one of them lives in Boston, maybe not. Maybe he's still using his real name, maybe not. Maybe he killed Al, maybe not. Maybe something to show for the afternoon, maybe not.

I stood up, folded the list like a business letter and slid it into my jacket pocket. I wedged all the files back into the drawers of the cabinet. I stiffly donned my jacket, thinking I could call J.T. tomorrow and ask him to put the names through the computer to see if there was anything current on them.

I opened the door. Ricker stood up. I didn't see his L'Amour novel. The clock said 19:15, 7:15 P.M. real time.

"Yessir?"

"I'm all finished, Sergeant. Colonel Kivens said I'd need you to lead me out of here."

Ricker grinned broadly. "Yessir. It's a real maze out there. Me, I was lost for weeks when I first drew duty here."

He went to a coat rack and got a regulation, olive-drab trench.

"Sir, you got transportation here?"

"No. Thought I'd just grab a cab."

Ricker chuckled. "These cabs, sir, they're tough to get out here sometimes. Where're you headin'?"

"Marriott, Key Bridge."

"Aw, hell, sir," said Ricker as he turned out the lights and closed the door. "That's right on my way. Let me give you a lift."

"Thanks, Sergeant, but I've already held you—"

"Please, sir, my pleasure, I insist."

I yielded gratefully. We threaded our way out down corridors dark and deep.

Ricker's vehicle was a spotless customized Ford pick-up, shiny even in the dark. We maneuvered through the vestiges of rush-hour traffic.

"Have you spent much time in Washington, sir?"

"No, not much. Weekend here or there."

"Fine city. Proud and powerful. But I'm a country boy myself. Four more years and out."

"That'll make twenty?"

"No, sir, thirty." He turned and smiled. "Thirty years with the Big Green Machine. Then a nice spread in Looziana, northeast corner."

He really looked familiar when he smiled. "You ever stationed in Saigon, Sergeant?"

The smile died, then rekindled. "Yessir. I had two tours in-country. First one in Saigon."

"When were you there?"

"Let's see," he said, rubbing his chin, "December '66 to October '67."

"Just before my time," I said.

"You were there with the Colonel, sir?"

I nodded. "For a time."

"Colonel's a good commander and a fair man."

"Then he hasn't changed."

Ricker smiled again. So familiar.

"Sergeant, are you sure we didn't serve somewhere together?"

"Well, sir, no I'm . . . uh-uh, what's this?"

I looked ahead and saw nothing. Ricker decelerated and began edging onto the shoulder.

"What's the matter?" I asked.

"Felt a shimmy from that left front wheel again."

"I didn't notice anything."

"Ach," said Ricker as we pulled to a stop, "truck ain't got four thousand miles on 'er and this is the second time she's done this." He looked at me. "Mind reachin' into the glove box there and gettin' me the flashlight?"

"Sure," I said, leaning forward and pushing the box button.

"Sorry about this, sir, but I don't want to press my luck."

"I don't see any—" I glanced up and over at Ricker, who squirted a cloud of something from a tiny spray can into my face.

I remember the sound of my forehead bouncing off the dashboard.

We were slogging through a rice paddy. The men were bunched up, though, in formation like on a parade field. I yelled for them to maintain their interval, maintain interval. They couldn't hear me because they were singing a Jody call. You know, "Jody, Jody, don't be blue, ten more minutes and we'll be through" and so on. They were marching through this paddy and singing to keep in step. Stupid thing to do, mines, mortars . . .

There was a flash of light and a tremendous explosion. The platoon was thrown up into the air and just burst. Rifles and arms and legs and heads flying outward and landing with a sploosh all around me. The little goat-girl, too.

I was kneeling behind an overturned jeep. It was on fire. A sergeant in full dress greens rushed up with a hose. But he had only the nozzle of the hose, there was nothing connected to it. He turned to me with it. It was Ricker, now in the uniform of a National Policeman.

"Sorry about this, sir," he said, "but I don't want to press my luck."

The water hit me in the face. I woke up shivering, but my face was dry. I was staring at a Sheetrock ceiling with some peeling pipes and crudely rigged rafter space. There were wide water skis, ancient fishing rods, and chipped wooden oars. It was dark, but not pitch black.

My eyes smarted and my head hurt worse than my mugging aches. I was tied spread-eagle on an old iron twin bed. My suit, tie, and shoes were gone, my shirt, briefs, and socks still on. My mouth was taped. I could move my head one hundred eighty degrees, my line of sight like the arc of an old protractor. I could just touch my chin to my chest, but the additional view wasn't worth the discomfort.

There were broken lawn chairs and a dust-covered old bicycle in one corner. Paint cans and a bucket with a rake and broom in another. Some army olive-drab canvas hung from a rafter. A magnified rectangle of indirect moonshine spotlighted a patch of concrete floor from a high, closed window. By arching my back and riding up on my neck like a wrestler, I could see, upside down, the top couple steps of a wooden staircase.

It was early March, and I was freezing to death in somebody's cellar.

I lay quietly for about fifteen minutes. I couldn't hear anyone walking around upstairs. In fact, no noise at all. No TV, radio, car, or even wind noise. Just a nagging, numbing cold.

The backs of my wrists were lashed palms outward to the top of the iron bed's headboard to keep me from grasping the railing with my fingers. My ankles were secured similarly at the other end. I tried throwing my hips ceiling-ward to see if I could rock the bed. It bucked a little, producing almost no noise or progress.

Then I heard footsteps above me.

The cellar door opened, and a light flicked on. High heels clattered lightly on the slat steps. I decided to play possum.

The shoes sounded more muffled on the concrete floor. A whiff of perfume preceded the accented, female voice.

"Open your eyes."

I stayed asleep.

"My husband put pressure thing on the bed. Wire upstairs. I know you awake. Open your eyes or I hit you in the nuts."

I opened my eyes.

She smiled down at me. She was Vietnamese, maybe thirty-five. Probably five feet tall without the heels. She wore designer jeans, a cowlneck sweater, and a baby blue parka. She held a short hunting knife in one hand and a short leather sap in the other.

"Better. When my husband come back, you talk. You talk plenty. But now you be quiet. O.K.?"

I nodded my head.

She looked me over, head to foot. "You good-looking man."

I didn't nod.

She set her knife down on the bed. She unfastened the top two buttons of my shirt and slid her hand in. It was warm against my cold skin. She ran the tips of her nails lightly over my right nipple. She spider-walked her fingers over to my left nipple and did the same.

"You like?" she said, licking her lips.

I nodded, very slowly.

She slipped her hand out of my shirt and drew it slowly down my front. She stroked and probed very gently around where my zipper would have been.

"Ah," she said huskily. "You like a lot."

There was a flash of brighter light through the window and the crunching of tires on gravel. She dropped the sap and used both hands to quickly rebutton my shirt.

"Too bad," she whispered as she snatched up her weapons and click-trotted away and up the stairs.

It looked to be a long evening.

"We're in Mexatawney. 'Bout fifty miles from the D. of C. Kind of a fishin' community come springtime. Probably nobody in a mile to hear you if you was to holler or anything."

I still had the tape on my mouth, so all I could do was listen.

Ricker shifted his butt on the creaky dinette chair. He'd brought it down the stairs with him. He sat on it backwards, the back of the chair toward me and him astride the seat, like a saddle.

"Yessir, you're in the house of a friend of mine from the 'Nam. Curly Mayhew. 'Nother Looziana boy. He's part of, oh, kind of a 'club' I belong to. Senior noncoms. Old Curl's a good man, helps another member out, just like in the 'Nam. Don't know how he stands this commutin' though. Fifty miles. Each way, each day. Whew!"

I blinked a few times. Ricker brought his wrist up to his eye level, exaggeratedly, like an actor in a kid's play. "Yessir, old Curl ought to be awingin' his way to Boston right now, havin' checked out of your hotel for you and havin' paid cash and all for room, cab, and airfare." Ricker tilted his head so his face and mine were on parallel planes. "Yeah, he don't really favor you a lot, Lootenant, but him and you are about the same size and he was wearin' your suit and all. Even got your overcoat back." Ricker righted his head. "For room clerks and cabbies and stewardi, I reckon he'll pass."

I heard the cellar door open and the clacking approach of my earlier visitor.

"Ah," said Ricker looking up. "Here comes the wife."

She came into my view, carrying a TV tray with a towel draped over it. I couldn't see what was on the tray, but I didn't smell any food. Despite the cold, I could feel the sweat forming in my armpits.

"This is Jacquie, my wife." He winked at me. "But then I understand you met a bit earlier."

Jacquie gave her husband a light cuff on the shoulder, then let her hand rest on the back of his neck. She aligned her body in an S curve like the Madonna statues in medieval churches, but without the spiritual aspirations.

"Hello," she said to me, smiling.

I nodded a greeting.

"Jacquie's a real helpmate, Mr. Cuddy. Yessir, we met when I was in the 'Nam, of course. I promised her daddy I'd take her back to The World and be real good to her." He looked up at her lovingly. "And once you promised her daddy something, you made good on it. He was a major in the National Police." Ricker let his gaze slide slowly, melodramatically over to me. "Interrogation specialist. He taught Jacquie everything she knows."

I tried to keep a poker face, but I expect that my eyes might have flickered toward the TV tray. My mind certainly went back to a different basement, halfway around the world, and the condition of Al's body.

"Haw!" Ricker slapped his thigh. Jacquie giggled. "Oh, Lootenant, you're a good one, you are. But you can relax." He signaled toward the tray. Jacquie stepped to it. She picked up a syringe and did a careful squirt test.

"Yessir," said Ricker, rising and stepping behind me. "We can't have another incident like Lootenant Sachs. No sir, that would be real suspicious. My orders, from another member of that club I mentioned, are truth serum for you. Yessir, I'd run clear out of old sodium P. Wouldn't you know it? Would've had to chase after some today, but fortunately old Curl had a bit of some new stuff in stock here. He got it through the club. Don't kill your memory or leave traces in the bloodstream. Now, how about that for progress?"

Jacquie crossed over to me as Ricker clamped down hard on my left arm, immobilizing it. "Good old Curl. He was Quartermaster Corps in-country. Like a squirrel, Curl is. Even now, he never lets go a nothin' that might come in handy."

Jacquie kneeled down on the floor alongside me. She pushed and bunched my sleeve past Ricker's grasp and above my elbow. She was wearing terrific perfume. She smiled a little more vividly as she jabbed the needle in. I felt the unwelcome, insistent surge of the drug into my arm. She pulled the needle out, and daubed my arm with a cold, wet cotton ball. Ricker let me go, and they rearranged themselves over by the chair. The perfect peacetime couple, a dream matching of cultures.

I began to float, and I grew warm. Even comfy. I sank deeper into my cot. It felt like a feather bed. Or more accurately, a bed of feathers, completely cushioned and completely conforming to my body. No matter which way I turned or settled I was equally, infinitely comfortable. I felt my eyelids closing, drooping really, to slits against the now bright-seeming light.

"You are feeling good, now?" asked Jacquie.

I nodded agreeably.

I smelled her perfume again. Her nails gently started a corner of the tape away from my mouth and snicked it, carefully and painlessly, all the way off. I didn't look up, but I bet she was smiling.

"Do you have any questions for us first?" she said sweetly into my ear.

They were going to let me ask questions. That was very considerate.

"Yes," I said honestly. "What kind of perfume are you wearing?"

They both laughed. Her laugh was closer and rose above his, like the clinking of fine crystal glasses over dinner conversation. I hadn't heard female Vietnamese laughter in a long time.

I felt marvelous. I was pleasing them.

"You are wonderful man," she said, stroking my eyelids and brow with the tips of her nails. It gave me goosebumps. "Now, what did Lieutenant Sachs tell you when you talk with him?"

I reported my conversation with Al as carefully as I could. I wasn't getting it quite right, and I apologized to her.

"That's O.K.," she said, soothingly, "that's O.K. Keep telling me."

I finished with Al. I told them all about the visit to the morgue, and I started to cry. She dried my tears with a handkerchief and gave me a little kiss on the cheek. Right away, I felt much better.

She asked me what I told the police. I filled them in on my talks with Murphy and my return visit to Al's hotel. I tried to tell them the names of the clerks, but I couldn't remember and she said that was O.K., they didn't need them. I started to tell them about the Coopers and started to cry again, but she used her hankie and brushed her lips over mine and said to forget about the Coopers, so I did.

We never reached Nancy Meagher or Marco or any of that. She asked about Al's family, and I told them all about my visit to Pittsburgh, Martha and Al Junior, and Kenny and Dale and Larry and Carol. Then she asked me what I told them about Al's death. I related the concerns in my talk with Carol and my promise to Martha to get the insurance payment.

Jacquie praised me for my efforts on my friend's behalf. She emphasized how much loyalty like mine meant to her. She slid her hand inside my shirt again. It gave me bigger goosebumps.

"You talk with Colonel Kivens, too?"

"Oh, yes," I said.

"Tell me."

I told her.

"How you make the list?"

"The list?"

"The names. On the list in your pocket. How you choose the names?"

"Oh," I said, "from the records that J.T. gave me. Excuse me, that he let me look at. The records from Vietnam, when Al was there. The list are people he knew, or arrested, or whatever. He . . ." I stopped for a minute. Thinking.

"Go on."

I was silent.

"Why you stop?"

A photograph materialized in my mind's eye. "I just remembered. That's where I saw your husband. That's why he looked so familiar. He was in one of the photographs. Smiling."

She seemed to turn away for a moment, then came back to me. "Oh," she said, nuzzling her face against my cheek. "That very good. Very good. You make me very happy now." She kissed my eyelid, licked my ear lobe with the tip of her tongue.

I was happy that she was happy. I was gloriously happy.

"Where is the list?" I asked.

"Don't worry about list," she said. "List gone."

I stopped worrying about the list. About everything.

"Did you call anyone about list?" she said.

"Call? No, no, I didn't."

Ricker said something. She hushed him.

She asked, "Did you *tell* anyone about list?"

"No one. No one but you."

"Ahh," she moaned into my ear. "That is perfec'. Just right."

Her nails pinched my right nipple, hard but exquisitely pleasurably. Her fingers trembled a little. She withdrew her hand and left my side.

I heard some noise but nobody talked with me anymore. I fell asleep.

Eighteen

My eyes opened. I was shivering, my teeth chattering inside the tape over my mouth. I clamped down on my jaws, but that just made my whole head shake, and it hurt enough as it was. My mouth was desert dry, like from a wine hangover. It was dark in the basement. Whether still dark or again dark, I didn't know.

I tried to shift around and remembered too late the motion sensor Jacquie had mentioned in her first visit. I heard her heels above me and then the cellar door. My mouth grew drier, but not from anticipation. The lights came on, and she came down the stairs. She walked up behind me.

I looked up at her. Her face was upside down and a bit haggard. Her right hand held the knife. No leather sap or other non-lethal weapon this time. A bad sign.

"You alla time so . . . active?" she said softly.

I shook my head.

"My husband go to call man in Boston. Not Curly, different noncom. Ricker no want phone bill to fuck up old Curl." She stroked my brow with her empty hand. "We all alone now."

The only noise I could hear was the faint scratching her nails made on my eyebrows.

"If I take off tape, you promise no yell, no scream?"

I nodded.

She peeled off the tape, gently. She ran her index fingernail around the outline of my lips. I kissed it. She moved it down to my chin.

"Ugh, you need shave."

"The price one pays for virility."

She giggled, but while she got it, I'm not sure she could have explained it.

"You have nice voice," she said. "I like talking with you."

"You made me feel very good with the drug," I said. "And with your fingers, and lips, and tongue."

She licked her lips, giving me just a peek at the tongue.

"Too bad I meet Ricker an' not you in Saigon," she said.

She positioned the knife, cutting edge up, just under my chin. Then she leaned over and kissed me, upside down, tongue thrust hard and often into my mouth. I'd never kissed a woman upside down before, but I did my best to respond.

"Mmmm," she said as she broke off the kiss. "Very nice." She pulled back the knife. Break off kiss, then withdraw knife.

She put the knife down next to my head and reaffixed the tape, testing it thoroughly. Careful woman.

"Yes, very nice. But I must wait for Ricker to get back. He want to watch."

She clacked away and started up the stairs. "You MP, like Ricker. He say he let me be 'double vet'ran' tonight. You know what that mean." She laughed, like glass breaking this time.

A double veteran was in-country slang for a GI who, after having sex with a woman, killed her.

She turned off the lights. I could still hear her laughing through the closed door.

Jacquie was watching something on television. Not enough music (and too much noise with the muffled voices) for radio. I was still shivering, wishing I'd hit her up for a blanket on her last trip. Fat chance.

I pushed the cold out of my mind and concentrated on Ricker. He, old Curl, and God knows how many other noncoms were members of a "club." Given the "fraternal customs" I'd seen, the club probably centered around contraband. Black market in Vietnam and elsewhere overseas, maybe drugs on-post here in the States. Far-flung, but tightly knit, with a high gross revenue since noncoms functionally ran almost every operation of any outfit I ever knew. Disciplined, savvy, competent. An impressive international organization, in whose Washington offices I was presently cooling my heels.

I was just about out of options. My bonds were no looser than when I had arrived. Even if I could get loose, my hands and feet were so numb it would be a while before I could move around or act effectively. My body ached, but probably more from the mugging and my present accommodations than from Ricker's spray can and needle. I couldn't see any way out. I couldn't see even a way to leave J.T. a message.

Mindful of the sensor, I arched my back as slowly as I could and rolled up onto my wrestler's neck bridge. I didn't hear Jacquie getting up to check on me.

I scanned as much of the room as I could see in the shadow light. Nothing new. No cutting edge, no communications device.

My gaze refocused on my hands. My right hand. My pinkie.

I remembered Jimmy Cagney and Al's little finger. I fought back a cold rush with reason. J.T. knew nothing of the special meaning of *13 Rue Madeleine.* Also, since Ricker used Curl to make it appear that I had left D.C., I couldn't imagine my body turning up in the foreseeable future.

I took a few deep breaths. I spoke inside with Beth, getting some advice. I said some prayers. I waited awhile, then said some more.

I saw the headlights' reflection and heard the gravel crunch and car door sounds again. Ricker's truck was the only vehicle sound I could remember hearing. He had said it was a deserted neighborhood this time of year, yet both of them seemed real careful about making noise. Knife over gun, taped mouth, promises and all. I had pretty well figured that Jacquie would remove the tape during her first efforts. I decided my last act (I couldn't quite characterize it as a hope) would be the best hollers for help I had left.

I heard their combined footsteps above. The door opened, and they descended the stairs, Ricker in the lead.

"Well, now," he said as he pulled up the chair, "I understand my bride here has sort of given away the rest of tonight's program." He smiled and raised his eyebrows.

I just stared at him.

He frowned. "Oh, come on, now, Lootenant, be a sport, huh? You realize how many guys go out a lot less happy than that? You forget how many grunts got killed on perimeter guard, floggin' their dogs when they should have been lookin' front?" Ricker spat on the floor. "Not to mention the insult you imply toward my wife's attraction level."

I looked up at Jacquie. She was a little unsteady. Drinks or drugs. A little slip by the careful lady?

"Anyway, there's nothin' you can do about it. I just talked to old Curl. He got into Boston and took a cab to your place. He used the keys you had to open your apartment—he said you don't have near enough security devices on your premises, by the by. He dropped off your suitcase and unpacked your stuff. He said he didn't have to mess up your covers none. Says you live like a slob. He opened your mail and put it on your desk." Ricker chuckled. "He even ripped up your junkmail and tossed it in the wastebasket. That Curl, he's a caution. I told ya, he don't miss a trick."

Ricker pulled a .38-caliber revolver from behind his back. He dug into his jacket pocket and took out a silencer. He screwed the three-inch muffler into place, then leveled the weapon at me.

"Take off the tape, honey."

She moved behind me, her hips rippling under the jeans. She peeled back the tape a little less gently and steadily than before. I puckered and bit on my lips to work the sting away.

"Well," prompted Ricker.

I just stared at him.

He arched an eyebrow. "Y'all gonna talk or what?"

I eyed Jacquie. "Maybe I'm just saving my tongue for your bride."

Jacquie stiffened a bit, as though only her husband could talk about her that way. Ricker just laughed, a low, throaty laugh.

"Lootenant, you're a better sport than I thought. You're tryin' to make me mad, so's I'll do something stupid." He shook his head, still smiling. "Good tactics, but what with you all trussed up like that, kinda bad strategy."

I smiled back. "Did old Curl happen to mention whether he played back my tape?"

"Tape?" said Ricker and immediately cursed, then laughed again. "You'da made a good boxer there, Lootenant. You had me alookin' at your right hand, and then caught me with your left." He made a tsk-tsk sound, then said, "Nope, old Curl never did mention any tape, and I shouldn't have let you know that, should I? Well," he paused for effect as he cocked the revolver and aimed it more specifically at my face, "maybe you'd best tell me about that tape."

I looked at the gun, then back up at him. "I think I'd prefer the truth serum."

"Five seconds," said Ricker, not smiling.

I waited three. "I have a tape machine attached to my telephone. It records all my messages. I've been gone since Thursday, the twenty-fifth. If your boy went through my mail but not my messages, it's going to be obvious to the police that I never got home."

Ricker closed his eyes for a moment, then opened them. "It was late when you got in, too late to call anybody back."

I shook my head, slowly. "First, some of the people trying to reach me are clients who would want to be called back at any time. Second, some of the other people trying to reach me are, ah, romantic interests who I would want to call back at any time. Lastly, the machine shows a little red light when a call has been received. It goes out only when the tape is played back. When the cops eventually get to my place, they'll see that red light, play back those old messages, and realize somebody tried to fake my return."

Ricker closed his eyes a little longer this time. "Damn." He snorted and slowly stood up. "Well, I guess old Curl will have to do a little more visitin' in Boston. Damned gadgetry."

Ricker looked down into my face. "If there's no machine attached to that telephone of yours, you'll wish old Alexander G. Bell had never been born."

He turned to Jacquie. "Honey, I'm gonna have to catch Curl in his hotel before he gets too drunk to walk. I'm gonna . . ."

Ricker noticed Jacquie was staring down at me, her breathing shallow and rapid. I didn't think she was paying attention to him, and he didn't either.

He slapped her. A snappy, short whack like a carpenter driving a nail.

She nearly tumbled off her heels. Her hand went up to her face. She rubbed her cheek with her knuckles. He now had her attention.

"Like I said, honey, I have to risk callin' Curl from here to catch him." He stuffed the revolver in her other hand. "You keep a close eye on this trophy, now, you hear?"

She nodded, her eyes downcast, and said, "Yessir."

Ricker leaned over, pecked her on the cheek. He

then scampered, no easy effort for a man his size, up the stairs.

She turned to me and licked her lips. There was a rosy blush where he'd hit her. She began to rub the barrel of the silencer slowly up and down one thigh, then the other. She licked her lips again and stared at me. Her eyes were glassy.

"How about a kiss," I said.

She assumed her behind-my-head position. She leaned over and put the business end of the gun in my right ear. Then she smothered me with a wet, tongue-driven kiss, moaning throatily. Her breath tasted sweet, like marijuana, but given hours of semi-consciousness, my palate wasn't exactly good litmus paper.

She came up for air. "You know," I said softly, "you could kill him and we could go away together."

She favored me with another kiss, still sloppy but shorter. She broke it. "No, my father promise me to Ricker. Beside," she said, straightening up as we both heard Ricker's footfalls upstairs, "I don't think you let me be double vet'ran like Ricker."

Her husband stomped down the steps. He was seething.

"That fuckin' drunk ain't in his room! Or he ain't answering his phone. And that fleabag he's staying in won't check on him."

"Which one is it?" I said. "Maybe I have some pull with the manager."

Ricker laughed, louder and longer than before. "My lord, Lootenant, you *do* have a set of balls. You surely do."

He took the revolver back from Jacquie. "The hell

with the machine. *If* you even got one. The more times Curl goes to your place, the more likely he is to get spotted. Besides, even if he got the machine squared away, he still couldn't very well call your clients and friends and pretend he was you. No, I guess we'll just have to risk it."

He took his seat and nodded to Jacquie. "You be good to my little bride, now, you hear?"

His wife shook off her parka and swayed over to me. She was trembling, but not, I thought, from the cold. I had stopped shivering and started sweating. Profusely.

Jacquie began undoing the last three buttons on my shirt. "I'd like to take a leak first," I said.

"No," said Ricker.

"Shower and shave then?"

"No."

"At least a little mouthwash."

"No, Goddamn it," said Ricker, his free hand awkward on his zipper. "Damnation, I never did see a man try so hard not to get laid."

Jacquie finished with the buttons and pushed my shirt tails under my back and behind my neck. She was humming and singing to herself in Vietnamese.

"Jacquie do a lot of this in Vietnam, Ricker?"

He had his own member in his hand, playing with it.

"Yeah," said Ricker. "Lots of guys. Lepers, mostly."

So much for even trying to get him mad.

Jacquie slid my briefs down to my ankles. She backed off half a step. She undid her designer jeans and shoe-horned her hands down between the pants and the rump. She worked her legs and hips alternately up and down until she'd shimmied her way out of them. She kicked off her heels and stepped out of the pants. Her legs were chunkier than the jeans and heels had suggested. There was a six-inch scar on her right thigh.

She smiled at me and reached down to tug up her sweater.

"Put your heels back on first, babe," said Ricker, a crack in his voice.

Jacquie complied. Her legs looked better again, dancerlike.

She pulled her cowl sweater slowly over her head. Her bra and panties were black and lacy. The panties were crotchless.

"You like?" she said to Ricker.

"Perfect," he said.

She turned to me, smiling and licking her lips. Her smile faded, her face darkened.

I had no erection for her. I had been picturing Beth, in her hospital bed and connected to a dozen tubes alternating life and death for her.

"Ricker, he not ready," she said.

"Make him ready, babe."

"Ricker . . ."

"Make him," he said sharply.

She slipped off her bra. Then she daintily plucked at the little bow that held her panties together. Her hand lingered down there a bit longer than necessary.

"Make him," he said, his voice more desperate than sharp.

She straddled me and lowered her shoulders. Her mouth was even with my navel, her breasts assuming the outline of my crotch. She began to move very slowly. Fingertips, breasts, lips, and tongue.

She was very good. I thought of Beth. And the tubes.

I heard Ricker groan and rise partly from his seat. Jacquie moaned to him and worked harder.

"He still no good." Now she sounded desperate.

"Shit," said Ricker, standing up and reaching to his back pocket. He pulled out a clasp knife and tossed it to her. "Finish him, then. Any way you want."

Jacquie opened the blade, slashing herself as she did so. She cursed, and the knife clattered to the floor.

She pummeled me in the balls with her good hand. I clenched my teeth and built up toward a hell of a yell. Jacquie hopped off me and onto the floor to retrieve the knife. Ricker said, "The hell with it," and leveled his revolver on me.

I heard the glass shatter but the tinkle of the shards was drowned out by the rifle coughing through its own silencer. Ricker's chest opened in three places, the size of peaches, as the high-velocity bullets tumbled through him. He dropped the revolver. One of the rifle rounds struck Jacquie in the shoulder as she straightened up with the knife. It knocked her off balance as Ricker dropped to his knees at her feet, his chest a fountain of blood.

She shrieked something in Vietnamese as her knife hand went up. She got rattled by the rest of the shooter's magazine. She fell across my groin area, draped lifeless except for blood and the release of the continency muscles.

I heard a door give way upstairs and more than one set of boots hit the floorboards above my head.

Two MPs in combat fatigues preceded J.T. down the stairs.

Kivens looked around at the mess and said, "God-damn fuck up."

"I'm fine, J.T. Thanks for asking."

He waved a hand at me absently and put the other to his face. "I know, I know."

Nineteen

THE DRIVER HAD STOKED THE HEAT UP IN THE PARKED car. My shoes had been under the iron bed. Even wearing a pair of old Curl's fatigue pants and one of his blankets around me, however, I was still shivering.

I also had a splitting headache. They had moved Ricker's pickup out of the driveway and replaced it with a nondescript Chevy van. There was a lot of quiet activity around the back of the van.

Casey came over to our car. J.T., who was standing outside, spoke to him briefly. Casey went back to the van, and J.T. got back in the car next to me. I still didn't have any real strength, or even feeling, back in my hands and feet. They had carried me out of the basement, cradled between two MPs like an oversized infant.

J.T. asked me his twentieth question, which I answered the way I had the previous nineteen.

By silence.

"Jesus, John, you might at least have thanked Casey. That was a hell of a piece of shooting he did."

I glared at J.T., then rested my head back against the seat to control my shaking. I hitched up the blanket a little.

"John, please—"

I broke. "You son of a bitch, J.T.! You *pulled* all those strings and *called* all those favors to get me a look at the files, and all the time you knew."

"John, we didn't *know* in the way—"

"Oh, c'mon, J.T. You knew like you were writing the script. You put me in that office like it was a clearing and I was a goat. You fucking staked me out to shoot a tiger."

J.T. turned gloomy. "We didn't want to shoot him."

"That's great. Terrific. Makes a big difference to the goat."

"You don't understand, John. I don't know what happened to Al. Truly I don't. He was more your friend than mine, but I want to find out who got him, too. We've known for a long time that there was something going on with the noncoms all through the corps. The MPs, I mean. But we weren't sure just what. Some kind of world-wide network, linked in with the quartermasters and probably set up during 'Nam, or even before. For all we know, it's damn near eternal, passed on from one corrupt sergeant to the next, generation to generation. I was pretty sure Ricker was dirty because of his lifestyle. Not crazy or flamboyant, just higher than it should have been with his army pay. I thought he might be part of the network. We figured to let him take you and then tap his telephone calls."

"You got a warrant for that?"

J.T. screwed up his mouth. "C'mon, John, this is the army, remember? We clean our own laundry."

"Go ahead."

"Well, he used only pay phones and a different one

each time. So we put a bug on the cellar window there, and we hoped he'd tip something while you kept him talking."

"But all he did was confirm that he, and Curl, and somebody else was in 'the club.'"

"Yeah, I know." The gloomy look again. "And now we've got two unauthorized bodies."

"What about old Curl?"

J.T. waved his hand. "We haven't touched him. He'll probably come back here sometime tomorrow. He'll find a broken window and door and a lot of blood sort of clumsily cleaned up in his basement. Then he'll try calling Ricker to piss and moan about it. When he doesn't reach Ricker, maybe our luck will change and he'll call somebody else in the network. Or maybe he'll panic and run. Maybe even run to someone else in the club."

"How do you plan to prosecute these boys with so much 'fruit of the poisonous tree' lying around in the form of wiretaps, and homicide, and—"

"We don't prosecute, John. We just get 'em."

I looked back over to the van. A subofficial graves registration. It all started to sink in.

"Can you take me back to my hotel now?"

J.T. tapped the driver, a slim blond MP in dress greens. "Go ahead, Squires."

"Yessir." He shifted into drive, and we pulled away from the house.

J.T. said, "You don't have a hotel anymore, or even luggage. Remember? Old Curl checked you out. I'll take you to a safe house we use sometimes. We can outfit and feed you there."

And debrief me and debrief me and debrief me. "Fine," I said and started thinking again.

Squires drove along the Interstate. I had a rough idea where we were. I saw a sign saying REST STOP, THREE MILES.

"We're going to have to stop at that rest area ahead," I said.

"John, we're only—"

"Now, look, J.T., goddamn it!" I snapped. "I've been knocked out, shot up, and stabbed at, and I goddamn want to go to the head. A real head. Now."

"O.K., O.K.," said J.T. "You're entitled, O.K.? Squires?"

"Yessir?"

"Pull in at the stop."

"Yessir."

A few minutes later Squires swung the sedan off the highway and into the rest area lot. There were only two other cars and a brightly illuminated log cabin with a small RESTROOMS AND SNACKS sign.

The MP parked curbside and turned off the engine. He pocketed the key. "Sir, if you don't mind, I'd like to go, too."

"Sure, Squires. Go ahead."

Good trooper, I thought. Knew enough to make coming with me seem his request rather than J.T.'s order. So I wouldn't feel "in custody." Squires was lifer material.

We got out, me leaving the blanket and walking quickly but uncertainly to the cabin doorway. A fat man, who wore a park ranger uniform none too well, sat behind a counter marked "Tuckville Rest Area." He barely glanced up from a magazine as we walked by him.

Squires held the door for me. I walked in and sagged a little against a sink.

"You all right, sir?" asked Squires.

"A little unsteady, but O.K. Thanks."

"Yessir."

I made my way to the nearest stall and clanged in. I dropped my pants, let out a groan, and smacked my hand hard, like it was my head, against the sidewall. I stumbled and shuffled to my left so that my right shoulder faced the door.

Squires knocked. "Sir?" He gingerly pushed the door inward.

I truly was groggy, and he was a lot younger and more recently trained than I was. I was slumped half against the toilet paper dispenser, using my left hand to clutch the toilet seat.

Squires leaned down. "Sir?"

I swung my right elbow up and out as hard as I could. It caught him on the right cheekbone and snapped his head back into the part-open stall door. I rose up and gave him a short, quick left to the nose, and he caved in. I didn't think I'd broken anything on either of us.

I buttoned up and stepped over him. I picked his pocket for his car keys and his holster for his weapon. I unloaded the weapon and dropped it into the next john. I clutched my stomach and dry-heaved my way out the door and toward the fat ranger.

"Hey," I said breathlessly, "the soldier and I are both sick as dogs. I think it's food poisoning. We got a buddy in the car outside. Get him. Quick, quick!"

The ranger bustled up and out a door next to the counter, the door locking behind him. As soon as he was outside, I grabbed a map and climbed over the counter. I unlocked and stepped out the back door, circling behind the cabin. I got around the corner just as J.T.'s heels disappeared into the cabin. The ranger was close behind him, snorting huge clouds of cold air.

I chugged to the car, got in, and turned the key. I eased away from the curb and slid back onto the Interstate.

The map showed a reasonably wide state road three miles on. I took it and headed east. Toward the town where a friend from college lived.

Cockeysville. Cockeysville, Maryland. A name that stays with you. Arnie had sent a Christmas card from there every year since we graduated. With any luck, he still lived there, commuting to Johns Hopkins where he taught philosophy publicly and railed against the military-industrial establishment privately.

As I drove toward the town, my mind kept switching around what I knew. From the photo in the file, I was pretty certain which case Al had stumbled on. The problem was, I couldn't see quite how. From his eavesdropping in the cellar, J.T. knew about the list, but if Jacquie had told me the truth, he wouldn't find it. Still, he'd be able to reconstruct it, and the photo with the younger Ricker in it should tip him off. Al, however, hadn't had access to the files, so he must have found the bad guy some other way. Since I didn't have, or particularly care to have, access to J.T. and the army's computers anymore, I figured probably there was only one way for me to find Al's killer. The same way Al had.

Whatever that was.

I hit Cockeysville and pulled up to three phone booths before I found one that had a book. I had the book open, shivering in my blanket, before I realized that I didn't have a dime anyway. The address would do. Arnie, or Arnold. Neumeier. The Ds, the Ls, Na, Ne . . .

There was something there, something fuzzy, vibrating in there with the headache and being muffled by it. My hands were shaking, and I was too tired to make sense of it.

I found Arnie's address. I got back in the car and crisscrossed streets till I hit his. I knocked on his door just as dawn was breaking. After he got over the shock of my being there and my appearance, what little I could tell him confirmed his view of the armed services. He led me in his car to an all-night supermarket eight miles south, where we parked the government car. Then we drove back to his house. Arnie fed me and loaned me fifty dollars and some winter clothes. He dropped me off at a bus station over the Delaware line and said "for chrissake" to stay in touch from now on.

I took a Trailways Scenic Cruiser to Providence, sleeping most of the way. I changed to the train and got off an hour and five minutes later at South Station in Boston. The cabbie told me it was 4:15 P.M. I thought about playing possum somewhere, but I needed more money and wanted a licensed weapon. I was willing to chance that J.T. or an allied paramilitary force had staked out my apartment.

They needn't have bothered.

The cabbie pulled to a stop and swiveled around with a shrug. "Hey, Mac. You sure you wanted Number Fifty-eight?"

I nodded, more at the blackened rubble than at him. My whole building was gone. As in blown up and burned down.

I had him drive me to Cambridge. I got off in Harvard Square, bought a "late stocks" edition *Globe* and had two screwdrivers in the Casablanca, an after-work and academic hang-out for the post-mixer set. I opened the paper. My building, or rather its destruction, made page one.

The explosion occurred at 10:00 A.M. On the nose. No doubt of it, because the antiques dealer across the street was just setting a mantel clock when the blast shattered his front windows. The resultant fire raged for nearly two hours. The manager of the drycleaner on the street level was badly shaken. All the residential tenants save one were accounted for, miraculously out of the building during working hours. One body, badly burned, was found that seemed to match the missing tenant's description. Police were "withholding any names until a positive identification could be made and relatives contacted." Due to the suspicious nature of the fire, the arson squad and other authorities were investigating. There was a photograph accompanying the story. In the corner of the picture was a hulking black man I'd bet was Murphy.

The anonymous tenant was, of course, me. The question then became, who was the guy everybody thought was me?

I had two candidates.

One was Marco. He'd gotten the Coopers. He'd try to get me. MO in the ballpark with explosion and fire. Marco just got careless with his implements.

Second choice was old Curl. Maybe doubled back, half in the tank, to rip me off. Maybe thought of something else he should have done. Marco has visited in the meantime, however, and bad timing cashiers old Curl.

I wasn't too broken up about either candidate. Whoever it was, however, I wanted to stay dead awhile. If Marco was dead, I still had to deal with Al's killer. If Curl was dead, Marco was alive, and I couldn't see any percentage in advising the elder D'Amico brother that he'd shot the wrong duck.

To stay dead, however, would require some immediate action.

Twenty

IT ISN'T EASY TO GET THROUGH TO A RANKING POLICE officer when you refuse to give your name. I ascended the scale, slightly disguising my voice for Detective Cross when she picked up. If confidential informants help solve only a few crimes, it may be because they spend most of their lives on hold.

"Murphy here. Who is this?"

"Lieutenant, when I tell you my name, I don't want it repeated by you on your end of the line, understand?"

"Shit. Mr. Lazarus, I presume."

I almost laughed. "That's pretty good, Lieutenant, but at the moment my sense of humor isn't what it might be."

"Christ, I can't see why. If I was you, I'd be jumping for joy about now."

"Listen, Lieutenant, let me connect a few dots for you and then ask you a favor, O.K.?"

"I'm listening."

"Since I'm not dead, the unidentified man is probably Marco D'Amico or an army sergeant from D.C. named Curly Mayhew. M-A-Y-H-E-W, I think. I'm not sure that Curly is his real name, but it might be."

"Go on."

"I figure somebody rigged my place to blow like the Coopers. Either Marco or someone else."

I heard some background conversation at his end. Murphy lowered his voice a notch. "I got a call from an ADA named Meagher who said you had Marco pegged for the Cooper killings. Where does the someone else come in?"

"I'm not sure. That's the favor part."

"Let's hear it."

"I need to stay dead a couple of days. That probably means that the lab report on the body has to be delayed awhile. Maybe lost in somebody's in-box, but you'd know better on that."

"Uh-unh, no way. I got Meagher on my ass on this one. She's been calling me every two hours since the office got word on the blast."

"I can let her in, too. No problem. She'll stop pressing you."

Murphy was silent.

"Murphy?"

"Yeah."

"Can you help me out?"

A shorter pause. "I don't like it. A body should be identified. Family and all."

"I don't like it either. But I'm not aware that Mayhew has any family, and if it's Marco, well, his parents at worst think they have a son for a few more days."

"I still don't like it."

"I don't like a lot of things, Lieutenant. I don't like my apartment getting blown up, or my neighbors left homeless, or my best friend from the army getting killed, or—"

"Awright, awright. But I got a job to do. And a job to keep, get me?"

"I got you. But I still need a couple of days."

Murphy grunted. "O.K. Two days. Then I've got to follow through."

"I really appreciate it, Lieutenant."

"Yeah. Listen, I want to hear from you. Use this number."

I wrote down the seven digits.

He continued. "I want to hear from you tomorrow morning and tomorrow night. Got it?"

"Yes. Thanks."

"Bye-bye."

"Oh, Lieutenant, one more thing."

"Yeah?"

"Can you lend me a few hundred bucks?"

Murphy laughed, a good deep roar. "Shit, man, with your present credit prospects, I wouldn't lend you a dime unless you were a cat!"

"As in nine lives?"

"You got it."

"Nice talkin' with you."

I dialed the DA's office asking for Nancy Meagher. Telling her secretary I was Lieutenant Murphy, I was put right through.

"Lieutenant?"

"Sort of."

"What?"

"You see I was a lieutenant before I made captain, but I'm retired now, or discharged if you want to be—"

"Oh my God," she said, followed by a cough and a little choking sound. "Is it . . ."

"It's me, Nancy. Safe and more or less sound."

"Oh, God, just a minute. . . ."

I could hear her snuffling and blowing her nose.

"John?"

"Listen, I'm sorry for joking like that. I didn't—"

"Oh," she said with one terminal sniffle. "That's all right. I'm . . . fine, now. What happened, who—"

I repeated for her my suspicions about Marco and/or Curly.

"How does the army fit into all this?"

"I can't tell you now."

"What can you tell me?"

"That I was pleased to hear you were ragging Murphy about me."

A short laugh. "Besides that?"

"Not much. Nancy, I'm sorry to have to ask this, but I need some money."

"Sure. Your bank'll think you're dead, so you can't cash a check."

"Right. Assuming I still had a checkbook."

"How much?"

I cleared my throat. "Seven or eight hundred dollars."

She cleared hers. "What do you want that kind of money for?"

"I'm going to have to buy some information."

"You going to buy anything else?" she asked cautiously.

"Nancy, I believe that whoever blew up my building is still around. As long as he thinks he killed me, I'll be pretty safe. As soon as he realizes he didn't, I'm going to need protection. I've got a firearms card, remember? I won't be breaking any laws buying a gun."

As she considered it, I realized that I should have

said I was *issued* a firearms card, since my wallet was probably ashes, either burned by Curl or with him.

"O.K.," she relented. "Just don't let this get out. I'd hate to have people know I was a shy for a private eye."

"Ogden Nash would be proud of you."

"Where are you staying?"

Her question made me realize that I couldn't be quite over the effects of Ricker and Jacquie. I had less than carfare left in my pocket, and nowhere to sleep.

"I'm going to try the Pine Street Inn," I said, a genuine charity that housed and fed homeless, often derelict, men.

"Forget it," she said. "In cold weather it's full by three P.M. You can stay at my place. Where are you now, I'll pick you up."

"Nancy, you don't—"

"No arguments. Where are you?"

I told her I'd be in the doorway of Elsie's, a Mt. Auburn Street restaurant and the most famous of the Harvard College hamburger hang-outs.

"I'll drive by in thirty minutes. Red Honda Civic."

"I remember."

"See you then."

"Nancy?"

"Yes?"

"Thanks."

When I got into her car, she smiled, her eyes no redder than a winter's evening should have made them. I felt the glow again as she squeezed my left forearm, then returned her right hand to the stickshift and kept it there.

"Put your seatbelt on," she said.

We got onto Memorial Drive, toward Boston.

"You look pretty shabby," she said.

"Borrowed clothes."

She moved her head in concurrence.

We drove on in silence, halted at the Stop & Shop traffic light.

"What do you like for breakfast?" she asked, glancing at the supermarket.

"Oh," I said, "whatever you have in the house will be fine."

The light changed. We eased forward with the surrounding traffic.

"What happened to the wise-ass PI who nearly gave me heart failure today?"

"He got nervous."

"About what?"

"About being a houseguest."

She laughed, then caught herself. "I'm sorry, John. It's just that . . . well, your place has been blown up, three or four people killed around you, and—" She shook her head. "Staying with me shakes you up."

I squirmed a little under the seatbelt. "I'm an odd one, all right."

"Pity there aren't more like you."

She negotiated the corkscrew ramps up and over the Longfellow Bridge, then down behind North Station. We drove along Commercial Street to Atlantic Avenue via the nameless byway under the Southeast Expressway. The Honda crossed over the Commonwealth Pier access road and then onto Summer Street toward South Boston.

I told her she was good at avoiding traffic.

She began to say, "Avoidance is . . ." then dropped it.

South Boston is one of the few residential neighborhoods in the city where residents can find a parking place on the street in front of their houses. Nancy maneuvered into a space, and we went inside and up the stairs.

At our footsteps, the door on the second landing opened.

"Hi, Drew," said Nancy cheerily.

"Nancy," said Lynch in reply, closing his door.

She opened her apartment door, and I followed her in.

"Make yourself comfortable in the living room."

"Fine," I said, walking by her.

"Would you like something stronger than ice water this time?"

"Do you have any vodka?"

"Yes."

"Then vodka and anything will be fine."

"Do you prefer orange juice or grapefruit juice for breakfast?"

"Orange."

"Then it's vodka and grapefruit tonight."

"Fine," I repeated, collapsing into her throw pillows, registering the aches in joints and organs from drugs and batterings and train and bus rides. I felt the way over-thirty quarterbacks have described themselves at the end of the season. I closed my eyes.

I opened them as Nancy came in with the drinks, hers a Scotch and water from the look of it. I didn't think I had dropped off, but Nancy had changed from suit to jeans and a red cowlneck sweater. A lot like Jacquie's.

I started to stand. She pushed me back and handed me my drink.

"To life," she said, lightly pinging her glass against mine.

"To life," I agreed.

We sipped. She nestled down Indian-style on the floor.

"Tell you what," she said, carefully placing her drink on the low table. "Let's pretend, O.K.?"

"Pretend?" I said.

"Yes, let's pretend that I've already fed us two steaks from my freezer, and plied you with liquor, and asked you if you were ready for bed. Let's pretend that you said you were and that I gave you the choice of my room or the couch and you chose the couch. O.K.?"

I grinned sheepishly. "O.K."

"Good. Now we can both relax and maybe even enjoy each other's company." She picked up her glass and took a long draw.

"Well," she said, replacing the glass and cradling back on her elbows, "tell me about what happened."

I told her. It took through dinner and beyond, but I told her. Most of it.

Twenty-one

I WOKE UP WITH A START. THERE WAS A LOT OF SUNSHINE in the room. Too much. Then I remembered Nancy's parlor would have southeastern exposure and get a lot of morning sun, even in winter. I wondered why she didn't grow more plants. I also wondered what time it was.

I didn't hear any stirrings in the apartment. I swung my legs out from under the covers and off the couch, sitting up. I felt about fifty percent better than I had the night before. I walked to the bay window and looked down at the street. Her car was gone.

I went into the kitchen. A pencil and a note were on the table.

> John, I'm going to the bank and one other stop. Be back by 10:30.
>
> N.M. 8:45
>
> P.S. I looked in on you twice. Your face is angelic when you're asleep. Maybe you can tell a book by its cover.

I smiled and glanced up at her wall clock. 9:10 A.M. I penciled a circle around the "10:30" on her note and wrote, "So will I."

The door to Nancy's bedroom closet was open, and she had a couple of oversized T-shirts at the bottom of it. She probably used them as nightgowns. Beth always did.

I tugged on a couple of T-shirts for insulation and tried not to notice her perfume or feel like a transvestite. I pulled on Arnie's clothes and figured I was warm enough for the short walk, even in March. There was a chance that somebody would spot me, so I rummaged rudely through Nancy's closet shelf till I found a watch cap that wasn't too feminine looking. I pulled the cap down and put the collar up.

I looked in the mirror. Only one person would recognize me. The only one who really mattered.

By the time I entered the gate, I was hungry. I walked up the main car path, then took the second right-hand walkway, as always.

As I approached her, I thought how most people felt that snow on the ground made places more dreary. Sorry, but that was not possible here. Neither spring flowers nor winter storms affect a cemetery. It's always the lost part of lost and found, even though labeled by marble markers.

I reached her, hunching my shoulders a little against an edge of wind from the harbor.

"It's been a while, Beth," I said.

She agreed.

"I saw Al's family, out in Pittsburgh. Martha, his wife, is taking it well. His son, Al Junior, is too young to realize yet. They're really strapped, though, so he'll realize it pretty soon. You see, Al let everything go. No insurance, no support from his company. Martha has some real close friends out there, a woman with a little boy older than Al Junior, and a gay guy across the street. With just a chunk of money, maybe twenty-five or thirty thousand, they'd be O.K. They could hold onto the house, at least long enough to sell it reasonably instead of at sacrifice. But that means finding somebody to pay, that means . . ."

Beth asked me about the "other woman" in Pittsburgh.

I winked and laughed. "Well, she was pretty cute. She hasn't had it too easy either, a bum for a husband, but that was years ago, the divorce, I mean, and now she's pretty solid."

I sighed and went on. "At least I hope she's solid. I had to tell someone out there what I thought about Al's death being a cover-up for something else. Martha was in no shape, she was just coming out of it, the shock and all. Dale—that's the gay guy—I think he was in the process of losing his lover, and I think he knew it. That pretty much left Carol, Al's boss being a schmuck on any list."

I paused to let her get a word in edgewise. I heard a car door slam behind me. An elderly woman and a small boy left the car, the boy bounding ahead.

"Washington? Oh, I had a ball in Washington. First I got mugged, then I got set up by J.T. From the army, remember? Then . . ."

I phrased my situation with Jacquie and rescue as delicately as I could. "You saved me, Beth. As usual. But I felt badly about having to deck the MP. I hope J.T. at least has the balls to own up and not use the kid as a scapegoat. I . . ."

The boy from the car pulled even with us and stared at me. Maybe I was talking a little loudly. It's hard for me to tell sometimes. The boy, who was about seven years old, twisted around and darted off, stopping briefly at each gravestone before running to the next.

Then a voice from behind me. "Harleee! *Harley*. You come back now, you heah? Right now. Harley?" The woman was dressed in a light blue pantsuit and a heavy, ill-fitting outer coat.

"He must be over here, Gram," Harley replied. The boy had none of the woman's strong Southern accent.

"Harley, he can't be over theah, boy! That's the Fs and the Gs. He's over theah. In the Ls, where he belongs. *Harley!*"

I was tempted to tell the woman that this cemetery wasn't alphabetical, that the assignment of resting places was a function of price and chronology.

"I see an L over here, Gram! In fact, two Ls."

"Harley, Gramps is over theah. He has been over theah for seventeen months. To the left, Harley, to the left. By the Ls."

"I see another L!" called Harley back, and continued his survey.

The elderly woman muttered none too sweetly under her breath. She began to stomp doggedly down the path to the left.

I looked down at Beth's headstone. Elizabeth Mary Devlin Cuddy. Would she be in the Cs for Cuddy, or the Ds for Devlin, or even the Bs for Beth. . . .

You jerk! The Bs. "I had a lotta luck with the Bs, John-boy." Al, who never expressed a liking for hockey, or betting on it, but who always loved looking through phone books for people he knew. Blowing half an R-and-R on the Honolulu directory. Now I knew how Al had found his killer.

And I knew I could find him, too.

I turned back to Beth. I started to tell her about Nancy, and the glow, but after a few sentences she could tell my heart wasn't in it. She shooed me off.

I got back to Nancy's place and realized I had no key to her building's front door. I debated pushing the Lynches' bell for about two minutes, shivering on the front steps and anxious to go through the telephone book. I was about to buzz them when I heard two quick honks from the street. It was Nancy.

She got out with a grocery bag in the crook of her right arm. She strode up to me. She had the spring of an athlete, even with the bag.

"You don't look any better in that hat than I do." She laughed, more with her eyes than her voice.

I smiled and thought about offering to take the bag. I decided not to, chivalry yielding to feminism.

"Here," she said, shoving the bag into my arms. "Hold this."

She keyed the lock. We went in and upstairs, me carrying the bag.

"Set it on the kitchen table."

I did. She tossed off her coat and crossed to the table. She rummaged around in the bag, producing a packet of disposable Bic razors, some shaving cream, a toothbrush, and some Old Spice stick deodorant.

I scratched elaborately under my arms. "That bad, huh?"

She laughed again, music.

"It occurred to me this morning that I wasn't too

well stocked for male guests with no luggage." She pulled out a package of nondescript briefs and two exceptionally cheap-looking dress shirts.

"I guessed on size but skimped on quality." She shrugged. "I didn't want to buy good stuff that wouldn't fit."

I thanked her and pulled off the watch cap.

Reflexively she put her fist in her mouth to stifle a shriek. "Maybe I should have favored a hairbrush over the toothbrush."

I popped in the bathroom. I looked like a punk rocker only halfway down the assembly line. I came back out and scooped up the things she'd bought for me.

"Maybe I should just shave my head while I'm at it."

"Oh, do. That'll certainly make you inconspicuous."

We both laughed. She gave me a quick, strong hug and asked if I'd had breakfast. I said no. She told me to shower and shave while she made it, and pointed to the narrow vertical shutter on the wall that hid the towels.

It was a simple, silly domestic scene. Maybe the best few minutes I'd had in a couple of years.

When I came out of the bathroom, we had bacon, eggs, orange juice, and English muffins with choice of jam or marmalade. The bacon was a bit overdone for my taste, but I wasn't shy about seconds.

I insisted on clearing away and washing the dishes. I started getting itchy about the telephone book, but didn't want Nancy to see it.

As I dried the last of them and turned around,

Nancy reached into her purse and put an envelope on the table. She nudged it toward me. I dried my hands and opened it. Mostly twenties and tens.

I arched my eyebrows at her.

"There's eight hundred dollars. In smaller bills, no higher than a twenty. And old ones. I told the teller I was going on a trip and didn't want to risk giving away too new bills on some Caribbean island. She recommended travelers' checks for safety, but I stood firm on cash and carry."

"Just an old-fashioned girl, huh?"

Nancy blinked a few times. "In most ways," she said, softly.

I felt dangerously close. Close to saying something and close to her. "Shouldn't you be getting off to work?"

She hid most of her disappointment with a good effort at a smile. She stood up and crossed to a cabinet drawer. "Yes, I should. I called the office and told them I had a doctor's appointment I'd forgotten and absolutely couldn't break again. I just drew bail appeal this morning, anyway."

She turned and tossed something to me. "Catch."

Two keys held together on a paper clip. "Big key, downstairs door. Little key, upstairs door."

I hefted them in my palm. "What do I say to Mrs. Lynch?"

Nancy disappeared into her bedroom to change. "Better tell her you're my cousin." She closed the door.

No, Nance, I don't think I'll tell her that.

Nancy had said she'd be home about six. I told her not to wait for me. She had asked if there was anything else she could do for me. I thanked her and said no.

I watched her get into the Honda and drive off before grabbing the telephone book. I dialed Murphy's special number as I traced down through the Bs to Ba, Be, Bea. . . .

"Murphy here."

Bee, Beg. "Hello, Lieutenant. Just reporting in."

Bek.

"Hold on a second." I heard him yell at Cross to close the door.

Bel! "Listen, one of my people fouled up. You better hear about it."

I looked away from the telephone book. "Fouled up? What do you mean?"

"A reporter was pressing Daley. Remember, the guy from the morgue?"

"I remember him."

"Well, it was a woman reporter and the damn fool sort of confirmed that the corpse in the building was you."

"So?"

"So you're on page fucking four of the morning *Globe.*"

"Photograph?"

"No, just a short three-inch follow-up, ID'ing you as the dead man. I'm gonna chew his ass good."

"You know, Lieutenant, he may have helped rather than hurt. I've got no family in the area to be upset, and I should be through before any friends volunteer to shepherd my remains through the formalities."

"I can hold that up anyway. Glad it's no trouble for you." Murphy grunted. "Course, I'm still gonna chew his ass."

"I'll call you tonight."

"You got anything?"

"Not yet. I'll still call tonight."

"Sooner if you get something."

"I will."

He rang off.

I went back to the Bels. Beldow, Belgrade, Bell, dozens of Bells, then Belson, then . . . wait a minute. K before L. I went back. No Belk's. No Belker. I threw the white pages across the room.

I went through the Yellow Pages. Nothing. They landed just to the left of the white pages. Some guest I was.

Guest? Al was a guest in a hotel. Probably just Boston white and yellow pages in the rooms, but the lobby?

I closed my eyes and could picture a bank of pay phones I'd used just outside the bar entrance at Al's hotel. With a library of phone books below them. Al, just killing time, thumbing through them.

I took Nancy's money and hopped a Summer Street bus to South Station. I cabbed it from there to my rent-a-car place. Luck was with me. The guy behind the counter had dealt with me before and didn't look like he read comic books much less newspapers. A ten persuaded him that I'd left my wallet in my other coat and that the license number I gave him was accurate.

I got into the late model Chrysler and drove to the hotel.

The clerk at the desk was the striking blonde the uniformed Keller had tried to pick up. I dodged her glance successfully and went to the phone bank out of her field of vision. Hanging under them were eight or ten phone books in those black, metallic, swivel looseleafs. I levered up one suburban directory after another. Nothing.

Till I got to West Suburban. There he was.

Belker, C. Bus. 73 Main Street, Weston Hills
Res. 149 Willow Drive, Weston Hills

I pictured him in that swank suburb. Tall, gawky, Alabama. Obnoxious. And a murderer.

Bingo. If he lived in Weston Hills, he was no pauper. Martha and Al Junior had won. Now I just had to collect their prize money.

Twenty-two

I REACHED INTO MY POCKET FOR THE LEFTOVER CHANGE from Arnie's stake to me. I fed a dime, dialed Belker's business line, and was told by an atonal voice to deposit another forty-five. I barely made it.

"Weston Hills Realty, may I help you?" A nicely modulated voice.

"Yes," I said, "may I speak to Mr. Belker, please?"

"Certainly, sir. May I say who is calling?"

"Certainly," I replied, "it's—" I scratched my last coin against the mouthpiece and clicked down the cradle in the middle of her second, concerned, "Hello?"

I beat it to the car and drove to Weston Hills as moderately as a man without a license should.

I wanted a look at Belker before I spoke with him. After everything else that had happened, I wanted to be sure it was him so I wouldn't scare the daylights out of some innocent citizen.

I passed slowly by 73 Main, a two-story, brick-front building, newish and typically suburban. WESTON HILLS REALTY was painted on the windows, and an apparently classy woman was seated at what seemed a reception desk. I parked a half-block past the building and adjusted the passenger outside mirror to focus on the front door of the building. A real estate broker should walk out and around often enough so I wouldn't be there all day. The clock outside the bank said it was nearly 12:30. Lunchtime. I hoped Belker was hungry, because a good cop or nervous operative would spot me after about fifteen minutes.

Of course, Belker had no reason to be nervous anymore, now that I was dead. Also, he never was a good cop.

A little voice in my head whispered, "But he was good enough to take Al."

"Al was away from it and out of shape," I replied.

"He was in good enough shape to bounce two Steeler fans around a sidewalk a few months ago," said the little voice. "And he would have been on his guard."

My response to the little voice's troubling logic was thrown offtrack by the short, red-headed, and bespectacled man who exited the realty door. He smiled and waved to someone. The someone said, "Hi, Mr. Belker." He said "Hi" back and walked away from me.

Mr. Belker. Shit. Five-foot-six and red hair was not the Clay Belker that I knew. But the coincidence. Belker's name in the phone book where Al—

"But there are dozens of names that you wrote down in Washington that appear in hundreds of phone books," said the voice. "Besides, you don't even know that 'C. Belker' stands for 'Clay Belker.'"

Neither had Al, of course, unless Al had called the

office. Or the residence. But then, so what? Even if it is "C" for Clay, it still isn't the right Clay Belker. The man I'm looking for is well over six feet and big-boned.

Wait a minute. The man who came to the clerk at Al's hotel. He was described as short. But, still, where's the tie-in? When Al talked to or saw this little guy, Al would have realized he wasn't the right Clay Belker. Besides, what would Al have had to blackmail Belker about? The only time Belker and Al were in the files was . . .

The little man was back in mirror-view again, politely walking around an older woman and saying something to her. He was carrying a take-out bag, and his smile was phony, a real salesman smile. Familiar, somehow, like an older . . .

Damn! I nearly hit my horn, slamming my hand against the wheel. The little man disappeared into the building.

So that was it. I could see how Al would have been taken and why he was killed. Had to be killed. And why Ricker wanted information first from me, too.

I started up and pulled out. I drove slowly as a plan I'd been mulling over took more definite shape.

The Button. Not his real name, of course. He was one of the first blacks to arrive (and therefore one of the last to be welcomed) in a predominantly Irish neighborhood in Dorchester, a working-class section of wooden three-deckers and family-owned stores south of Back Bay and the South End. The Button had spent twenty years in the navy and was known to almost every cop, private investigator, and industrial spy in eastern Massachusetts. If he'd located ten years later in a classier part of town, he'd be a consultant, not a parts supplier.

The Button, you see, is in *e*-lectronics, accent on the first "e." He sells nothing that is *per se* illegal, only components that a knowledgeable pair of hands can assemble into just about anything. Occasionally, the Button can be cajoled into giving even a professional a little advice. He also has a brother who runs a gunshop in predominantly black Roxbury down the road. While the brother is competent, however, the Button is a genius.

I pushed open the door, and the wind chimes attached to it tinkled and sang. A few steps later, the Button appeared through a dark red curtain across a doorway behind his main counter. The chimes were a little masquerade the Button played for the rest of the world. Behind his drapes was the control board of a sensor and closed-circuit TV system that had picked me up as soon as I left my car half a block away.

The Button nevertheless feigned surprise and delight at seeing me. Perhaps he had forgotten he once had shown me the control board. Or maybe somebody finally had ripped it off.

"Why, John Francis. It is so good to see you." His face was deep coal in color and cracked with his wide smile. A fringe of short-cropped white hair rode up in front of his ears, then slid down as he dropped the smile. "I just realized I haven't laid eyes on you since your wife's passing."

"I got your card. It was good of you to think of me, and poor form for me not to acknowledge it."

The Button smiled again, more mellow than bright.

He dismissed my confession, like an admiral forgiving an aide's blunder. "Please, no apologies are necessary. Perhaps, though, an explanation?" The Button put an index finger to his chin, creasing and raising his eyes thoughtfully. "I could have sworn I read something quite disquieting about you in the *Globe* this morning."

I shrugged. "Surely you don't believe all that you read."

The Button dropped his hands and fussed with the arrangement of a few small gizmos on the countertop. "No, but it is good to see that Mark Twain's response is applicable to an old and valued customer as well."

I smiled at the "Reports of my death . . ." allusion and began to explain what I wanted. He stopped me at one point and brought a clipboard with graph paper out from under the counter. The Button diagramed and labeled a bit as I talked. He was like a secretary taking a visual form of dictation.

I pointed to one part of the diagram. "I need this to be mountable inside the engine compartment of a car."

"Hmmmm," went the Button, as he sketched and scribbled a few extra parts specifications on the margin of the diagram.

"It'll also have to be simple enough to be set up entirely by me."

"Hmmmm," said the Button, "*that* simple, eh."

"Uh-huh."

He scratched out a few connecting lines on the diagram and drew some more direct ones.

"Lastly," I said, "I need a special kind of triggering mechanism."

"What kind?" he said.

"I want a trigger that will activate when I release it, *not* when I depress it."

The Button frowned. "When you release it?"

"That's right."

The Button doodled a bit on the diagram and looked up. "Like what they use on a subway train?"

"Subway train?"

"Yes. They call it a dead-man's switch."

I exhaled a bit longer than usual. "Exactly," I said.

The Button crossed to the door, swung the gone-to-lunch side of the sign outward and pushed a red plastic square at the baseboard. He came back and beckoned me through the curtain. There he assembled and demonstrated each component, including the two-step arming of the switch. When he was satisfied I was familiar with the system, he slipped it into a brown shopping bag along with four mounting braces of varying angles and metal screws of varying diameters.

I pulled out some money, and he asked if that was it.

"Almost," I replied. "Now I'd like to call your brother."

The Button wagged his head. He didn't even look surprised.

An auto graveyard is a busy place during a New England winter. The average car-owner now keeps a car something like seven and a half years. That's a lot of road salt, sand, and skids to work on a car. Toss in drunk middle-aged drivers and inexperienced teenage drag-racers, and you have a junkyard's bonanza.

I followed two late-model Japanese cars being towed inside Eddie Shuba's gate. Eddie was from Lithuania, and in 1945 he was seventeen years old.

That was when Eddie and thousands of other refugees were sandwiched between the Red Army pushing west across Germany and the American forces pushing east. By some miracle, he'd had a little English and got enlisted in our army. He received citizenship, served in Korea, and qualified for a disability pension which he parlayed into the auto yard.

"Johnnie, Johnnie, good! Very good to see you now!"

He came humping over to me, his war leg inflexible in the cold. He wore a brand-new olive-drab field jacket with a U.S. flag stitched carefully where a unit patch should be. The driver of one of the tow trucks honked to get his attention, but Eddie ignored him.

"How are you, Eddie?" I said, shaking the hand that pumped mine.

"Oh, good, good. Stiffer in the leg and older is all."

He had a crew cut more gray than white and a few facial scars, but still a grip like one of his mechanical car-crushers, screeching and grinding off to the right.

"So how are you?" he said, openfaced and smiling.

I smiled back. No need to worry about Eddie reading "disquieting" news in the papers.

"I'm fine, Eddie, but I need a favor."

"A favor? For you, anyt'ing. You t'ink I forget? My arm, my business, what you need?"

About seven years ago, some high-level car strippers were using Eddie's yard, through a dishonest foreman, to shelter some of their skeletons. My old employer, Empire Insurance, was underwriting a lot of theft and vandalism policies then, and an overly eager assistant DA tried to connect Eddie to the ring. Eddie was clean, but he also knew that I was the one who steered the assistant straight with some help from a Holy Cross classmate who was one of the assistant's superiors. The only time I ever saw Eddie in tears was when he became convinced that his foreman had betrayed him by fronting for the ring.

"Just a small—" I said, when I was cut off by the tow truck driver, who shoved me aside and started to beef to Eddie. The driver was maybe thirty, at 220 about thirty pounds overweight. He came complete with a freely running nose and body odor, even in the cold, like a month-dead moose.

Eddie just swung his wrecking ball of a left fist fast, hard, and upward into the driver's stomach. The driver went down on his knees, gagging, and Eddie cuffed him alongside the head with the heel of the same hand, toppling him over into the slush and mud.

"Swine!" bellowed Eddie. "You wait until Eddie Shuba ready for *you*. Now, get your rig and get out. Forever, move!" Eddie kicked him rather gently for punctuation, glared at the other driver, who was obviously in no mood for the same, and then gave me a forward march gesture with his right arm.

"Come, Johnnie, we go into my office. Where there is peace and men can talk."

I followed him into the shack. The driver's dry heaves weren't quite drowned out by the compressors that seemed never to stop.

Eddie closed the door behind us, which shut out most of the noise. He offered me vodka.

"Only if I can sip it," I said.

He roared laughter and an epithet about how I had to learn to drink vodka properly. He poured us each about two ounces of 100 proof into styrofoam cups.

He handed me mine, we toasted the U.S. of A., and then he threw his drink off in one gulp, smacking his lips without a hint of coughing.

I took a polite slug. He seated himself in a big worn leather office chair, using both hands to position his bad leg at a more comfortable angle.

"So, Johnnie, how can Eddie Shuba help you?"

I prefaced my request with an abstract explanation of how I was helping the widow of a war buddy and was dealing with a very bad man. Eddie nodded gravely.

"So basically I need an old car that'll drive maybe thirty miles competently at highway speed. I'll also need a key to your front gate."

"Sure t'ing. I got a four-door Chevy Nova that run."

I shook my head. "No, I need a bigger car, preferably a two-door, with a long engine compartment."

Eddie poured and tossed another shot, wiping his mouth with the back of his hand. "I got maybe two cars so. One a Pontiac, '67. The other a Buick, '69. The Buick run better maybe, but it's four doors. The Pontiac got only two."

"Make it the Pontiac then."

Eddie looked grieved when I pulled out my bankroll. "No, no," he said, "favor to good friend. Eddie—"

I held up my hand. "I insist," I said, counting out three hundred. "By the way," I asked, "do the cops in this town come by here much at night?"

Eddie, rummaging around through some dog-eared, stained paperwork, gave his lion's laugh again. "Hoo, sure, Johnnie, sure. Just like they go to church. Ever' Christmas and Easter."

He gave me a registration and a set of car keys, then tossed a gate key on top. "Come, we try this beauty for you."

"Oh, Eddie," I said. "Two more things."

"Yeah?" he said, turning at the door as I finished my vodka.

"We're going to talk some more, but if anybody asks you about today, you tell them I just asked you if I could use the driveway beyond the gate as a meeting site. I never got any old car or any gate keys from you."

"Okay," he said, a quizzical look on his face.

"And, Eddie?"

"Yeah?"

"After I use it, I want the car crushed."

"Crushed?" said Eddie.

"I'll be leaving it here tomorrow night, and I'll want it crushed first thing in the morning."

Eddie fixed me squarely. "I show you where to park it. I work crusher Friday morning myself. First t'ing."

We went back out into the yard.

After Eddie Shuba, I saw the Button's brother. I barely had time to catch the post office before it closed. I decided to let it and the stationery store go till tomorrow morning. I looped and skipped as much rush-hour traffic as I could, buying an evening *Globe* from a kid at an intersection just as it hit the street a little after 5 P.M. At the next three traffic lights, I leafed through it. My identification as the corpse was dumped to page six by two flareups in the Middle East, a political corruption case, three fires, and a schoolbus accident. I pulled off into a Seven-Eleven store parking lot and called Lieutenant Murphy.

He picked up on the third ring.

"It's Mr. Lazarus," I said.

"Who?"

"You know, the Charcoal Kid?"

"Hold on," he said, bellowing something at someone on his end. I thought I heard a door close.

"Where have you been, Cuddy?"

"I've been busy," I said.

"What have you got?"

"Nothing definite."

"Let's hear about the maybes."

"I'd rather not."

"Now look, mister," he said, the telephone growing warmer from his voice, "I am out on a limb for you. I have an as yet unidentified—"

"Misidentified," I interjected.

He growled but drove on. "*Un*identified body in the morgue and I have to either confirm or deny the *Globe* article."

"Tell them that no positive identification is possible until my prints come in from Washington."

"The hands were too burned. I got Daley calling dentists. You know how many—"

"I haven't been to the dentist since mine died two years ago."

"That's all right. Boring him is better than chewing his ass for the reporter slip. Now, what have you found out?"

"Al Sachs was killed by a guy he'd met in the service. Al had blown the guy's cover somehow."

"How? What's the guy's name?"

"I'm not sure of that yet."

"You're not sure of the name?"

"No, of how Al found out."

"What difference does that make? Do you know who the killer is?"

"No, not as such."

Another growl. "What do you mean, 'not as such'?"

"Look, Lieutenant, I'm at a pay phone, and there are three teenage thugs looking to—"

"Fuck the thugs. What's his name?"

"Sorry, Lieutenant, I can't hold—" I jiggled the cradle five times, then held it down. I'd have to be straighter than that with him next time.

I got back into the rental and drove it to Nancy's house.

"You know," she said, lazily swirling the wine in her glass, "it's kind of nice coming home to a cooked dinner."

I had stopped at a small grocery and bought four split chicken breasts and some Shake 'n Bake. I tossed it together, and it was ready just fifteen minutes after she'd come in the door.

"In my opinion, it's the Green Giant Niblets that set the whole tone of the meal."

She laughed. We were both half kneeling, half squatting around the low table in her living room, throw pillows under our rumps.

I sipped some of my wine. She pushed some corn around on her plate.

"Are you getting close?" Nancy said, eyes down and casual.

"Close to what?"

"Close to whoever or whatever you're after?"

"Yes."

"Can you tell me about it?"

"Not ever."

She nodded. She finished her meal in a subdued, but not sulky, manner. She cleared the dishes while I finished my glass of wine.

Nancy came back into the room. "How about a walk on the beach?" she said peppily.

"The beach?"

"Yeah, Carson's Beach."

"Nancy, it must be zero with the wind chill."

"So, you can use some of my sweaters."

"They wouldn't fit."

"I'll ask Drew Lynch for some of his then."

"I don't want him to know I'm here," I said lamely.

Nancy came over and put her hands on my shoulders gently, as though lecturing a slow learner.

"John, you won't have to show Drew any identification for me to borrow a sweater from him. Besides, he certainly knows you're up here by the sound of your footfalls."

I thought back to Jacquie and Ricker above me in old Curl's house. I shuddered.

"Chill?" she said.

"No," I replied.

"Well, then, let's go."

"What about the numerous ruffians who no doubt frequent the area?"

She laughed. "Don't worry, it's too cold for them."

I yielded.

Drew's sweater was a thick-ribbed, oily burgundy turtleneck that closed out the cold. The stars were bright over the patch of inky black harbor we could see as we strolled along the beach. A couple of joggers in ski masks thumped by us, looking like terrorists and flicking their mittens at us in salute. Nancy swung her arms conservatively at her side. I kept my hands in my pants pockets, thanking whoever had given Drew the sweater for Christmas.

"It's tomorrow, isn't it?" she said. She spoke quietly, but the air was so cold and the night so still that I was sure the joggers, at least a quarter mile behind us by now, could have heard her. We kept walking.

"What's tomorrow?"

"Whatever it is that you're going to do."

I exhaled heavily. My breath clouds never got started because of the wind coming off the harbor.

"Probably," I said. "If all goes well."

She dug her hands into her pockets and watched her feet. "Would it do any good for me to argue that the court system is the better way to resolve disputes like this one?"

She made me smile in spite of myself. "No, it wouldn't."

"John Francis Cuddy," she said wearily, "you are too old, too recently drugged, and probably too damned decent to deal with these people."

"You left out too loyal, too arrogant, and too stubborn to quit now."

She stopped and punched me in the arm, harder than I was ready for.

"Don't!" she cried out, then dropped her voice. "Don't you dare make fun of yourself."

"O.K.," I said, feeling the little glow inside again. "I won't."

She shook away the tears beginning to form in her

eyes. She went up on tiptoes and threw her arms around my neck, drawing her face up into the side of my throat.

"Please come back," she said. No sobbing, just an even, reasonable request.

I stroked her hair and began to realize just how much I wanted to.

We walked back to her house, Nancy's left arm slid into the crook of my right. We climbed the stairs. We both knew I'd taken a step out there on the beach. She had the good sense to realize that a step wasn't a leap.

"Couch?" she said lightly.

I nodded.

"I usually set the alarm for seven," she said in the same tone.

"That'll be just fine."

She walked into her bedroom. "Why don't you take the bathroom first," she said, closing the door behind her.

Twenty-three

My agenda for the morning was short, and the first two items took no time at all. I drove to Newton, a city about eight miles west of Boston. I obtained a large General Delivery mailbox for a month at the Newton Post Office under the name of "J. T. Davis" and bought ten dollars' worth of stamps. Then I stopped at a stationery store and bought five large book-mailing envelopes with the legend "Books—Fourth Class Mail" already printed on them. I put these in the trunk of the rent-a-car, just above the blanketed shotgun I had bought at the shop of the Button's brother. I got into the car and drove to Eddie Shuba's junkyard.

I drove by slowly and counted off the five side streets Eddie and I had agreed upon yesterday. I turned right and spotted the old Pontiac slumped into a parking space next to a weather-beaten house and across from a nonoperational auto body shop. I pulled in ahead of the Pontiac and walked back to it.

I got in and found the keys on a wire just under the glove box. I pulled off the ignition key and turned the engine over. The car started on the third try. I let it warm up while I went back to the rental and transferred my cargo from it to the Pontiac's cavernous trunk. I put the Pontiac in gear and drove it into the driveway of the auto body shop and behind the building itself. The old car still had effortless power steering and crisp, albeit squeaky, braking.

I turned off the engine and sat in the car for a few moments with the front windows rolled down. No noise, no voices. I got out and walked to the back of the car, my footsteps crunching the unshoveled snow. I reopened the trunk, taking out the tools Eddie had left there for me, and returned to the front of the car. I opened the hood of the Pontiac and went to work.

It took less than an hour.

Oh, I had to push a few wires and hoses out of the way. Also, I spent fifteen awkward minutes cutting a hole through the engine side of the glove box and niggling into place a doubled-over shirt to take the powder burns. Three of the Button's braces were perfect, though, and the wire to the dead-man's switch was easy to attach. I ran the wire down through the dash and mounted the switch itself on the floor next to the headlights' dimmer switch. I armed the switch with the shotgun empty and did a few trial runs. Then I tossed my remainders into the trunk and folded one of the mailers into the glove compartment. I reset the system and took the Pontiac out for a bouncy test drive of about two miles. I came back in behind the auto body shop and tried it again. I heard the satisfying click from under the hood. I reset the switch and loaded the shotgun. Then I paused a few minutes to think things through one more time. The only flaws I could see were those of timing that I had already anticipated and those of chance that I could not predict.

I started the Pontiac and headed toward Weston Hills. I stopped at a pay phone in Newton and dialed Murphy's number.

"Lieutenant Murphy's line, Detective Cross speaking."

I tried to disguise my voice. "Lieutenant Murphy, please."

"I'm sorry but he's not available. Can I take a message?"

"No," I said, "I can call him back." I paused. "Just tell him Mr. Lazarus tried to reach him."

"All right."

I hung up. I walked several stores down and bought a paper, a tuna sub, and two root beers. I walked back to the Pontiac and killed nearly three hours before I drove on.

I got to Weston Hills about 3:30 P.M. I found a parking space across the street and three doors down from the real estate agency. It struck me that the Pontiac was the oldest, cruddiest car on the street but I passed that worry and found another pay phone just across from "Belker's" office.

I dialed the number and got the Mount Holyoke receptionist again.

"Weston Hills Realty, may I help you?"

"Mr. Belker, please."

"May I say who is calling?"

I had given the answer to that question a lot of malice aforethought. It was luck that he was in, but as much as I wanted to twist the knife in him, I couldn't let "Belker" and Al's death, and therefore me, appear connected in any traceable way.

"This is the Board of Registration of Real Estate

Brokers and Salesmen. A former customer of your agency has, ah, expressed some concerns to us, and I wanted to speak with Mr. Belker about them before the situation got out of hand."

"Yes, certainly. Hold on, please."

Nicely done, Cuddy. Too flustered to remember to ask about your name again. There was an outside possibility that she would monitor the rest of the conversation or that he would tape it, but that was a risk I would have to run.

A click and then, "Hello, this is Clay Belker." Another perfectly modulated voice.

"Hi, this is Al Sachs calling."

Silence from his end.

"Or would you prefer Sergeant Ricker?" I continued.

"Who is this please?" he said gamely.

"Or maybe a heroin pusher named Bouvier?"

"I'm sorry to disappoint—"

"Listen, I really think we should talk."

"I don't know—"

"Today."

"I'm afraid I'm pretty well jammed for—"

"Two hours. In front of your house. I'll be in a yellow Ford station wagon."

"I'm afraid that's—"

"Perfect for you? Excellent. See you then." I hung up and walked over to an army/navy surplus store, keeping my back to his building and watching his door in the store's reflecting plate glass window.

The next five minutes must have been bad ones for him. A few notches up from an annoying consumer complaint lodged with the Real Estate Board. I was dead sure he had a stash of contingent money and identification somewhere. Maybe at home, or in a safety deposit box, or with an attorney. Perhaps some fail-safe combination of all three. My gas-guzzling dinosaur was the ace in the hole there: no matter where he ran, its engine was big enough to catch his car and its body heavy enough to force him off the road.

I had just moved my window watching from the surplus store to a video shop when my man slipped casually out the front door, an attaché case swinging lightly at his side. He smiled and waved to a couple of people as he made his way up the sidewalk. As he crossed the street to my side, I checked my watch and strolled over to the Pontiac. When he got a block ahead, I started up and slid into the stop-and-go traffic, slowly trailing him.

There have been lectures given and volumes written about methods of following subjects. Two-operative, three-operative, street-zigzag, vehicle-parallel, etc. If you're alone, you can follow almost anyone for a short time without help. However, you can follow almost no one, even a complete boob, for a long time without a lot of good, and not a speck of bad, luck. I wanted my man to be unaware of me only until he had cleaned out his hidey-hole. After that, I wouldn't need to follow him anymore.

He weaved leisurely through the sidewalk throngs, still nodding and waving like a candidate on the stump. The flow of traffic cooperated nicely; only once did I nearly pull even with him.

About two and a half blocks down, he turned into a bank's main doorway. I checked around for cops, then eased over into a yellow loading zone. I waited. And worried.

Probability said he was going into the bank to take a huge chunk of cash from a safety deposit box. Possibility said I had caught him just before a scheduled real estate closing at the lender's, and he was merely intending to collect his six percent check. Nightmare said he was cleaning out his cache but would smilingly prevail on the security guard to let him out a back entrance.

I sweated for about seven minutes. Then he emerged from the bank. A bit quick for a closing to have concluded, and the attaché case seemed to swing a good deal less lightly at his side.

I put the Pontiac in gear. I pulled into the bank driveway just as he was drawing even with the sidewalk.

"Mr. Belker," I called in an artificial, Southwestern twang. "Yo, Mr. Belker."

He turned, looked at me impatiently and turned back to continue on his way.

I called a bit louder. "Yo, I do have that name right, don't I? It is *Clay* Belker, from Vietnam, isn't it?"

He froze and looked around. He didn't think anybody had heard me either time, but he was afraid my next decibel level might call attention to us.

I expect he decided then and there he'd be having to kill me.

He turned toward me again, smiling and giving his little wave. He walked up to the driver's side window, unbuttoning his coat and glancing into the empty back seat. He leaned down a little. "I'm sorry," he said pleasantly, "but I'm afraid you have the better of me."

I smiled back. I said, softly but in my normal voice, "Get in the car, Sergeant Crowley."

"I don't know—"

"If I intended to turn you over to the authorities, I wouldn't have forewarned you. I'm talking private deal here. Now get in the car."

"But I have to get some papers back to my—"

"I have a feeling those papers will figure prominently in our negotiations. Now get in."

The wheels must have been spinning furiously in his crew-cut brain. There were two alternatives.

One, I was working for the authorities, who had staked me out to lure him in. If so, they were probably within sight and/or sound and could thwart any attempt by him to run. If I were with the authorities, he couldn't risk reaching into his unbuttoned coat and acing me, since I was probably being filmed, recorded, or at least watched.

The other alternative was that I wasn't working for the authorities. In that case, there was at least a chance I was alone. If so, he could play along with the blackmail until he could kill me. The Clay Belker cover might be potentially too dangerous to resume, but he'd be free and away with the contents of his briefcase.

"Well," he said, "at least you can give me a lift to my office while you explain yourself." Alternative Two.

"Come around. Front seat," I said, depressing the switch with my left foot.

"All right." He walked around to the passenger side and got in, case placed on the floor between his legs. "My office is . . ."

I shifted to reverse. I backed out and headed down

Main Street in the eventual direction of Eddie's junkyard.

"My office is back the other way," said my passenger evenly.

"We're taking the scenic route," I said and glanced at him. He sat slightly sidesaddle, Walther PPK in his right hand. He held it low, out of my reach, and angled up at my chest.

"Fine weapon, the Walther," I observed.

"Take the next right," he said.

"Of course, without a silencer, kind of noisy." The next right slid by.

He advanced the weapon an inch or so toward me. "I would take the next available right if I were you."

I smiled. "Take a look at my left foot."

He looked down and tensed. "You're wired. I knew that. . . ."

"It's a wire, all right, but not to a tape machine. My foot's depressing an armed switch. The switch is connected to enough explosives in the front of the car to send both of us back to Saigon."

He didn't offer any reply.

"Therefore," I continued, "if you shoot me or don't cooperate, I let up on the dead-man's switch, and we both blow."

"That's crazy," he said, still evenly. "Either way you lose."

I tried to sound resigned. "I'm a down-and-out private investigator, boy-o. I lost my wife to cancer and my best army buddy to you. Al Sachs has a widow and infant son that I sure as hell can't provide for. I don't see that anybody is so much worse off if I lift my foot except you."

"You're bluffing," he said, still with no emotion in

his voice. He must have been a great real estate bargainer. "Nobody is that suicidal."

I shrugged and ignored the next available right.

"Nobody," he repeated.

We drove on for a bit. Neither of us said anything.

"Where are we going," he finally said, not quite so evenly as before.

I tried not to sound relieved. "To someplace quiet where we can talk about Al's family. And their future."

We traveled in silence after that.

I drove past Eddie Shuba's gate on the right and counted five blocks before turning in. It was 4:35 and already dark.

"I don't like this," said my boy.

"I don't much care about that," I replied.

My rental was still across the street. From a windshield appraisal, it didn't look like anybody had stripped it. I turned left into and behind the auto body shop. My passenger's head whipped nervously left and right.

He said, "I hear a sound or see anybody, and you're dead."

"Relax," I said. "There's just the two of us." I turned off the engine. It was perfectly, almost serenely, quiet in the derelict neighborhood. "Besides, if I'm dead, so are you."

I watched him steadily for a minute or two. The car was still warm from the heater, but he was perspiring a little more than the temperature alone would have warranted. He was pale, like a grunt from the bush during the rainy season in Vietnam.

His gun hand was steady, though. Quite steady.

"You wanted to talk," he said. "So talk."

I shifted carefully to face him a little more directly. He stared at my left stationary foot until I stopped moving.

"I figure that by now you're convinced I'm not working with the cops, the army, or anybody."

"I don't know what you're talking about," he said.

"O.K.," I said, "so you're not convinced. Let me do the talking, then, till you get bored. Then feel free to jump in."

He said nothing, so I continued.

"My guess is that you were up to your eyes in something, probably black market. Covering for shortage investigations, helping launder the skim, whatever. Anyway, you sensed that somebody was on to the operation, but was still a few turns or steps away from you. I figure it was like a chess game, and you could see checkmate in maybe a few moves."

"I don't know—"

"So," I talked over him, "you had to set up a safety valve for yourself. An out. But a big problem. You're in Saigon, not the U. S. of A. If you want to get back to The World, you've got to get out of the country and then back into this one. Shipping out of 'Nam other than with Uncle Sam's blessings is touchy and expensive. Slipping out with Uncle Sam focusing especially on you is touchier and *very* expensive. So you set up a trap door as your out."

I paused. His jaw worked a few times, but no sound.

"You arrange a meeting between yourself and one Bouvier, a ballsy, reasonably connected holdover from the colonial heydays. But there's a double cross, and a bit of explosive takes somebody's head off. Your double cross, my friend, but, more's the pity, not your head. You and Bouvier are roughly the same size and coloring, and with everybody thinking he killed you, attention is shifting from the crooked noncom to the dastardly drug dealer. Of course, you need some help there, but it doesn't have to be much. Just one man really. The MP who takes the prints off the corpse. No head means no face or dental charts for identification. So you draw Belker into it ahead of time, and after he roll-prints the corpse, he switches fingerprint cards for you. No big problem. The prints on the switched card match the ones of yours on file, and you just lay low for a couple of weeks, then fake enough ID to come out as, what, a British journalist?"

He stared hard at me. "Canadian," he said.

"Ah, of course, no accent for you to fake. Anyway, you get back to the States, but you realize then, or maybe you realized beforehand, that you'd be short one important item without which you'd be doomed to menial, unpleasant jobs and frequent relocation."

He swallowed hard.

"You also had a loose end dangling. A potentially dangerous one. The absence of the item and the potential of the loose end would make it tough to enjoy your profits much."

I gave him my best smile. "The item was a social security card. The loose end was Belker. My guess is that you decided to kill both birds with one stone."

My passenger laughed. It startled me. The noise was like a little creature chirping, then stopping to listen. "You know," he said, almost nostalgically, "it was a stone I used. I mean, I could have bought a social security card, you know, but you never really know whose card you're buying. Then some computer or compulsive, low-level auditor spots some discrepancy and where are you? Nowhere, except the slammer or back on the run. No, Belker was perfect. I knew about him, you see. I checked his 201 file very carefully. Neither of us had any family. To know him was to dislike him, so no friends to worry about coming to look him, or me, up. Just in case, though, I went through everybody's 201 file who had anything to do with him. That left me with quite a choice, geographically. I decided I liked Boston the best." He frowned. "How did I miss you?"

"I wasn't in Saigon then. I arrived a few months later."

He smiled. "Well, even so, you would have been no danger. I changed my appearance, and good God, there must be dozens of Clay Belkers in this country anyway. If somebody did stumble on the name, I just wasn't *that* Clay Belker."

"To avoid even that, why didn't you just change your name? From Clay Belker to something else, I mean?"

"I looked into it, but it required a birth certificate. I was older than Belker and, well, applying for a driver's license or broker's license is one thing, going before a judge is another. Besides, like I said, there didn't seem to be much risk."

My passenger was doing an excellent job of lulling me. He came across as a reasonable, thoughtful man. A sweetheart of a guy who had tortured and mutilated a good friend.

"You used a stone?"

He blinked.

"You used a stone, you said."

"Oh, yes. To kill Belker. I arranged for him to meet me in San Francisco when he got rotated back to the States. I told him that I wanted to wait till he was discharged, so that he could take off without leaving any tracks that would be followed. He was discharged on a Thursday. He had all his gear in a duffel bag and met me in Golden Gate Park. We drove out to a place called Muir Woods. Heard of it?"

"No."

"It's a stand, actually I guess nearly a whole valley, of redwoods only about an hour's drive from San Francisco. Someone, not Muir, saved the valley from being developed. Nobody ever does anything there except maintain the trails. We hiked about half a mile off one. I hit him with a stone. A few times. Then I used a folding entrenching tool to bury him. The ground was pretty soft. It didn't take long."

"Then?"

"I came to Boston, sent the army a change of address so I could do my income taxes correctly as Clay Belker, and lived happily, conservatively, ever since."

"Until last week."

His face clouded. "Yes," he said. "The fool. How can one contemplate that a moron from the army would go through telephone books looking for . . . Oh, it's simply too ridiculous."

"He tried to call you, thought it was the wrong guy, but—"

"Oh, I handled it badly. My receptionist was out getting coffee. I took the call, and I realized who it was but feigned ignorance. He told me later that he recognized my voice. That was arrogant of him. I think instead that he just could not believe that he was wrong and came to the office to see me. Apparently he spotted me getting into my car and followed me to my home. He knocked on my door." He gestured with the gun. "Can you imagine that? He actually knocked at my door and came in. I told him I would have to gather the money. We arranged the drop-off for the next day. A warehouse area"—he swung his head around slowly—"not unlike this one. He was very nervous. And not too smart, after all." He sneered at me.

"How did you take him?" I asked.

"I rigged a bundle with a gas trigger. Not unlike the substance Ricker said he used on you. In any case, the baboon opened the bundle at the drop-off. He keeled over, and I waited till he revived and then interrogated him."

"Were you acquainted with Jacquie's father, too?"

"Jacquie?"

"Ricker's wife."

"No. Outside of 'Nam I barely knew him. Ricker, I mean. Or Mayhew. They were just people in the network. Ricker told me on the telephone that you recognized him from a photo . . . oh, of course. That's how you recognized me, too. From the photo in the file."

"No," I said, shaking my head. "I recognized you from the photo in Al's package."

"Package?" He looked pained. "What package?"

"After Al spotted you, he sent me a package. Photos of you. From Weston Hills. With a little chronology of how he found you by flipping through the telephone book."

"You're lying," he said evenly. "You're definitely lying. He never had time for that."

"Sure he did. He wrapped it up for me. Fourth-class mail. It didn't arrive until after I left for his funeral. In Pittsburgh."

"You're lying. He never mentioned anything about a camera or a package to me." Again the sneer. "And believe me, he would have, he told me everything else. After what I did to him, he begged me to let him tell me."

I took a chance. "If you were so good at interrogation, how come he never mentioned me?"

Crowley caught himself and lied. "He did."

I shook my head. "No, the first time you heard about me was when you decoyed the hotel clerk and saw the message in Al's box. Just after you tossed his room."

"How did you—"

"No," I interrupted, "Al never mentioned me to you. I was his insurance policy. I was the one who would see to it you paid the debt if he couldn't make you."

Crowley ground his teeth a bit. "Where is the package?"

"No," I said. "First we open your bundle. Then we open mine. Just like at Christmas."

"Where's the goddamned package?"

"You first," I said.

Crowley lowered his weapon till it was pointing at my crotch. "Where's the package?"

"I'm afraid you're going to have to play it my way. If you shoot me, I lift my foot and the sanitation men draw some overtime. If you open your package first, at least you're still in the game."

Crowley smiled suddenly, in a superior manner. "You said that his package arrived after you left for Pittsburgh?"

I sighed. "That's right. At my post office box. It and three bills are the only other paperwork I've got left after my apartment was leveled."

Crowley dropped the smile and looked a little queasy.

"By the way," I said, "did you arrange that?"

"What?" he said, lost in thought.

"I said, did you plant the bomb at my place?"

"No, no. That would have been stupid, an unnecessary risk. I had no reason to believe Sachs had told you anything. He never mentioned you. I found your message at his hotel, and then I held my breath for about three days, poised to run. I . . . well . . . I assumed that Ricker had taken care of you. When I then read in the paper about your apartment building and the corpse that was supposed to be you, it all seemed so . . ."

"Fortunate."

"Yes." He snapped back to the present. "Now where is—"

"Short memory, my friend. You first."

He gritted his teeth and worked his jaw and started twice to talk. His left hand, shaking badly, levered the attaché case up and between us in the suicide seat, latches and handle toward me.

"Go ahead," he said. "Open it."

I thought back to Al's alleged mistake at the drop-off. "You open it."

Crowley smiled. "You are either much more clever or far more stupid than I thought." He seemed to relax. "My judgment is for clever. If you had begun to open it, then either you were too stupid to recall how your friend failed, or could ignore it because you knew that switch under your foot was a dummy, attached to no bomb." He reached forward and turned the case over, back to facing him. He was no longer the nervous killer but again the cool, methodical businessman. He fingered two catches, and the lid popped up, the case relieved of the pressure of being stuffed to bursting.

"If you had done that," he said, wiggling his finger at the latches, "you'd be dead now."

I winked at him and pointed to my left foot. "So would you."

He winked back.

I tipped the case's lid back against the hinges and toward me. It was full of rubber-banded stacks of old bills, tens and twenties showing.

"Rough estimate?" I asked.

"Sixty-five thousand." Then, more wistfully, "All I've got in the world."

I grinned. "More likely one-third maybe of all the old, passable cash you've got in the world."

He laughed, a real laugh. "You're good, Cuddy. Maybe good enough."

"Bet on it."

"Oh, I am, I am." He sank back into the door behind him more, easing what must have been a stiff back. "I'm betting that you're even clever enough to realize I have no reason to kill you. Even if you turn to the police. You see, after tonight, Clay Belker just drops off the earth, through another trap door. I take off, so I don't care who you go to with your information. You, and the widow and the kid, get sixty-five thousand dollars. I get a twenty-four-hour headstart.

I'm not a vindictive man, really. Belker, the real Belker, and your friend, were genuine threats to me. You're no threat, not after this time tomorrow. Gentleman's agreement." He smiled ruefully. "Sorry, poor taste, in view of Sachs', ah, derivation. I meant agreement as in officers and gentlemen."

"Let's say I'm clever enough to get out of here alive, with the money. Why should I wait for twenty-four hours?"

"Because—and I really believe this, after talking with you—you intend that money for Sachs' widow and kid. Based on what Sachs told me about his motives, they really need it. No, if you blew the whistle on me, it would be tough for you to wash that money and get it to them. Tough enough for you that I think you'll keep your end of the deal."

"And if you're wrong?"

Crowley shrugged. "If I'm wrong, I'll find out about it. And the first thing I do, perhaps the last thing too, but the first thing I do is get to Pittsburgh and kill Martha and the boy."

He threw me with that one, and my face must have shown it.

He laughed his good laugh again. "Oh, come on now. You thought of everything else. Don't feel badly. Your revenge has to be financial, that's all. Just strictly financial." He dropped his voice to a low, authoritative tone. "Let that be enough."

"It's a deal," I said. "The package is in the glove compartment."

His eyes narrowed. "What package?"

"Al's package. The one he sent me."

"What the fuck are you talking about? I searched

his room and his car. Sachs had no camera. He couldn't have sent you any package."

"Okay, he didn't. Step out of the car and dive off to the right. I'll drive the hell out of here and you'll have your twenty-four hours."

Crowley stared at the glove compartment.

"He couldn't have. He wasn't that smart."

I thought of the broken pinkie and *13 Rue Madeleine.* "Oh, he was that smart. He was scared shitless of you, and I can see why. But he was that smart. Now take the package and go, or don't and go. Either way."

"Open it," he said in the authoritative voice.

"Open what?" I said.

"The glove compartment! The goddamned glove compartment! Open it!"

I shrugged and leaned over. He put the barrel of the Walther in my right ear. He smelled acrid, worried. He was breathing shallowly. He started to say, "If anything, if anything at all—"

I popped open the box, Crowley tensing as the lid bounced a few times. He relaxed, and I straightened back up.

"When I felt the barrel of that Walther, I nearly got a cramp in my left foot."

His breathing edged toward normal. He glanced into the box.

"The envelope," I said.

He frowned at me, then peered down into the box and reached with his left hand.

I relaxed my left foot and sensed the switch come up. The car quaked as Crowley caught the full blast of the 12-gauge squarely in the face. His Walther went off, the slug whacking me in the fleshy part of my right upper arm, wrecking some tricep.

I yelled once in pain. My arm burned like hell, but there was no more noise or sensation except for the urinating sound of Crowley's blood as it drummed onto the vinyl upholstery. I looked over at him and tried not to think of how Marco must have felt as he watched the Coopers' house burn.

Twenty-four

I GOT OUT OF THE CAR AND LISTENED. NO VOICES, NO sirens, nothing. The Walther bullet had torn up some of the driver's seat behind me. I ignored the upholstery and packed some snow up under my sleeve as best I could to retard the bleeding. I reached back into the car and pulled Crowley's case toward me. With some effort, I latched it back down. Then I sprang the hood of the Pontiac and, with a lot more effort from one and a half arms, tried to free the backward-facing shotgun from its braces in the engine compartment. I finally yanked it clear, parallel to the course the pellets had taken as they traveled through the barrel, past the hole and cloth in the engine side of the glove compartment, and into Crowley's face and chest.

I set the shotgun down and opened the passenger's door. With my left hand, I grasped Crowley's coat at the neck and dragged him out of the car onto the snow. I examined his face and mouth for as long as I needed to. The features were a pulpy mess, the teeth too shattered for a dental chart comparison. I stripped him of all other ID, taking the cash from his wallet and using a pen-knife on his clothes labels. When I was finished, I left him on the ground.

I closed down the hood of the Pontiac and carried the shotgun to the back of the car. I opened the trunk and fished out the blanket for the shotgun. Then I tossed Crowley's handgun and wallet in the trunk.

For the tenth time I thought of tossing Crowley's body into the trunk, too. After all, Eddie was going to crush the car; the corpse could be crushed just as easily. The problem was that I had already involved Eddie more deeply than I cared to, and I was not about to make him that active an accessory.

I walked back to the driver's door and retrieved the attaché case. I brought it back and opened it at the trunk. I divided the cash stacks into four piles of roughly equal weight. I then put the piles inside the book mailers and sealed them. They were addressed to J. T. Davis' box at the Newton Post Office.

I closed down the trunk of the Pontiac and walked out from behind the building, cradling the wrapped shotgun in my bad arm and carrying the mailers under my good arm. I stood in the shadow of the side of the building and listened. It was only 5 P.M., but the street was cathedral quiet. I carried my bundles down to the rental car. I opened the front door and tossed the mailers in on the floor of the passenger's side. I unwrapped and laid the shotgun gently on top, spreading the blanket over everything. I locked the door and returned up the driveway and around to the Pontiac. My arm was beginning to throb. I'd been wounded more seriously in the past, and I was pretty sure I wasn't losing enough blood to cause shock.

I started the Pontiac and moved it back and forth a few times to ball up whatever tire tracks might be in the snow. Then I drove down the driveway and over to Eddie Shuba's place. Very light traffic.

I pulled into his driveway and opened the gate lock with the key he had given me. I drove the Pontiac around behind some compressed wrecks and in front of some likely candidates. As I got out, I patted the steering wheel twice. I'm not sure I believe in animism, but the car had come through like an old, loyal farm dog. Fearing powder burns from the Walther and blood stains from Crowley, I stripped off Arnie's old jacket and tossed it into the trunk. As I trudged back toward Eddie's gate, I looked behind me. No way anybody would spot the car from the street. I stopped at Eddie's shack and slipped the keys to the car and the gate through the slit in the lockbox on the shack wall. I edged through the gate, squeezing home the clasp of the lock from the outside.

I looked around as casually as I could manage. I saw no one. I started hiking the half mile or so back to the auto shop and the rental. I stumbled two or three times, but I made it.

I unlocked and turned the key in the rental. It coughed and grumbled twice, but it started on the third try. I mouthed a silent thank you and drove off slowly, stopping at four different mailboxes over a seven-mile, patternless stretch, dropping one book mailer in each. Then I drove back to the auto body street.

I got out of the car, carrying the shotgun. I walked behind the auto shop, ejected the first, spent shell, and fired twice more, one into the snow near Crowley's body, a second up at the concrete and wood wall. Then I braced myself, tore up the area of my wound a bit and dropped down, rolling around in the snow.

I staggered, part for show and part for real, back to the rental. I drove, as erratically as possible, into the center of the town where I carefully selected a parked municipal vehicle, plowing into same at about twenty miles per hour. At impact, I struck my forehead on the steering wheel a bit more forcefully than the laws of physics required and slumped sideways into the suicide seat. I heard some yelling and footsteps. I tried to nap while I awaited the arrival of the police and ambulance.

I gave the impression of fading in and out for as many hours as I thought I could get away with it. It was probably 4 A.M. when I finally decided to awaken and a bleary-eyed cop named Wasser was called by the nurse to my side.

While I had no mirror, I was willing to bet I looked better than Wasser. He wore a patched and taped Baxter State parka whose red-plaid lining clashed with the purple dot matrix plaid of his double knit sports jacket. He had battled a shaver at some point in the last thirty-six hours, but the skirmish hadn't reached the right side of his chin. He carried the remains of a vile-smelling sub sandwich in off-white butcher paper in his left hand and a pad and pencil in his right. He was overweight, probably thirty-two though he looked nearer fifty. I was willing to bet this was his first shooting. He pulled out a filthy card that looked as though it had figured prominently in the making of his sandwich. He began to read from the card.

"You have the right to remain silent. Anything—"

"Cut the rights recital, will you. Is he dead?"

Wasser blinked at me. This was not a member of the Boston Police Homicide Squad. This was a member of a small-town, selectman's nephew, incompetent detective squad. I had picked the site carefully.

"Is who . . ." he started to say, then shook himself and ran through the rights as though there were no spaces between the words.

I acknowledged I understood them and asked if there was anything he'd like me to sign.

He turned the card over and back a few times.

"Not on the card," I said, "there's a separate form."

He blinked some more.

"If I were you," I said, "I'd call for reinforcements."

He stopped blinking and took a bite of his sandwich. Then he hurried out of the room, and I dozed off for real.

"Are you awake?" said a voice with some juice behind it.

I looked up into the eyes of a hard-chiseled face. Short black hair, not much gray. Wasser stood behind him, chewing.

"My name is Lieutenant Parras." He spelled it for me. "I understand Detective Wasser read you your rights and while you understand them, you want to speak to us anyway. Is that correct?"

"Yes."

Parras said, "We didn't find any identification on you. What's your name?"

"John Francis Cuddy."

"Address?"

"It's not there anymore."

His eyebrows knitted. "What?" he said.

"It's gone, my apartment house. Somebody blew it up."

Parras smiled condescendingly. "Is that how you got hurt, Mr. Cuddy?"

I looked down at my right arm. The bandages showed, bulged even under the loose-fitting hospital johnny.

"I wouldn't expect Deli-Master over there to recognize it, but surely the doctor who treated me told you that I'd been shot."

Wasser, incredibly, was still chewing on something.

"Mr. Cuddy—" Parras started.

"Your questions also mean you haven't been down behind the auto shop yet either, have you?"

Parras' eyebrows knitted a few more stitches.

"What auto shop?"

I sighed. "Where am I?" I asked.

"St. Jude's. The hospital, I mean."

"You have a street named Breston in this town?"

"Yeah, about . . . Why?"

"On Breston Street, in a warehouse district, there's a deserted auto shop. Fender and body work."

"Maybe. Why?"

"Oh, for Christ's sake." I said. "I'm a private investigator. I turned an old Pontiac that was following me and trailed it there. I got suckered into leaving my car and walked behind the place. I got ambushed. I got one of them, right at the car as he was getting out of it. The other guy drove off."

"What the—"

"I got back to my car and made it to some kind of shopping area when I blacked out."

"Do you mean that you . . . That there's a body . . ."

I put my good hand up to my face and did a slow burn which shut him up. "Lieutenant Parras, I'm not sure who or what is where, but I've got a pretty good idea you ought to start at that auto shop." I shifted and grimaced. "I'm sure as hell not going anywhere for a while."

"You, you mean—" Parras broke off. Not as much juice as I thought. "Wasser, better call the Chief."

Wasser checked his watch. "It's four-forty-five A.M., Lieutenant. Maybe you better call him."

I closed my eyes and smiled on the inside. Perhaps I had underestimated Wasser.

Chief Kyle was stocky and bald, and bore a striking resemblance to Edward Asner, the actor. He arrived just before 6 A.M. I elaborated for him the story I had summarized for Parras, who stood where Wasser had, Wasser having disappeared. Kyle did not much like my story and said so.

I shrugged, then clenched my teeth from the resultant pain in my arm. "Sorry, Chief, it's the only story I've got."

Kyle looked like he wanted to spit but was barely civilized enough to refrain. His next remark was cut short by a knock at the door and the head of Wasser around it.

"Chief?" said Wasser.

"Yeah?" said Kyle.

"He's here."

Kyle nodded, gave me a disgusted look, and said to Parras, "Stay here but don't talk to him." Kyle didn't wait for an acknowledgment. He just banged open the door and left.

I made faces at Parras for about ten minutes before the door banged open again. Kyle came back in with one Lieutenant Murphy, Boston P.D. Wasser shuffled in behind them, dragging a couple of hard plastic chairs but carrying no obvious forms of nourishment.

"Cuddy."

"Lieutenant."

Murphy and Kyle sat in Wasser's chairs. Parras and Wasser stayed standing. Murphy looked to Kyle, who motioned him to go ahead. Murphy said thank you and turned to me.

"Why don't you tell me what you say happened, Cuddy?"

I did.

Murphy leaned forward a bit, resting his chin on his upturned palm, elbow on his knee. The Thinker.

"You turn the tail and follow him to the auto shop. You didn't make the plates?"

"Like I said, no front plate and no light on the back."

"And you're not sure which model or year either?"

"It was a big, old Pontiac. It was dark, and I didn't want to get too close."

"How long were you in claims investigating?"

"About eight, nine years."

"And you couldn't ID a car better than big, old, Pontiac?"

"Big, old, *dark* Pontiac."

"Big, old *dark* Pontiac?"

"That's right."

"And after all the shit you've been through in this case, after somebody bombing your place and all, you followed somebody into an alley—"

"Well, more like a business—"

"I *been* there!" snapped Murphy. "It looks like an alley."

"Okay, an alley."

"So you followed somebody into an alley all by yourself?"

"With a shotgun."

"That you got through a guy whose license to sell firearms is hanging by a thread."

"I try to support marginal but vital—"

"Oh, cut the shit, man! You blew a guy up last night."

"I did."

"With a *shot*gun."

"That's right."

"Where'd his gun go?"

Nice shift of gears. I hoped Parras and Wasser were learning something.

"I don't know. He threw a shot at me from the passenger's side, then I pumped two shots at him as his partner hit me. I was close, maybe six feet. I let fly another shell, but I think the guy was already on his way. I got up and got only close enough to the guy I shot to know I'd finished him. I never saw a gun."

"How do you know he had one?" snapped Kyle.

"Because he shot at me, Chief."

"Ah, how do you know it wasn't his partner?" ventured a hesitant Parras.

"Two different reports."

"Whose reports?"

"Not written reports, Parras," I said. Though he had the same rank as Murphy, he didn't belong on the same level in my mind, so I accorded him no title. "Report as in sound of the shots. Two different weapons."

"What kinds?" said Kyle.

"Sorry, but I'm not that expert, Chief. I could just tell there was a difference in the noises."

I stole a look at Murphy. He was not pleased at the useless tangents being pressed by the locals, but politely played invited guest. He waited till it was quiet, then resumed.

"So you didn't take any gun from him?"

"No."

"Or anything else?"

I shook my head.

"Cuddy, the man had nothing on him. No keys, no wallet, not a label in his clothes."

"I can't explain that."

Parras broke in. "You see anybody in the area who could have stripped him?"

"Shut up, Parras," said Kyle.

Murphy didn't bother to let me answer.

"And you figure that the dead man is the guy who killed your friend?"

"That's what I figure. Matthew Crowley. The dead man is about the right size. I spotted him in the files I reviewed in Washington. You can call a Colonel Kivens at—"

Murphy closed his eyes and held up his hand. I stopped. "If you volunteer it, it'll check out."

"It should just be a matter of checking his fingerprints," I said.

"Chief?" said Murphy.

Kyle shook his head, then stood and slouched toward the door. Murphy got up, too, and Kyle followed him out. Parras muttered something to Wasser, who nodded. Parras followed the first string out of the room.

I looked over at Wasser.

"Deli-Master, huh," he said.

I drooped a little onto my pillow. "I'm sorry about that. I was a little pissed off."

"Forget it," said Wasser, digging around in his parka pocket. "You were in 'Nam, huh?"

"Yeah."

"Me, too."

I looked at Wasser. "Outfit?"

"First Cav."

The First Cavalry, Airmobile. The helicopter unit that was caricatured in the "Death from Above" sequence in *Apocalypse Now*. A unit that in real life caught a lot of tough fights.

"You?" he said, trying another pocket.

"MPs."

He squinted at me, as though trying to judge something. "Tet?"

"Yeah."

"Your friend, too? The guy the stiff killed?"

"Yes."

Wasser came up with a candy bar. He gestured with it toward me the way soldiers probably have since the Caesars. The gesture that said "you-want-half?"

"Thanks, no."

He shrugged, unwrapped it, took a bite, chewed thoughtfully. "You know," he said, "one thing I don't figure."

"What's that?"

"I seen a lotta dead guys."

"Yeah?"

"Yeah. Mostly in 'Nam, I admit. But a lot." He took another bite of his bar. "Never saw anybody hit as bad as that stiff leave so little blood."

I thought about the volume of blood Crowley must have left in the Pontiac. "It was pretty cold out there. Retards the bleeding."

"Probably." Just kept chewing. "Only thing is"—he swallowed—"that round the partner threw at you, shoulda been in your left arm, not your right."

I thought about it, felt a little flush around my ears. "I must have turned or something." I sounded hollow.

He finished the bar, sucked on his finger. "Maybe," he said, "but you weren't dressed warm enough for this time of year and I don't see the partner stripping the stiff, especially not cuttin' the labels and all. I also don't see the missing gun. And to top it, I sure don't see you being close enough to ID the stiff but not the car before you took his face off."

"So?" I said, not liking the turn our talk was taking.

He didn't reply immediately. He examined his fingers for any missed traces of chocolate, then focused on me. "So, I figure you set the guy up somehow."

"No way."

"The black guy, Murphy, he figures it that way, too."

I shook my head.

Wasser didn't continue.

"So, what are you going to do about it?" I asked.

"Me?" he said, then giggled. A faraway giggle. "The stiff, he aced your buddy, right?"

"Right."

Wasser yawned, dug around again but fruitlessly in his pockets. He moved to the door. "Fuck it," he said and walked out.

Twenty-five

I SLEPT, FOR REAL, FOR A FEW HOURS AFTER WASSER left. A nurse awakened me so that a doctor could speak with me. Fortunately, he happened to be both my "admitting" and "treating" physician. After a brief exchange of information about hospital room rates, the effect of shock and blood loss, and my absence of medical insurance coverage, we agreed I could be discharged that afternoon. He also told me there were several reporters interested in an interview with me. I declined, but said I would love to see a newspaper. He said he would ask the nurse and departed.

I spent the next thirty minutes or so wondering if I should call Nancy, since I had already decided that I would wait to confirm Eddie Shuba's compaction of the Pontiac. I resolved against using any nonpublic telephone for a while.

I was about halfway through the mental accounting of where the "J.T. Davis" money would go when the nurse popped in with an "early stocks" edition of the *Globe.* Crowley and I had made the small box on the right lower corner of page one. Few details, and those given were misleading. They got the hospital's name right, however.

A different nurse looked in on me an hour later and changed my dressing. She gave me a printed list of instructions for further "outpatient care," interlineating a few suggestions of her own. I promised her I would come back in two days so the doctor could check my progress. She helped me on with my clothes, the local constabulary not having impounded them. She said an orderly would be by somewhere between ten minutes and two hours later to wheel me down. I thanked her and waited patiently (no pun intended).

A Bahamian man, in white togs and about thirty, came by for me half an hour later. I settled in the chair, and we left the room. No police outside my door, no reporters. His name was Bragdon Bailey, and he was as sunny as a Caribbean morn.

"Somebody here to fetch you, my friend?" he asked.

"No. I thought I'd take a cab."

"My cousin, he have a taxi. I can call him, no problem."

We pulled up to the elevator. "Thanks. I'd appreciate it."

"Hey, my pleasure. The gentlemen of the press, they real interested in you. We can go out the back way. Avoid them."

"That would be a blessing."

The elevator doors opened. Bailey pushed me in and hit a button.

"The chap you shot?"

"Yes?"

"Must have been a bad fella!"

"He was."

"The police letting you go?"

"I haven't heard otherwise."

He chuckled. The elevator lurched to a stop and the doors opened. He wheeled me down a corridor into a small office.

"You don't have no insurance, you settle up here. I'll call my cousin."

I thanked him. I gave the cashier's clerk Nancy's address and telephone number. The clerk was a lot more courteous and understanding about the situation of a homeless, ID-less man than I expected, and I told her so.

She smiled and tapped the news account folded open on her desk. "You're a celebrity. They're always better treated."

I returned her smile.

"Where are you headed?" she said.

"To see my wife," I said softly.

"That's good. Kids?"

"No."

"Too bad. My Sam and me got three. What's your wife's name?"

"Na—" I stopped, blinked. "Beth," I said, a little thickly.

She reached over, patted my hand lightly. "Don't worry, you've been through a lot. She'll understand."

She always has, I thought, but just nodded.

Bailey stuck his head around the corner.

"Ready, Mr. Cuddy?"

The woman and I both said yes at the same time. We all three laughed.

Bailey wheeled me through a rear corridor, making small talk. We hit the back door and cold, bright sunlight.

We went down a ramp toward an orange and white taxi.

"Mornin', Mr. Bailey," beamed a heavy-set man who got out of the driver's side and came around to help me.

"Fine mornin', Mr. Delton," replied Bragdon. "This gentlemen is Mr. John Cuddy. He had a tough time of it last night, and I want you to be good to him." Delton held the door as I got up from the wheelchair and entered the back seat.

"My pleasure," said the driver. "Where are you headed, Mr. Cuddy?"

"East Fourth Street, South Boston."

Delton and Bailey stopped talking and exchanged questioning looks.

My mind was turning to mush. After the school busing controversy, South Boston was a part of the city where a black was not safe, daylight or dark, even in a car. "I'm sorry," I said, "it never crossed my mind . . ."

Bailey held up his hand. "No problem. My cousin can take you there. No worries."

Delton stayed silent, coming around to the driver's side. I started to protest, Bailey shushed me and closed the door. I rolled down the window jerkily with my left hand and stuck the hand through the opening.

"Good meeting you, Mr. Bailey," I said.

He took my hand, shook it sideways. "Good luck to you, Mr. Cuddy."

"If I still had a card, I'd give you one. Private investigator. Call me if you ever need—"

Delton had started the car. Bailey mock saluted, and we pulled off.

At the first traffic light, I rapped two knuckles on the Plexiglas shield between the driver and the passenger compartments.

Delton turned his head.

"Mr. Delton," I said loudly, "make that police headquarters instead. Berkeley and Stuart streets, downtown. There's someone I want to see first."

The light changed. Delton strained his neck to watch the road.

"Look, my friend, I stand by what my cousin promised."

"I appreciate that, honest. But I still have to stop there first."

Delton smiled, bobbed his head, and turned on the radio. The station was playing some Reggae music, and both of us were able to enjoy the ride.

Cross told me to wait. As she walked away, I thought about asking her whether she had heard back about her "probationary check-up," then decided that the way my mind was working, I would reserve the question. She beckoned to me from Murphy's door.

"He'll see you."

She moved back toward her desk. I entered Murphy's office, closed the door, and sat down.

Murphy was behind his desk, running the index finger of his right hand rapidly down the lines of some report while he sipped tentatively at probably too hot coffee in a cracked mug.

"Well?" he said, without looking up.

"What do you think Chief Kyle is going to do?"

Murphy stopped tracing but kept sipping. "Why ask me and not him?"

"Because I think you know what he's going to do and will tell me. I think he doesn't know what he's going to do and wouldn't tell me even if he did."

Murphy put his coffee down between the files on his blotter. "You take a hell of a lot for granted, Cuddy," he said, raising his head.

I made no reply.

"Do you remember what I told you when I gave you a ride from the Midtown?"

"I think so."

"I told you never to tell me another lie."

"You did."

Murphy slammed his hand flat smack on the desk, like a ref in a wrestling match. His coffee mug danced but didn't tip over. "Then what the fuck was that ration of shit about following the dead man into the alley and being ambushed?"

"Back there, in the hospital, you asked me to tell you what I *said* happened, not what did happen."

Murphy just stared at me, no emotion in his voice. "You realize that if you ever pull a wordgame like that in one of *my* cases, in this jurisdiction, your license is gone?"

"I know. I'm here to apologize and level with you."

Murphy just stared, thinking.

I continued. "If you want me to, I mean. If you really want to know what happened."

Murphy stared a little longer, then reached for the coffee cup. "The gun shop you used. The owner's got a brother."

"I know him."

"Was the Button involved in this?"

"Unknowingly."

"If all you did came out, would any of your shit stick to him?"

I thought a moment. "Maybe. I know what I told him. I don't know what he guessed or should have known."

Murphy took a hesitant, then longer drink of coffee. "The Button and I grew up together," he said. "He was older, he looked after me."

I just watched him. He grunted, put down his coffee cup.

"Chief Kyle doesn't like your story, but his cops so fucked things up at the scene and with you that the medical examiner and lab can't bust your version. I don't see Kyle pressing his county's DA for an indictment. He says self-defense and his foul-up doesn't get attacked by your defense lawyer and spread across six columns in the paper."

"Thanks, Lieutenant."

"Is this Crowley guy going to be missed by anybody?"

"I don't know."

"Was Crowley the name he'd been using?"

I had thought about that question a lot. "If I tell you that I know, and how I know, you might get deeper into this than you want to be."

Murphy turned that over. "Was he living or working in Boston?"

"No," I said, "well outside the city limits."

"Cuddy, if you *ever—*"

"I won't," I interrupted, "not ever."

He rotated the fist with the mug, swirling the coffee. I anticipated his question.

"I had to kill him, Lieutenant. Finding out I was still alive, he would have killed me."

"Or run," said Murphy. "Man like that, probably had an escape route planned."

I anticipated him again. "With a chunk of money to help him along the way."

Murphy drank. "What do you suppose would happen to that?"

"Maybe he was decent enough to leave it to Al Sachs' widow and child."

"All of it?" asked Murphy.

"Most of it."

Murphy shook his head. "Cuddy, if you are for real, I may actually have found something to believe in again."

I was starting to thank him when he told me to get out of his office. I got.

It was 2:45 P.M. when I walked back down the steps of police headquarters. I walked up Stuart Street past the bus terminal and used a glassed-in public phone to call Eddie Shuba.

"Shuba," answered the voice.

"Eddie. John Cuddy."

A pause at the other end.

"Eddie?"

"That Pontiac all taken care of," said Eddie a little strangely. "On its way to glue factory."

I laughed. "Thanks, Eddie."

"I did it myself."

"I appreciate it."

"Johnnie," he said, lowering his voice, "I ain't seen no cops, but that front seat. There was a lot of . . . like somebody spilled paint on it, you know?"

"Yeah. Somebody had an accident."

"You O.K.?"

"I'm fine, Eddie. Just fine."

A sigh of relief. "Anybody asks me, I don't know not'ing."

"You're a good friend, Eddie."

"I old-country man, Johnnie. You no do this without good reason. I know."

"The best reason, Eddie. For a friend."

"Take care, you."

"Take care, Eddie."

I hung up and decided to call Martha in Pittsburgh, to let her know everything was all right. I still remembered my credit card number, so alternating with directory assistance, I tried her, then Carol. No answer at either home. I obtained Dale's number and got a pick-up on the third ring.

"Dale Palmer." There was a disjointed tinkling of piano keys in the background.

"Dale, it's John Cuddy."

"Oh, John, it's good to hear from you. Are you still in Washington?"

"No, no, I'm home now. How's Martha doing?"

"Fine, really. She's out at a job interview now, and I'm minding Al Junior." He paused and the disjointed music sounded briefly louder. "Can you hear him at the piano?"

"Yeah, a budding Chopin."

Dale laughed.

"Dale, how are you doing?"

"Pretty well, considering. Larry is—has moved out."

"I'm sorry."

"That's all right. I've just got to practice saying it. Better now, though, than after a year of unhappiness. I've been that route before. The lame excuses, the dark suspicions, the emotional scenes. Better a clean break."

"I wish I were there to drink to it with you."

"Actually, I've . . . I'm going to make a clean break there, too, if I can. I was beginning to get a little worried about . . . it. You know what I mean?"

"Yeah, after Beth—my wife—died, I came close to . . . it."

He paused, I thought, to move off a subject I hadn't handled well with him in the past. "John, Carol told me—I know you told her not to, but I'm the one who's really home, around here, that is, to keep an eye out—she told me about your, ah, qualms. Is everything *really* all right? For Martha I mean?"

"Everything's fine. No danger. And with luck, a payment is coming through soon that will, well, that she can use to . . ."

"Square things?"

"Yes."

"Bless you, John. She should be home tonight. Do you still have her number so you can tell her personally?"

I said yes. We exchanged closings and rang off.

I put in another dime and tried Nancy at the DA's office. Her secretary recognized my name and told me Nancy had gone home early. I thanked her and hung up.

I walked two more blocks to the rent-a-car place. The kid who had "helped" me was there and took a lot of soothing before believing that I really was going to square things for him on the car damage. I told him I'd call him as soon as I had a new place.

I walked back outside and hailed a cab.

"Where to, pal?"

"East Fourth Street, South Boston."

Twenty-six

I RANG HER BUZZER ONCE, WAITED, THEN RANG IT again. The cabbie had been tipped enough not to honk. I heard her steps on the stairs. The door swung open. She was still in her work suit, carrying the towel at her side.

"I'm unarmed," I said, glancing down at my sling.

She frowned. "Not funny. Come on up anyway." She turned. I gestured to the taxi and followed her up the stairs.

To make conversation, I said, "How come you're still in your lawyer clothes?"

"In this case, they're funeral clothes. We buried the Coopers this afternoon."

Shit. Where was my mind? I'd never even asked her about them.

"Why didn't you tell me it was today?" I said, an unwarranted whine creeping into my voice.

She turned, looked at me with a poker face. "I figured you had other things on your mind."

She turned away and opened the door for us.

"Drink?" she asked as we entered the kitchen.

"Thanks. Screwdriver, light on the vodka."

I went into the living room. The arm was starting to

throb, the last painkiller from the hospital wearing off. I dug out a vial of pills the nurse had given me. I thumbed it open with my left hand and rolled one out into my right palm. Nancy appeared with our drinks.

"Controlled substance?" she asked, but she wasn't in a mood to joke, and it didn't sound quite right.

I took the pill from my right palm, tossed it into my mouth, and choked a little on the booze with which I chased it.

"Are you all right?"

I nodded as I coughed. "Just awk . . . ward with the . . . left hand. I usually . . ."

She kneeled down and put her hand on my knee. She waited out my coughing.

"Awkward is about how I feel right now, too."

I started to talk but she wagged her head and drove on quietly.

"You did something yesterday. I'm sure the *Globe* screwed up the details, but I have a pretty good idea what happened. I thought about going to the hospital, but I had one dealing with Chief Kyle in the past, and . . . So anyway, I called the hospital instead, and a nurse assured me you were doing fine. I stayed away from Murphy because I was afraid he'd figure it out."

"He did, but . . . well, it's not O.K. with him, but he understands."

Her eyes welled up with tears but she kept them from her voice. "He 'understands'! I wish I could, but . . . I can't. Not really. I see the vendetta stuff all the time, John, from cafeteria brawls in schools that end up in knifings to the big boys, the no-hands and no-teeth level. What scares me is that it changes the people in ways they can't change back. It hardens them, John. It also never ends. There's always—"

I put my fingers on her lips. "This one's over, Nancy. Finished. The guy was basically a loner. A psycho. No family, probably not even a friend."

She shook her head and my fingers away. "You can't ever be sure and even then . . . oh shit! I pictured this like a jury opening and it's coming out all wrong, all tangled up." She sniffled and resumed. "Even if you're right, there's still the . . . the . . ."

"The fact that I set someone up to be killed."

"Yes."

"And then killed him?"

She lowered her face to my knee and cried noiselessly, dipping her head haltingly.

I stroked her hair very lightly with my fingernails and spoke very softly. "Nancy, I don't like having to say this, but please listen. The man I killed was scum. He murdered a string of people before Al, and he tortured and mutilated him first. He left an unemployed woman in Pittsburgh with a three-year-old and a hopeless mortgage situation. And he was smart enough and quick enough to kill me or blow the country before our revered legal system could have begun to make him pay, in dollars or anything else, for what he did."

Nancy looked up at me. "But you're not . . ."

"God, or a judge, or authorized by anybody to square accounts. Absolutely right. But Al was my friend, and the man I killed had wronged him. Do you see?"

She gnawed her lip. "I know what your words mean, but . . ."

"But what?"

"But I don't see how this is different from Marco killing the Coopers. They helped you get his brother, so he gets them. The man you shot, what was his name?"

"Crowley."

". . . Crowley gets your friend, so you get him."

I thought back a lot of years. "Sounds like a good law school point, Nancy."

"So?"

"So law school is law school, and the real world is different."

"I'm not in law school anymore. I'm in the real world, every day."

"That's a start," I said, feeling the painkiller lift and blur me a little.

Nancy rubbed at her eyes like a seven-year-old in need of a nap. She dropped the debate and put on a smile. A real smile, full of warmth and hope and . . .

I said, "If you're not too beat, I'd like you to take a walk with me."

"Now?"

"Yes."

"Sure. But why?" she asked.

"There's someone I'd like you to meet."

"I'll get my coat." She stood and turned away from me. Back over her shoulder, she said, "You're a good man, John Cuddy."

"No, but I used to be."

She stopped at the doorway but did not turn to face me. "Sometimes that's enough," she said.

I went to the bathroom while she bundled up. The walk would probably dispel the dull buzz I was experiencing from the painkiller, but I had fourteen more of them.

When we hit the sidewalk, Nancy locked her right

arm into the crook of my left. The early evening was clear and bright, a little damper but a lot warmer than Pittsburgh. The last few working people were pulling into their virtually reserved parking places in front of their three-deckers. Here and there, one waved to her. She waved back with a name and a greeting.

"You grew up in this neighborhood?" I asked.

She gestured behind her toward the massive Edison plant, puffing impossibly high and full clouds from numberless stacks and vent holes. "Two streets over. Dad died when I was three. Mom died my last year in law school." She shook her head. "We rented, you see, and she worked so hard to put me through. Oh, I had scholarships and loans, and part-time jobs, but it was her effort really, and she never got to see it."

"Oh," I said, "I think she saw it." I took a deep breath. "I know I have."

Nancy pressed her forehead into my shoulder for a few steps. Then we walked up the hill. We got to and walked through the gate. Nancy never broke stride or hesitated in any way.

"They're pretty good about leaving the place accessible," I said.

Nancy nodded, patted my forearm.

"Usually either this gate or the K Street one is open." We climbed the car path for the forty yards or so to the second walkway that cut right. Except for a car that I heard pulling onto the wide path behind us, the place was empty.

We walked the right path, then eased left. We stopped a few steps later at the familiar marble stone. Nancy slid her arm out from mine.

"Beth," I said, "this is Nancy."

Nancy didn't say anything. She didn't look at the

stone or at me. She just stared down at the ground, where I used to look. Where Beth *was*.

I said nothing. Nancy glanced up at the inscription, then down again.

"Thirty was too young, Beth," she said. "Way too—"

The first shot hit her high on the left shoulder, spinning her around and down. She bounced off the marker of Edward T. Daugherty, d. 1979. I dropped and felt the stitches tear out of my right arm. Not much pain, just the parting sensation and a feeling of warmth flowing outward. My blood.

I skittered crablike in an arc five or six headstones wide. The second shot took a chunk from an angel's granite wing, and I quick-crawled three or four more monuments away, leading the shooter away from Nancy.

He spoke to me. "I wanted her first, shithead. I wanted her down so I could come after you."

I recognized the voice, and I rubbed some snow on my face. It stung away whatever painkiller effect the adrenaline was missing.

"Just like you hunted my brother, shithead."

I moved three headstones more, quartering toward the gate and further away from Nancy.

"Your brother was the shithead, Marco," I yelled and dived, a round pinging off my former cover.

"Keep talking, big man," said Marco, sounding closer. "I torched that nigger and his whore. And I thought I got you."

I zigzagged twelve paces. "I've got nine lives, Marco," I said, diving again as he fired twice at my voice.

I heard him clicking new bullets against a cylinder,

so I moved as fast and as far as I could. Still toward the gate. His next round sprayed stone shards into the left side of my face.

"Closer that time, wasn't I, asshole?" he called. "I read about you in the paper but I missed you at the hospital."

I rolled three or four yards, came up in a crouch. I still hadn't spotted him, but his voice was moving with me.

"Since when do chickenshits like you read, Marco?"

I slipped on a patch of ice and his shot caught me in the left calf. I clamped down hard and swallowed a scream. I dragged myself on elbows as fast as I could. If he saw the blood, he'd have a perfect trail and pick up his pace.

"So, no piece, huh, asshole?" said Marco, sounding a lot closer than I wanted to place him. "That's how I found you, you know. I told the woman at the hospital office I was your partner and was bringing you your gun. Hah. The stupid clit told me you was meeting your wife. I thanked her real nice."

I tried my left leg. Gingerly. It wouldn't push me at all. I shifted over to my right leg and raised up to a three-point stance. I could hold it only for two counts. I sagged back down into the snow.

"You know," said Marco, maybe twenty feet away, "I checked around on you. After the trial. I found out you went to Pittsburgh. I also heard in a bar down the street that your wife was dead and buried here and that you was queer for her." His voice was circling me. "After what the hospital broad said, I froze my ass for hours out in the car, by the gate back there. I knew you'd come."

He stopped talking, he was where he should have seen—

"Blood? Oh, did I get you, asshole? Or still bleeding from last night? Either way, don't matter. It's like Hansel and what's her face, followin' the bread crumbs."

A giant 747, on its declining approach to Logan, passed in majestic thunder three hundred feet above our heads. It drowned out everything. I edged around the headstone I'd picked, keeping it between Marco's last position and me.

The plane roar subsided. I didn't hear anything. Couldn't hear anything but my own heart, pounding in my ears and pumping life out the holes in my arm and leg.

"Behind you, asshole," he said from four feet away.

I stayed rabbit still.

"From where I stand, I can see a hole in your left leg, just below the knee."

I exhaled.

"Come on, shithead, turn around. I wanna see your eyes when I do you."

"Marco—" I said.

"Turn around!"

I turned but my right arm gave way, so I flopped over, like a fish struggling for air on top of a frozen pond.

He was standing, looking down at me, long-barreled revolver in his right hand and pointed at me.

"Oh, this is good, asshole, this is very fuckin' good."

"When I had your brother like this," I said, weakly as I could, "I stepped on his shoulder, on his *wound,* Marco, till he did what I wanted."

Marco's expression screwed up in rage. He took a step toward me, then stopped. His face relaxed. Sort of.

"Nice try, shithead. You had me going there for a minute. Joey told me about what you did. He told me, all right. But I'm just gonna chip away at you, a part at a time, till I only got one bullet left. Then I'm gonna drill you. Dead square in the face," Marco jeered, cocking his revolver. "In your *face.*"

The barrel mouth slid toward my good leg. I was out of ideas. I thought of Nancy and Beth, Martha and Al Junior. Of unclaimed book envelopes gathering dust in a post office. The waste of it all.

I heard a shot and a second, and a slug thumped the ground next to me as a third and a fourth and . . .

Marco pitched toward me, the monument between us throwing a stationary hip-check on him. There was a clicking noise behind him as he slumped and tumbled over the stone. His face crunched into a small marker at my feet. There were two gaping, burbling holes in his back. I released a long breath and raised unsteadily to face the clicking.

She was propped against a waist-level cross. A bloodstain the size of a baseball cap was spreading on her shoulder. Her clothes looked like she'd been the mold for a snow-woman. Her eyes were open, but her trigger finger kept driving home the shrouded hammer of the Bodyguard, methodically, reflexively.

I limped over to her. I put my hand on her gun arm. She stopped pulling the trigger. I gently pried the weapon from her clamped fingers. A police car, lights flashing, no siren, came barreling into the cemetery and up the car path. "Oh, my God," she said, sinking down on her knees, "oh, my God . . ."

I tried to support her, but instead my leg gave way, and I sank down with her. I heard the cruiser doors open and slam. "Over here," I called, dropping the Bodyguard to the ground. "Get an ambulance."

"Oh, John, oh my God, I killed him . . . oh Jesus Mary, I killed a man."

I drew her face toward me and mourned for the time when I would have felt as she did.